"AN EXCITING COMBINATION OF MYSTERY AND ROMANCE"

—*Syracuse Herald-American*

JONAS SMITH thought he had a bright new medical career stretching out before him. He had no idea, when a car pulled up to the cottage next to his, that its honey-blonde and beautiful occupant was to help turn his life into a nightmare of suspicion,

suspense,

and murder . . .

"A fast-moving killer-diller"

—*New Orleans Times-Picayune*

DATE WITH DEATH

ZENITH BROWN

Writing as Leslie Ford

WILDSIDE PRESS

Date with Death

Published by Wildside Press LLC
www.wildsidepress.com

The young man lying at the end of the pier, over the moonlit water of the creek, adjusted his lank loose-jointed frame to co-operate with the uneven oak plank under him and shifted his pipe to the other side of his wide mouth. The Llewellyn setter stretched out beside him raised his head and thumped the boards with his feathered tail.

Jonas Smith M.D. put his hand out. "Not yet, boy. It's our last night. Look at that moon. Just look at it, boy. Where's your soul? Don't you like solitude? You're as bad as Agatha."

The dog put his head down between his paws again. Jonas Smith drew a long satisfying breath, filling his lungs with the cool soft fragrance of pine and swamp magnolia as his soul was filled with all the intangible loveliness of marsh and woods, fields and moonlit water in the Spring. He was happy; he had never been anywhere near so happy when he was in love with Agatha Reed as he was now, out of love with her. What a break, he thought, for both of them, that they hadn't waited too long to find it out. In less than the month since it had happened she had faded almost completely out of his mind, coming back only when something happened that reminded him of her lacquered unyielding conformity. Agatha was beautiful, but Agatha was a snob. Agatha laughed but Agatha had the sense of humor of a rachitic newt. Crisp and positive, Agatha had been hurt and querulous before they'd quarrelled and broken the engagement for the second time. And Annapolis, Maryland, was the third time, the last time, and for keeps, Jonas Smith was thinking . . . whether Agatha knew it or not. Agatha wouldn't come to An-napolis. She wanted to stay in Baltimore, Maryland. It was in-comprehensible why anybody who didn't have to should want to start his practice in a one-horse town. Particularly in Annapo-lis.

"A civilian in Annapolis has no prestige, darling. Now if your father had been an admiral, or your grandfather . . . Or even if you'd been more than just a lieutenant in the Reserve . . ."

Jonas Smith propped his head up on his arm and looked over toward the little town, quietly asleep at the mouth of the Severn, eight miles away over the silvered rim of oaks and tulip trees that fringed the south side of Arundel Creek. On the one radio tower at Greenbury Point visible above the woods, the red beacon light went on and off like an aerial Cyclops genially winking his solitary eye.

"—Maternal and Child Care Clinic!" Agatha's adrenalin turned on easily, like tap water. "You don't have to go to Annapolis for Public Health clinics. What you mean is the sailing, and fishing, and crabbing and duck shooting. And if that's all the ambition you have then it isn't me you want to marry!"

Jonas stretched his long legs and winked back at the bibulous red eye over the trees. He took his pipe out of his mouth. Agatha was so right. The question now was whether he wanted to smoke another pipeful before he went to bed, or whether he'd just lie there on the little pier a few minutes longer, watching the moonlight that softened the outlines of the shore and made the broad creek look like an isolated mountain lake, infinitely secluded and remote, no one there at all but himself and his dog, and an occasional muskrat crashing in the silent night across the shimmering surface to the other wooded shore. It was their last night. Tomorrow, Sunday, he and Roddy would leave their borrowed cottage retreat and go in to Annapolis, Monday they'd open shop. It was all set, his office and living quarters in the wing of the Blanton-Darrell House in Darrell Court, his nameplate already on the door. He fished in his pocket for his tobacco pouch and sat up.

"One more and then to bed, Roddy," he said.

He looked back at the cottage, and then across the marsh, farther along the creek. The other cottage there belonged to some people he'd just met. Some day he'd get a spot on a creek like this. There were hundreds of places like it, little arms of the Chesapeake, hidden off the main roads, unbelievably remote and quiet. In the week he and Roddy had been here, the only people they'd seen were the watermen, crabbing from their dingy boats along the shore, poling silently with their slow rhythm by the shallow margins where the soft crabs lived under the shore grass and seaweed. No one else had come at all.

Then, as he put his pipe in his mouth and reached in his pocket for matches, he was suddenly aware it wasn't true. A car was coming up the road of the other cottage along the creek, the place across the marsh. He could hear it before he could see the lights through the trees.

The dog raised his head and growled.

"It's all right, Roddy. We couldn't have it this way for forever."

The yellow glow of the headlights came out of the wooded lane into the clearing and stopped a little way from the Milnors' cottage there on the point. Jonas looked at his watch. Even without the illuminated hands he could have read it easily in the high white brilliance of the waxing moon. It was just after twelve-thirty, and it was an odd time for a car to be coming in. It wasn't the Milnors. They were with the Fergusons, whose house he was using for the week, in the Fergusons' car and not leaving Cambridge until after lunch Monday, according to the phone call he had had around five o'clock. Because they had asked him to keep a casual eye on the place, he waited, mildly interested.

The headlights went off. He heard the car door slam. Then, in the utter silence of the night he heard a girl's voice, as clearly as if she were on the screened porch of his own cottage on the shore fifty feet behind him.

"You said they were expecting us. Look—they've gone to bed."

"They're on their way out. They said to go in and have a drink and wait for them."

The man's voice answering her was cultivated and easy.

"—Oh, baby, what a night! Isn't that a honey of a moon? Come on down and look."

Jonas saw them, first through the gap in the hickory and gum and holly trees fringing the Milnors' shore, and again when they ran hand in hand down the steps on the bank and out to the end of the Milnors' pier. Except for the sound of feet on the oak planks in the still night, he could have thought the girl was a disembodied spirit. She was slim and ethereal in a long filmy white dancing dress that floated out behind her as she ran. The man was very tall, in dinner clothes, his shirt front gleaming.

It was all right. They were obviously friends of the Milnors. Jonas relaxed, still wondering a little about the phone call at five o'clock from Cambridge.

"Let's go for a row."

"Oh, we can't, Gordon! We've got to get back."

The girl moved toward the shore. "Come on, Gordon, please. I shouldn't be here unless the Milnors are. Sis would hit the ceiling."

"Oh, don't be like that." The man's voice was abruptly impatient. "Let's have a drink. A snort'll do you good."

7

The moonlight gleamed on the silver flask. The girl moved farther toward the shore.

"You know I don't drink. And you've had enough, Gordon. Please don't drink any more . . . and please come on."

The flask raised to the man's lips, his head tilted back. It was a long snort.

"Gordon!" The girl's voice rose abruptly. "We've *got* to get back! *Please!* If you don't take me I'll go by myself!"

"Okay, baby, okay."

The man put his flask back in his pocket, his voice suddenly amiable again. Jonas reached for his matches again. He had even wondered, for a moment, if there would be any point in making himself known. It was no real business of his. The two people over there, on the pier across the marsh, seemed to be friends of the Milnors. If gals would wander at night, they ought to be able to take care of themselves.

"Okay," Gordon said again. "Give me one kiss and we'll go."

The girl hesitated, and stepped quickly forward into his arms. Jonas waited. When the man spoke again his voice was smooth and highly content. "I guess I've changed my mind, honey child. I guess I don't want to go home right now."

The girl broke away, stumbled, caught herself and ran, back along the pier toward the bank. Gordon stood where he was. The moonlight shone again on the flask. Then he was standing there brilliantly visible in the yellow glare from the headlights of the car, his shirt front and blond hair shining. The car door slammed violently shut again, the white figure of the girl appeared between the trees and on the pier again.

"Give me the keys, Gordon—please! You stay and wait for the Milnors if you want to. I've *got* to get back. They can take you in. Please give me the keys!"

"Okay. Here they are." Gordon's hand reached in his pocket, reached out toward her.

"Toss them here. I don't trust you."

"Don't trust me . . . or don't trust yourself, honey?"

Jonas Smith moved slightly. The voice was unpleasant then. Something new, or something very old, had been added.

"I certainly trust myself."

The girl's voice was sharp with anger. She went forward and held her hand out. Jonas heard the splash.

"For the love of God!" the man said. "Look what you've— Now neither of us can get in. You couldn't take them without knocking them in the water, could you?"

Jonas took his cold pipe out of his mouth and looked at it thoughtfully.

"This," he said, "is time for us to sound off, Roddy."

He got to his feet and stood there hesitating. The girl could have knocked the keys out of his hand. It could have been an accident.

Gordon's voice was angry. "Stop blubbering, for Heaven's sake. I'll get you home. I always have, haven't I? Just shut up and come on in. I'll call up a taxi, and you can call your blasted sister and tell her we've had a flat and you're out at the Milnors'."

They went back along the pier in the full glare of the headlights, and up the steps to the top of the bank.

"Wait till I turn off the light, I don't want the battery to run down.—Or go on in, the key's over the screen door. Phone for a taxi while you're at it."

Jonas put his pipe in his pocket and bent down to roll up the mat. When he started up the pier to the house, the yellow path of light from the car was gone. He stopped a moment until he saw another light spring up in the window of the cottage.

The dog followed slowly at his heels.

"Come on, Roddy. It's Life, boy—in Annapolis same like any place. People ought to keep their kids at home."

As he reached the screen door he stopped to look back over the silver shimmer of the water. In the hushed silence of the wooded slope across the creek something of the enchanted loveliness of the night had died.

"Let's turn in, Roddy."

He dropped the mat on the bench by the living room door, went inside and switched on the table lamp. He stood looking down at his own telephone. Something stirred vaguely in his mind. It was something connected with a telephone. It escaped him . . . escaped but stayed with him, troublesome in spite of all his effort to put it out of his mind and quit worrying about it. It was still there when he turned off the light and went out with the dog into the end wing to go to bed.

It kept pricking at his mind after he turned out his light there and closed his eyes. Someone he was supposed to have called and had forgotten about? Something about the phone at his new office in the wing of the Blanton-Darrell House in Annapolis . . . He lay looking up at the ceiling, listening to the setter peacefully snoring on the floor at the foot of his bed. He gave it up and closed his eyes again.

When he woke abruptly the setter was over by the door, growling, the moonlight full on his spotted coat. Jonas sat up in bed.

"Quiet, Roddy."

He pushed back the blanket over him and felt around with his feet for his sandals on the floor.

"*—There is no telephone in the Milnors' cottage . . .*"

It was in his mind as clearly as if he were actually saying it aloud in so many words. That was it. It was how he'd met the Milnors. They had come over to use the phone out in the living room because they hadn't put a line in.

But the awareness of that was not what had waked him, and certainly not what had waked Roddy.

2

He looked at the clock on the table by his bed. It was eighteen minutes past one. He must have barely dropped off to sleep. He went over to the door and motioned the setter to his pad at the foot of the bed, left the door closed, stepped through the long open window out onto the screened porch and went quietly along it, keeping in the shadow of the sloping roof. He listened intently, stopped and drew back against the wall. The sound he heard was the creak of leather, oars dipping in the water. Then he saw the boat through the branches of the willow on his own bank and the white figure of the girl rowing. She turned her head to look, gave one long pull and raised the oars. As the boat slid noiselessly up the shallow beach she caught her filmy skirts in both hands and jumped. She came running up the bank. Jonas could hear her breathing, a strangled sobbing, as she ran up to the screen door.

He took a step forward, and stopped abruptly. The girl thought she was alone. Everything about the way she moved, silently, the passionate intensity of her breathing, showed it, even to the swift concentrated dash she made to the old lantern on the right hand side of the door where the Fergusons kept the key to the house. She thrust her hand in for it, drew it out and ran to the door. He heard it strike the metal in frantic fumbling haste before she got it in the lock, not knowing the door was already unlocked.

As she went inside he moved back so the light when she turned it on would not let her see him. Then he realized she was not turning on the light, and remembered the phosphorescent dial number card he had put there himself. She spun the dial around. When she first spoke her voice was shaking and inaudible. Then it was raised, compelling with some desperate urgency.

"—Tom! It's Jenny, Tom. Listen to me. I'm . . . I'm in a mess, Tom. I can't tell you what it is, but you've got to come. I'm out at St. Margaret's, at Natalie's. Only I'm really next door. No—I *can't* call her! I don't dare! Tom, I'm afraid . . . I've *got* to have help! I know, Tom, but you've got to help me! No —they're away, they're all away—both the Milnors and the Fergusons. I'm all alone. You've got to come out, Tom—and please, don't tell *anybody! Please*, Tom!"

Jonas heard the convulsive sob as she put the phone down, missed the cradle and got it into place. Then she was moving inside, coming into the bedroom wing. He flattened himself against the wall, wondering how he could come out and offer to help her without frightening her still more. She was in the room next to him, Natalie Ferguson's bedroom. As the shaded light on the dressing table there turned on, he took a step to the window. She was going quickly to the closet door, in her stocking feet, a pair of mud-blackened evening slippers in her hand. The filmy white net skirt hung in torn and bedraggled rags around her legs, the bodice was ripped. It was not the moment, Jonas saw, to let her know the house was not empty. She was pulling with her free hand at the fastener under her left arm, and as she reached the closet door the dress fell to the floor. She stepped quickly out of it.

As she pulled the closet door open, he stared at her with a feeling of pity, and anger.

"Good God," he thought, "she's a baby. She's nothing but a kid."

The small pointed face, drained white, the flesh sticking paper-tight to the high cheekbones, the frightened trembling mouth, the dark terror-ridden eyes so deeply circled they were almost lost under the white forehead with its cloud of smoky black hair . . . no single feature, but all of them added up, made her pitifully and tragically young. Seventeen, he thought; maybe less than seventeen.

She was struggling with a black dress she'd taken out of the closet, trying with trembling fingers to find the fastener. Then

11

she was in it, took shoes out of the closet, slipped them on, bent down again and brought out a striped canvas beach bag. She scooped up her evening dress and slippers and jammed them in it, ripped the fastener closed, thrust the bag back in the closet and closed the door. She turned the light off and was gone. Jonas went quietly along the wall in the shadow of the roof, in time to see her run down the bank to the boat. She stepped in and pushed off. Then she was rowing with quick strokes back along the shore to the Milnors' pier.

Jonas took a deep breath. "I'll be damned," he said. He went back to his room. His clothes were on the chair by the bathroom door. Without turning on the light he felt his way across the room, took off his bathrobe and pajamas and dressed. He reached down and patted the setter.

"Good boy," he said. "Stay here, boy, I'll be back."

Roddy, hating it, would be there until the crack of doom.

"You didn't know it, Roddy, but old Jonas Smith is going to be the White Knight of Arundel Creek."

Outside at the back of the cottage he stopped, thinking. He could get to the Milnors' quickest by swimming or rowing. Either seemed out of the question, being a frontal approach in plain sight. That left the long way, around the marsh, or the middle way, across the marsh—risky, but possible if he kept his footing on the slippery bulkhead the Milnors and Fergusons had put up with the hopeful idea of making a fortune out of terrapin if and when they ever got around to it. He had crossed once in daylight. He hesitated, guessed he could make it at night, and guessed right, with only one narrow margin halfway across when an owl hunting for frogs rose on ghostly silent wings with a malignant hoot barely ten feet in front of him. Unstrung but undaunted, he kept his balance, made the shore, remembered the vicious thickets of poison ivy along the bank and climbed up.

It was too late to go back to the lane, poison ivy or no poison ivy. He went on, looking for the path leading into the old unused wagon road that was a short-cut to the Milnors' orchard. He came on it in a few steps through the undergrowth, a narrow silver ribbon in the dark woods. Along the curving back road he could see the banks of laurel blossoms glowing in the moonlight sifting through the oaks and dogwood trees. As he stepped through them he thought of the poison ivy again. It was all through the violets and honeysuckle that covered the old tracks and flourished down the middle of the road.

"Forget about the ticks and the ivy, Smith," he said to himself. "Get on with whatever it is you think you're going to do."

As he looked around before starting out for the oyster-shell lane that led to the cottage he started violently, and relaxed with a grin. The bulk there was only the Milnors' old black jalopy, standing forlorn and abandoned by the woodpile in the curve of the road. He went on toward the lane, through the orchard. What exactly was it he did plan to do? He shook his head. Nothing, except stand by, in case there was more trouble from Gordon, or whatever the trouble was, until Tom came, whoever Tom was, and took the Baby home. It would be simple. Through the top of the orchard he would come to the big three-pronged-tulip tree a hundred yards from the cottage. He could stay there, quietly, on hand if needed, unobserved if not needed.

He went through the orchard, across the meadow, and stood by the big tulip. The lights were still on in the cottage. The girl was nowhere in sight. He waited, and heard her. She was pulling the boat up on the muddy beach.

"The poor little devil," he thought. She must have been sitting down there in it, ready to pull out into the creek if she had to. He had a sudden impulse to go over to the cottage and let her know he was there, to help her if he could. He took a few steps from the tulip tree. She was coming up from the beach then, tiny and fragile in Natalie Ferguson's black dress. As she came onto the lawn in front of the cottage she pushed her hair back from her head with a gesture so tragic and hopeless that he stopped. She crossed the lawn to a group of painted wood chairs and sat there, small and lonely, watching the lane.

As she sprang up suddenly Jonas took a quick step into a clump of dogwood. A car was coming. He could hear the motor, the tires grinding on the oyster-shell, and finally see the lights through the trees. The car swung around the bend into the clearing and braked to a sharp stop. Two doors opened and slammed shut. A man and a girl were running toward the cottage. The girl on the lawn stood, waiting for them.

"—Jenny! Jenny baby . . . what is it?"

The girl stood speechless, her hand raised, pointing at the cottage.

"*Jenny!*"

It was the man speaking. Jonas saw the glint of the insignia on his cap, the glint of the single gold stripe of an ensign in the United States Navy on his sleeve.

13

He heard Jenny's voice. "There . . . inside. It's Gordon. I . . . I've killed him . . ."

Three people stood rigid . . . Jonas Smith as blank and dazed as the young ensign and the girl by him.

"—I tell you, it's Gordon. He's in there. I've killed him."

The girl said it again, quietly. Then, as if their shocked immobility was more than she could take, she threw her hands out to them.

"Oh, don't just stand there! Do something! Can't you hear me? Can't you hear what I'm saying? It's Gordon. I've killed him—he's dead! Oh, do something! *Please . . . do something!*"

The two turned quickly then and came running up the path to the cottage. Jonas Smith took a quick breath. The girl Jenny was standing there on the lawn, her head down, her arms hanging limp at her sides. The ensign and the other girl were running across the porch. He himself was standing there. He was Jonas Smith M.D. He was a doctor. He had an obligation to himself and to his profession. It was his duty to dash in there, see if the man was dead, save him if he was not, do everything he could to save him. And he hadn't moved.

The ensign had opened the cottage door. He stood there motionless, one arm held back to stop the girl coming up behind him. Jonas heard her voice.

"Don't be a fool, Tom. *Is* he dead?"

She pushed his arm away, stepped quickly into the doorway, and stopped.

"Oh, dear God!"

She turned back, brought her clenched fist to her mouth and stood, shocked and perfectly still for an instant, before she went slowly across the narrow porch to a chair. She stood holding to the back of it with both hands.

She straightened up and turned back. "Tom—what'll we do?" Her voice was controlled. "Where's Jenny?"

"I'm here."

The girl came around the end of the cottage and stood there by the screen door.

The ensign's voice was curt. "Keep out of here, both of you."

"No. I'm coming in. I did it. It was——"

"Shut up, Jenny."

"But I did. I tell you I *did* it."

"All right, Jenny baby."

14

The other girl's voice was quiet and reassuring. "We'd better go in, Tom, and shut the door. We'll wake everybody in St. Margaret's."

Jonas Smith moved out of the dogwood. The ground was carpeted under the pines. He went silently across to the end of the cottage. A dim light showed through the window there. He went up to it. Through a tiny kitchen and the open door across it, he could see into the single living room. As he saw the thing lying there on the green composition-tiled floor, he felt a sudden guilty sense of relief. No matter how he had acted, there was nothing he could have done for Gordon—nothing anyone could have done for him. Gordon had been shot through the heart. It was not pretty, but final. The look of surprised horror on the handsome face staring up from the floor was evidence enough, more evidence than the bright crawling stain still moving through the white string rug in front of the fireplace.

"—And quit riding her, Sis."

Jonas could not see any of them, but their voices came through clearly.

"She's not riding me. She told me not to go out with him. She told me what he was like. And I didn't mean to. I did go to the hop. I went just so I wouldn't have to go out with him. I didn't know he was going to meet me at the gate. I couldn't say no, I didn't want him to take me home. And then——"

"But your note said you were going to the dance at St. John's——"

"That's where we were going, Sis! You've got to believe me! We were going to the dance. But he said he had to pick up the Milnors and take them in too. That's why I came. It's true, Sis —it really is!"

The girl's voice was rising, dangerously near the hysterical breaking point. Jonas tried to piece it together. The two were sisters, the ensign was their brother. The hop would be the dance at the Naval Academy. He had sisters who'd been hop girls in their day. The gaps in what Jenny had said were simple. If she'd had to leave the Yard to go home alone, it meant the midshipman she'd gone with was a last minute date who hadn't signed up for liberty to take her home. Jonas knew about late dates too, an old Annapolitan custom, deplored by the midshipmen who brought them down and fed them but whose hops ended at midnight, enjoyed by the St. John's students who danced on till two and didn't care what time they said good-night. He looked through the little kitchen down at the body on the floor. This was no St. John's student. There was nothing of the college man about him, not even of the returned veteran. There was an aura of sophistication that was not like Annapolis. Gordon was too experienced, too worldly, by far too well dressed.

"But you knew the Milnors are in Cambridge——"

"He said they were back, Sis. They'd called him up."

"Skip it," the ensign said.

"No. I've got to tell you. You've got to listen to me. And don't look at me like that, Tom—don't! I didn't mean to do anything I shouldn't. I tried to go home, but he wouldn't let me. He threw the car keys away, in the creek. He did it on purpose—he told me he did when we got in here. He said we'd come in and phone for a taxi, and I . . . I forgot till we came in that they don't have any phone. Then I . . . I couldn't get out, and . . . he said horrible things. He said I wanted to come. And then he pulled out that gun, and threw it to me, and said I could . . . I could shoot him if I wanted to, it was one thing or the other. And I was so scared I did. I did shoot him, and he fell over. He fell over just like that——"

"Oh, Baby, stop! Stop it, Jenny. It's all over now. We do believe you, Baby."

The poignant tenderness in her sister's voice sent a sharp thrilling warmth up from the roots of Jonas Smith's spinal column.

"—He's dead. There's nothing we can do about that. He was no good—he shouldn't have brought you out here.—What do we do now?"

The ensign broke in crisply. "Who saw you come out here, Jenny?"

"I don't think anybody. We didn't even pass a car on the road. That's when I first began to get a little scared."

Jenny's voice was muffled and streaked with tears.

"Who saw you get in at the gate?"

"Everybody coming out of the Yard could have. I wasn't trying to hide. George took me to the gate. I was going home, and——"

"Who saw you leave the house?"

"Nobody. Nobody was home. That's when he said why didn't we go over to the dance at St. John's and maybe Sis would be there."

"All right. You didn't leave the house, Jenny. You got to the house and said good night to him and went to bed. That's all you know, and that's the last time——"

"No. I won't do it. I'm going to tell them I did it. I'm not going to tell a lie about it."

"You want to go to jail, and be tried for murder, and have everybody——"

"Oh, no! They——"

"Let her alone, Tom," the other girl said quietly. "I'm afraid you'd have to, Jenny. But it's not jail so much. It's Grandfather."

Jonas heard the younger girl's short terrified cry. Her voice was hardly audible then. "That's why I didn't call you, Sis. I didn't want him to find out I was . . . I was in a jam. He'll be furious!"

"Oh, the hell with him."

The ensign moved into the space visible from the window. He was tall and erect, the part of his face not shadowed by his cap hard and intense. He reached down to the small snub-nosed automatic on the floor.

"You shot once?"

"Yes."

He held the gun to the window curtain and wiped it.

"Oh, please don't, Tom! I'm not afraid . . . you'll just get in trouble——"

"He's already in trouble, Jenny. Terrible trouble. You know he is. You might as well face it. And stop crying. It's too late to cry."

"—You know what'll happen, Elizabeth," the ensign said. His voice was curt and cool. "And it's not going to. He was a louse, he had it coming, let him take it."

He stepped over the dark stain on the floor, picked up the dead man's hand, pressed the gun into it, brought the hand back to the floor.

"Where did you go in here, Jenny?"

Her sister's voice was controlled. Jonas Smith shook his head. She'd weighed the consequences, decided to play it with her brother, not as Jenny wanted it. It was wrong. He knew it was wrong. "—But if it were my sister . . ." He shook his head again, remembering the small pointed face, the hollow terror-stricken eyes and trembling young mouth.

"Try to think, Jenny! What did you touch? Did you go out in the galley?"

17

"No. Yes. No, I didn't. He went out, to get some water for his drink. I didn't. I didn't touch anything—I didn't move from here."

"All right.—Your dress, Jenny . . . that's not your . . ."

"It's Natalie's. Mine's over there, and my shoes. In the beach bag in her closet."

"We'll get them in the morning. Nobody'd think of going there even if they find him. It's Tom we've got to think about now . . . he's got to get back in—Leave the light on, Tom Oh, Tom . . . there's blood on your cuff. And look at the mud . . . Jenny, go on out. Both of you. I'll get the mop. Be quiet."

Jonas moved to the side of the window. She was coming into the little kitchen. He saw her hand reach behind the icebox for the mop. Then he saw her face. It was reflected, for a tiny but to Jonas Smith indelible moment, in a round piece of mirror of the kind women put on the table to set a bowl of flowers on. The mirror was propped up between a pair of glass candlesticks at the back of the linoleum-covered shelf under the wall cupboard, and it held the reflection of the girl's face for a brief instant that transmuted itself in the mind of Jonas Smith into a fragment of eternity. She was lovely, and as different from her younger sister as dawn is from dusk and flame from smoke. She was blonde, her fair hair drawn back and tied with a black ribbon at the neck, slender and thoroughbred, with a pale intent oval face and calm grey eyes. There was something else that shown out from behind the grey eyes and that had the same warmth and moving tenderness that her voice had.

Jonas Smith realized slowly that he had changed from a man alert and watching to an automaton, walking as if in a dream, without conscious awareness, back to the great tulip tree. Or he knew, when he thought of it, that he must have walked there. He was there when she came swiftly out and hurried to meet her sister and the ensign by the dead man's car. He heard a door open and close, saw the three of them go quickly to their own car at the end of the clearing, saw its red tail light disappear along the oyster-shell lane into the woods. It was the way he would have seen them if it had been a dream.

He stood motionless, in the now utterly quiet night, looking unseeingly down at the cottage on the moonlight-flooded point. He was gripped by a curious sense of some new kind of reality that was the most profound experience of the twenty-eight years of his life. It had come quietly up out of some deep inner

18

recess of his mind, a kind of intuitive knowledge, admitting neither question nor doubt.

"That's the girl I'm going to marry," he said.

3

He heard himself saying it aloud in the quiet of the whispering woods and the lap-lap-lap of the water on the shore, and as he said it he felt a glowing sense of confidence and warmth that made him feel, suddenly, as if he had moved all his life half-asleep to come now to this abrupt and vivid wakening. He took a deep breath and stepped out of the shadow of the tulip tree into the moonlight. Then he stopped short. The lighted cottage across the clearing on the point was still there in front of him. A man named Gordon was in there on the floor, dead. In a few timeless moments his own inner life had been changed and illumined. The fact of the dead man's body in there had not changed. It was solid and incontrovertible. Something had to be done. Jonas Smith was the man who had to do it.

What he had to do was go at once to the telephone in the Fergusons' cottage across the creek and call the police. There was such a thing as law. He believed in it. His duty was clear and tangible. It was to find the nearest officer of the law and report what had happened . . . everything that had happened. The nearest officer of the law was exactly as near as the Fergusons' telephone. It was all simple, and no problem whatever. On the other hand . . .

He shook his head. "There is no other hand, Smith," he said to himself. "There's only one hand, and you've got hold of it."

He went through the pines to the cottage. Two other facts were solid and incontrovertible. The sister of the girl he was going to marry—the girl whose last name he didn't know, whose face he had only seen reflected for a tiny instant in a piece of mirror propped up against a kitchen wall—was legally guilty of homicide. The girl herself, Elizabeth, and their brother the young ensign, were legally, technically and in fact accessory to it. A third fact just as solid and incontrovertible came suddenly into his mind. He was himself accessory, as of the last fifteen

19

minutes. He would continue to be as long as he did nothing about it.

He shrugged his shoulders, went inside the cottage and looked down at the motionless figure on the green-tiled floor, his eyes resting on the surprised and horrified face staring sightlessly up into nothing.

"—He never expected her to shoot. He never had any idea he was going to die until he got it."

The impression on his mind was so vivid that it seemed audible, and he looked around involuntarily to see if by some chance there was another person in the room saying it to him. There was no one there except himself and the thing on the floor. He looked down at it again. The face was handsome, the wavy blond hair as neatly in place as if Gordon had smoothed it back just before his last fatal gesture. His dinner clothes, messed up now, were perfectly cut, of silky finely woven midnight blue cloth. His hands were soft and well manicured, with colorless polish on the nails. There was a green scarab ring on one finger, and on the left wrist a watch in a wide flexible gold bracelet. Jonas did not like men who wore gold bracelets, but he knew there were places—not Maryland—where they were considered fashionable and in good taste.

Jonas shook his head. All in all Gordon did not look like a fool, like the kind of man who sober or drunk would toss his only set of car keys in the creek or toss a loaded gun to a terrified hysterical girl and say "Shoot me, baby." And he had done both. Was he an actor, used to dramatic gestures, so experienced he believed he was irresistible, so convinced of his own charm that he was hardly taking a chance? Jonas gave it up; stepped back carefully and opened the door. Outside the air was clean and cool. It washed the reek out of his nostrils and cleared out of his mind the momentary anger at what had happened, at what he himself had done. If he'd only stayed in the Fergusons' cottage, gone to bed when the dog had wanted to . . . He might have known nothing about all this, Jenny and Elizabeth and the young ensign Tom might have got away with it. But he hadn't, and there was nothing he could do except one thing.

He went down to the beached boat, got in and rowed out into open water. The single red eye by the Navy Experimental Station winked at him over the trees. It was a sinister wink now, not friendly and bibulous as it had seemed when he was lying there on the Fergusons' pier, at peace with himself and all the world, before Gordon and Jenny, Tom and the future Mrs.

Jonas Smith had shattered everything. He pulled across the shimmering silver saucer of the creek. All he could think about was her. The second girl, the one who was a conscious and determined accessory after the fact of the killing of Gordon. The girl he knew he was going to marry. It was not until he was in the living room of the cottage, switching on the light on the table by the telephone, that he thought: "What a hell of a way to begin marrying her."

He stood looking down at the phone with as much distaste as if it had been a dead weasel curled up in front of him. Then he picked it up and dialled the operator.

"There's been some trouble out at St. Margaret's, on Arundel Creek. Who do I call?"

"Is it a police matter? You call the County Police in Eastport. 4526. Or do you want me to call them for you?"

It was a straw. Jonas clutched for it. "Will you? Tell them it's the Milnor cottage on Arundel Creek."

He put down the phone. Then as if he had figured it out from the moment everything began and had known precisely from the beginning what he would do, he went across the room, gathered his records into a pile on the top of the phonograph and went swiftly into the bedroom wing.

Roddy was lying on the floor at the foot of the bed.

"Boy, we're going."

He put his gear in his suitcase. It was twenty-two minutes past two o'clock. At twenty-five minutes past two he switched off the light, closed the windows and went out. He stopped at the door of Natalie Ferguson's bedroom. There was a beach bag in there, in the closet. He went in quickly without hesitation and got it. As he came out he stopped by the door, listening, wondering if it was a car he had heard out somewhere behind the house. He went through the living room and out onto the screened porch. If the County Police had got there already, from Eastport ten miles away, someone had called them before he did. Or they could have had a radio patrol car out on the Ferry Road, he thought suddenly. He stood listening, watching across the marsh, waiting for the glow of headlights through the trees. There was nothing. No sound, no light except the pale yellow glow through the Milnors' side windows. The whole place was as quiet as the grave it was.

At twenty-five minutes to three he was headed down the dirt road toward the paved highway into Annapolis. A mile down the highway he saw the suffused glare of headlights reaching out toward him, and turned left into the winding remnant of the old St. Margaret's Road. It could be headlights on the green police sedan he'd noticed in town, coming toward him from the Ritchie Highway, headed for Arundel Creek. He kept on, swung down the last curve of the old road and shot up to the left onto the approach to the Severn River Bridge. The stop sign at the intersection before the Bridge, the right of way belonging to the old vehicle rattling down the main highway from the still empty site of the Ritchie Memorial, were matters he noted automatically as he went by.

He slowed down as he crossed the deserted bridge. Behind him now, the red Cyclops eye had become a twinkling figure in a whole rose-colored ensemble dancing a stately minuet high above the woods of Ferry Farms. To his left the Severn widened out into the shimmering stretches of the Chesapeake. It made a silver girdle along the twenty-seven square miles of the United States Naval Academy, the walled reservation where twenty-eight hundred midshipmen were sleeping in the great granite pile of Bancroft Hall. He rounded the sharp bend at the Post Graduate School and kept on into Annapolis, not concerned with the Academy that had been there since 1845 or its small Liberal Arts neighbor St. John's College that had been there since 1785, though he was going along the street that separates them.

He was deeply concerned about other things, thinking of the small tortured face of the girl Jenny as he'd seen her in Natalie Ferguson's bedroom, ripping off the torn mud-stained dress now in the beach bag on the seat beside him . . . of the agony of terror he knew now she'd been in, knowing what she'd fled from on the floor of the Milnors' cottage. It was unfair, pitifully unfair, in some way; she could pay all her life for something that had started out as just fun, ended as catastrophe. Maybe it was old fashioned for her to defend her personal dignity and honor. It was all right with him. There were infinitely more people her age, and Elizabeth's and Tom's, to say nothing of his own, who had the same code, in spite of all the talk that made juvenile practically synonymous with delinquency these days. He'd known when he left the Fergusons' that he was all for her. He'd never have brought the beach bag along, with the telltale dress and mud-caked shoes, if he had not known it. He'd have stayed to meet the police if he had not been in it, in it as far as the ensign and Elizabeth.

It was a funny thing what a difference two hours and one unleashed libido could make in people's lives . . . in Jenny's, in Elizabeth's and the ensign's. To say nothing of Gordon's.—To say nothing of Jonas Smith's, he thought. He remembered himself lying there on the pier in the moonlight. Then he grinned quickly in spite of everything, thinking of his landlord in Annapolis. Professor Darrell owned the Blanton-Darrell House, the right wing of which Jonas had leased, if the maze of restrictions and prohibitions he'd signed could be called a lease. So far as he could remember, there was nothing among them about coming in at three o'clock in the morning. On the other hand, from certain indications he felt definitely it would be a good thing, as he'd said he would be there Sunday evening, not to get Professor Darrell out of bed to see who was there now.

He parked the car on College Avenue and went the rest of the way on foot. The Blanton-Darrell House stood in the center of Darrell Court, the only Georgian house in the heart of the old city still enclosed in its own brick wall, the only one left whose grounds had not been sold off to have frame houses and stores built up to meet or enclose it. Randall Court was to the west, the Chase House and Ogle Hall and the Hammond-Harwood House to the east and south—all distinguished monuments of the past glory of Annapolis, all within a long stone's throw. Jonas stopped in front of the old house, filling the square block between College Avenue and Tabernacle Street, where Prince George divides to become Princess Anne Street on one side and Queen's Street on the other. He looked across the open garden at the mauve brick façade sleeping quietly behind the magnolia grandiflora, guarding on either side like a pair of glossy and gigantic Nubian slaves. A fan of frail yellow light shone above the carved white wood, and the slate roof glistened like hoar frost in the slanting last rays of the moon. The floribunda roses were moonlit too, their blossoms transmuted into a bank of drifting lemon-colored snow high above the ragged black outlines of the old yew trees.

He went quietly along the narrow brick walk to his own front door. A stray shaft from the street light over the brick wall lighted the brass plate there. "Jonas Smith M.D." It had been his father's. Seeing it, he felt a small tightening in the cords of his throat, remembering the years of his life it had been on another door. What would his father have done if he'd been at the cottage on Arundel Creek? You could never say how any older generation would act about a younger generation's problems. Maybe, he thought, that was what Elizabeth had meant out at the cottage when she said, "It's Grandfather I'm thinking about," and the younger girl had cried out suddenly. It was certainly when the ensign had made up his mind and picked up the gun.

He went inside and switched on the light. There was a small parlor off the vestibule that was to be his waiting and reception room. He turned on the lights, put his suitcase on the old leather sofa that had been his father's and set the beach bag on top of it. He went back into what had been a dining room wing, opening out into a small garden now fitted up as office and consulting room, and turned on the lights there. His two sisters had moved him in and arranged things. His bag was on the desk in front of the windows, the calendar was torn off to Monday, May 17th, when he would presumably start the practice of medicine.

He looked around with a sense of satisfaction and contentment, in spite of the last hour, and groaned suddenly as Roddy scrambled to his feet off the hearth, growling, his tail out, pointing toward the front of the house.

He should have ' pulled the curtains so Professor Darrell could not see the lights. It was too late now. He could hear the footsteps himself, coming along in front of the wing from the main house. He looked at himself in the mirror just as he heard the knock on the door, reflected that he looked more like a deck hand than a doctor of medicine and there was nothing he could do about it, went out into the vestibule and opened the door, a vision in his mind of an irate and plethoric landlord, in pajamas and dressing gown probably, as mad as a hornet undoubtedly, demanding who the hell he was . . .

He stood there staring for an instant at the girl whose face he had last, and for the only time, seen reflected in the mirror on the kitchen shelf of the Milnors' cottage. He pulled himself quickly together as she stared at him for an instant before she took a quick backward step.

"Oh, I'm sorry . . . I'm terribly sorry! I thought Dr. Smith . . . I thought perhaps the doctor had come."

She spoke quickly, the color flushing up from her throat and warming the pale oval face turned toward him in the lamp light. She took another step back.

"I beg your pardon. I didn't mean to disturb you."

He found his voice as she turned to go, making it as matter of fact as he could.

"That's all right. I'm Dr. Smith."

He smiled down at her. "I guess I don't look it, but that's the way it is."

She had turned back and was looking him up and down, her eyes as incredulous as her voice. "You mean *you*—" Her color went a quick shade deeper as she broke off. "I'm sorry. I'm being awfully rude. I just thought you were going to be . . . going to be older, I guess."

"I am," Jonas said. "Every day I'm going to be one day older."

"I mean I thought you were going to be middle-aged. Anyway, it doesn't matter. I'm Elizabeth Darrell, I live next door——"

Sudden involuntary laughter bubbled up like champagne in her voice and lighted her grey eyes.

"You rent the wing from my grandfather, Professor Darrell. I don't see it's any more surprising than for you to be Dr. Smith."

"It isn't," Jonas said.

It wouldn't have been, except for the last hour, and even then it was not half so surprising as the job she was doing, covering up what he knew was an acute and desperate fear. With no prior knowledge, she would have seemed only naturally worried about an emergency situation that was sending her out to hunt a doctor at that hour in the morning.

The laughter had gone out of her voice and faded from her lips and eyes.

"I came over to see if I could get you to help me. My sister's had a . . . she was in sort of an accident tonight, and she's pretty upset. She can't get to sleep. I thought when I saw your lights on maybe you'd give me something to quiet her down."

"Would you like me to come over and see her?" he asked quietly.

Her lips parted, the pulse in her throat throbbing.

"Oh, you're nice, aren't you? But you don't have to do that. She wasn't hurt. She's just sort of . . . shaken, is all. She'll be all right if——"

The glance she shot back toward the main house seemed to him to be sharper and more apprehensive than her fear he might insist on going back with her. She took a step inside the doorway where she could not be seen from her home.

"I'll be glad to come if there's any point in it," he said.

"No, *please!*"

She caught herself quickly. "I'm sorry, I didn't mean to be

25

abrupt. I couldn't let you come. I . . . don't want to disturb Grandfather. I mean . . . well, he doesn't like to be disturbed. You'll find that out if you're going to live here. He's really an angel, if he likes you . . ."

"And vice versa?" Jonas suggested.

She nodded, looking toward her grandfather's house again. The warm color had faded out of her cheeks and throat.

"He wouldn't like it if he knew Jenny was upset. So if you *will* give me something for her I'd be glad if you wouldn't say anything about it. And . . . I've got to hurry."

"Come in," Jonas said. "I'll get you something."

She followed him through the vestibule and stopped. "Oh, it's pleasant in here, isn't it?"

He looked back at her. Under the outward calm she was desperately frightened. It was all so mixed up, he thought, wondering what he ought to do. She was standing at the end of the sofa by the vestibule door, looking around with an interested air, without the remotest inkling that he'd been out at the Creek and had seen and heard everything, or nearly everything, that had happened. It was also plain that she seemed to have no remote inkling of the fact that some day she was going to be Mrs. Jonas Smith. It was all so mixed up, some elements of it so palpably absurd, in spite of the pathetic tragedy underneath, that he found himself smiling a little as he opened his bag. He got out a tube of pills, put six in an envelope and sat down at his desk to write out the directions.

He pushed back his chair and got up "Give her two now," he said as he came back into the reception room. "Another one if she wakes up. And call me——"

He came to a halt inside the door. "What's wrong——"

"I've got to hurry. Grandfather— Oh, give them to me, please—I've got to hurry!"

She took the envelope out of his hand and was gone. The door had closed behind her before he could get the picture of her white face and wide panic-stricken eyes straight in his bewildered mind. He stood blankly, listening for an irascible voice through the wall that divided the two houses. There was no sound except an occasional creak of the arthritic joints of the old mansion, and the setter asleep on the hearth, audibly dreaming of the open fields.

Still puzzled, he went over to where she had stood and looked around the room, wondering what could have alarmed her. Then he stared down at the sofa. The striped beach bag was there on

26

top of his suitcase, tipped over on its side. He saw what he had not noticed before. The name "Natalie" was printed diagonally across the lower left hand corner in red, white and blue letters two inches high. Among all the beach bags in Christendom, nobody could mistake Natalie Ferguson's.

"This," he thought soberly, "is a big help."

He picked the bag up and opened it. It was empty, the bottom still stained with the muddy seepage from the sodden evening shoes.

He glanced out toward the vestibule. It was an easy matter of the couple of minutes he'd been at his desk, and a handsome tribute, he thought ruefully, to his own stupidity. It was just a matter of quick thinking on her part; she could have them out of the bag, toss them out the front door to pick up on her way back, in an instant. If she hadn't been standing there at the end of the sofa when he looked back at her, he might have remembered. If he hadn't been dazzled and dazed by her sudden appearance, and her identity, he might have used his head. As it was, matters were different, suddenly, and more difficult.

He wondered what was going through her mind now, whether she wasn't perhaps already regretting it. It was folly; it was almost like a second unconscious betrayal. Coming for the sedative was the first. Taking the dress and shoes was in effect painting the arrow already pointing to her sister a bright brilliant red, making it a dozen times its original size and significance. But the important thing was the danger to them that the knowledge he had must seem to her, the agony of doubt and apprehension she must be in, over there, fearful of how much he knew, how much she had given away without meaning to do anything but help her sister.

Sober-eyed, unhappy and angry at himself for being a stupid fool, Jonas moved around, turning off the lights to go to bed. Something apart from the immediate problem of Elizabeth Darrell and how she was going to take the fact of his being there, just underfoot, on her own doorstep, came vaguely back to him, shapeless and persistent, gnawing at his consciousness, the minute the lights were out and he was there in the dark alone with it. It was like his first unformed memory that there was no telephone in the Milnors' cottage, a nagging, worrying, even frightening sensation, somewhere in the back of his mind. Darkness and danger seemed to associate themselves with it, sharpening it into something ominous and menacing.

27

It was hidden in his mind in a maze of dimmed and blurred impressions, connected with Elizabeth and Jenny but not anything he could put a name to or say came directly from either of them or both of them together.

It was not the dead man, though his face was there abruptly in Jonas Smith's mind, a visual after-image, the look of surprise and horror as vivid and startling still as it had been in actual fact. Nor was it the ensign, Tom.

Though there was something about her brother too. "He's already in trouble. Terrible trouble . . ." He remembered Elizabeth saying that to Jenny out in the cottage.

He let Roddy out in the small enclosed garden for a few minutes, thinking about that. What terrible trouble could an ensign get into in Annapolis, Maryland? Trouble usually reserved itself for the brass and the gold braid. Jonas had never heard of it stooping to the lowliest rank.

4

Jonas Smith shook the dazed cobwebs out of his head and sat up, looking around him for a bewildered moment. Outside the air was full of the noisy clamor of bells and the sound of the marching feet of the midshipmen on their way to church in the town. Nearer at hand there was an insistent intermittent buzz that he finally recognized. He reached his hand out for the telephone.

"Hello," he said. The next instant he was wide awake, everything that had got mixed up with a nightmare fantasy that had dogged his sleeping mind back again, not at all a dream but very real and very clear.

"Dr. Smith? This is Elizabeth Darrell. My grandfather, Professor Darrell, asked me to call you and ask if you'd like to come in after church."

She was making it sound as if she had never seen him and only barely heard of him before. Then, as if he might possibly misunderstand her, she added quickly, "It's an old Annapolitan custom if you don't know. You go to church and then you have a mint julep. My grandfather would be happy if you'd come, if you aren't busy, but——"

28

"I'd like to very much. Thanks a lot."

He interrupted her before she could say anything that would make it awkward for him to accept. "And she doesn't want me to come," he added to himself as he put down the phone. That was evident through the clipped forced cordiality in her voice, if it could be called cordiality at all. Ten to one her grandfather was there by the phone listening. So that was that. He was going to see her whether she wanted him to or not.

He sat thinking things over. What he was acutely interested in knowing about was what had happened in re. the body of the man Gordon out on Arundel Creek in the Milnors' cottage. How he was going to find out was another matter. There was nothing about it on the radio. Annapolis, he knew, had no Sunday edition, either of the *Capital* or the Southern Maryland *Times*. It was too late for it to have made either the Baltimore or Washington papers even if he had wanted to go out and find one. But there was no doubt he would find out, sooner probably than later, as towns without a newspaper at all always seemed to have the most effective grapevine.

He was thinking of that as he went along the Court to Professor Darrell's house just as the last moving notes of the Sailors' Hymn died away and the chimes under the green copper dome of the Naval Academy Chapel were silent again for another week.

He was not to be the Darrells' only guest. A flashy and expensive maroon convertible with the top down was negotiating the narrow curve of the cobblestone drive that the carriage and pair of bays it had originally been constructed for could have done with less damage to the magnolias and ancient shaggy yew trees. It drew up in front of the door as Jonas reached the iron hitching post set in the granite block to the right of it. The young woman who eased herself out from under the wheel and across the leather seat out onto the cobblestones was as expensive looking as her car and as strikingly un-Annapolitan, a product of nature and art that Jonas took one look at with happiness that he had come. Her hair under an exhilarating creation of brown and beige silk poppies was a rich tawny gold. Her skin was warm and suntanned, and she had on a sleek-fitting silk suit, toast color, that flared out, gracefully bell-shaped, around a pair of long and elegant legs. She paused on the second step and gave Jonas a gay and friendly smile that lighted up her brown eyes like sunlight sparkling through a glass of sherry wine.

29

"Hello," she said. "You're Jonas Smith, aren't you, our new cutter-up and general medico? I'm Philippa Van Holt. I heard you were coming in today."

The sherry-bright sparkle in her eyes seemed to Jonas to be doing the business of a slightly mocking adding machine, taking him in and totting up the score of his various points with an experienced and intelligent accuracy.

"How do you do," Jonas said. He looked at her with an easy grin. "Don't tell me you're an Annapolitan."

"Good Lord, no." She laughed. "You have to be born here, or live here forty years, before you can call yourself that. I've only been here a month. And if I stay another it'll only be because creeping paralysis is infectious. Or is it contagious? I don't know the difference. Anyway what I mean is catching. No, Dr. Smith, I'm not a native crab. I'm a writer. I'm here getting what we laughingly call local color."

"Oh," Jonas said. He glanced up past her at the open door of the Blanton-Darrell House. The slight sinking feeling in the bottom of his stomach was nothing a mint julep wouldn't fix— he hoped. "What kind of a writer?"

"Oh, bad, very bad, I guess. But it pays, and the nice thing about it is people never recognize themselves in print."

The sherry eyes were giving him another critically detached summing-up.

"Of course I don't mean you," she added calmly. "You're an outlander same like me. I mean these characters you see in houses like this, that . . . oh well, you know. They're dead but they won't lie down, as Gracie Fields puts it."

"They've got nice manners, though, haven't they?" Jonas asked. "I mean it's nice of them to invite us vipers in to drink their liquor on Sunday morning."

Philippa Van Holt laughed and shrugged her shoulders. "Oh of course. I forgot. You're going to *live* here, aren't you.— Oh, how do you do, Professor Darrell?"

One thing about Philippa Van Holt, Jonas decided then and there, was that she must be radar-equipped, though it was difficult for the naked eye to see where she carried it. Unless, he thought, it was hidden under the large hunks of rose tourmaline set in gold medallions around each of her wrists, that he saw now she had stripped off her beige doeskin gloves. Or perhaps looking at them had deafened him as well as blinded him to the approach of his landlord-host.

"You're sweet to ask us here!" Philippa Van Holt was up the

third step and inside the door shaking hands with Professor Darrell. "It's always such a privilege to come inside this *lovely* old house. If I owned it I'd never let a barbarian like me or Dr. Smith put a foot inside it."

Barbarian or no barbarian, Jonas thought, there was certainly nothing of the classic Greek visible about Professor Tinsley Darrell. He looked like a schizophrenic evil-eyed old horse. His pale bulging grey eyes glared at them, his nose looked less like sculptured marble than a bulbous lump of slightly cyanotic clay thrown off-center at his face and left to harden there with no attempt at shaping. He was tall, heavy-set and wheezingly short of breath. There was, however, one thing Greek about him. Barbarian though she might be—and Jonas thought she conceivably had something—Miss Van Holt had struck his Achilles' heel with a true and deadly aim. The glare in his eyes gave way to a watery glint.

"Barbarian, ha! It's a pleasure, Philippa. It's always a pleasure!"

He shook hands with her, brusque, but deeply pleased.

"Good morning, doctor. You've met Miss Van Holt, I see. Come in, Philippa, come in, doctor. I want you to meet my granddaughter."

As he moved across the wide airy hall in his wrinkled grey seersucker suit he looked like a huge bag tied up for the laundry.

"Oh, this heavenly room—I simply adore it!"

Jonas wondered if Miss Van Holt wasn't slightly overdoing it. One look over her sleek sweet-smelling shoulder as she paused ecstatically convinced him she was so far as Elizabeth Darrell was concerned. She was standing erect and poised across the room. As her eyes met his she looked quickly down, a faint flush showing for an instant. He saw Jenny at the same time. She was there beside her sister so quickly from where she had been sitting that he would hardly have known she had moved, if she had not brushed a section of the Sunday paper off a chair onto the floor. Jonas thought of a frightened fawn springing to its mother's side. The contrast between the two of them was more striking than he'd remembered—outwardly, at any rate, for he knew Elizabeth was not as calm and self-contained as she looked. She was taller than he had thought, honey-blonde with a quality that some way made Miss Van Holt a little too glittering. By comparison Jenny seemed a changeling gypsy child, burning with a dark flame-like intensity, with her blue-black

31

hair and small pointed face. The only thing about them that indicated blood relationship was in the grey-violet of their eyes, and it was less in their eyes than in the long dark curling lashes each had.

Philippa Van Holt said, "Hello, Elizabeth—hi, Jenny." It was evident that she did not waste her charm on her own sex, and more apparent as she turned to a woman Jonas did not see until he was inside the room. She was sitting primly on a stiff sofa against the inner wall, white-haired and pink-cheeked, dressed in her Sunday best, with innocent china blue eyes, as mild and happy-looking as a small sweet-tempered child at a birthday party.

"Hello, there, Miss Olive," Philippa said. "How on earth did you get here?"

"I walked," Miss Olive said.

"My granddaughter, Elizabeth Darrell, Dr. Smith," Professor Darrell said. "Now let's have a drink. Where's Wetherby? Wetherby!"

He glared around at the doorway.

"And this is my sister Jennifer, Dr. Smith," Elizabeth said. Jenny put her hand out, small, tense and very cold in Jonas's. "How do you do, Dr. Smith?"

"And Miss Oliphant, Dr. Smith," Elizabeth said.

"It's a great pleasure to meet you and welcome you to Annapolis, Dr. Smith," Miss Oliphant said happily. "My father had a great friend who was a Dr. Smith, but I don't expect you're any connection of his. He lived in New Orleans. I don't recall his first name, but he——"

"Jennifer!"

Jonas released Miss Olive Oliphant's plump soft little hand with a start and turned around. Professor Darrell was standing over the section of the morning paper that had slid off the love seat, glaring as if it were a coiled snake.

"Jennifer, haven't I told you——"

"That wasn't Jenny, Grandfather. That was me."

Elizabeth's warm beautiful voice that stirred the roots of Jonas Smith's spinal column also slightly staggered him with its calm disregard for palpable truth.

"I left that there, dear. Not Jenny."

"It doesn't make any difference anyway." Professor Darrell bent down and picked the paper up. "It's the way they fold the damned things these days. Won't stay together five minutes. Where's Wetherby with those juleps?"

32

He glared around at the door again.

"I'll go get him, Sis."

Jenny ran across the room and out. Jonas looked at Elizabeth. She had put all the papers on an ottoman by the fireplace and sat down where they'd been, smiling up at her grandfather. He wondered if it was a brief but vivid picture of life in the Blanton-Darrell House. Anything that Jenny did that was wrong was right if Elizabeth did it. Jenny was terrified of the old man, Elizabeth had no fear of him at all. He wondered about it, in terms of what had happened the night before.

"Goiter is six times more common among girls than among boys," Miss Olive said. "It tends to occur chiefly in adolescence. I read that in a magazine the other day. I cut it out, and I have it here in my bag somewhere. My father always encouraged me to read a great deal and to cut out and keep items of great interest."

She fished around in her rusty black bag, smiling happily at Jonas.

"Although you probably saw it yourself. And I should think one of Elizabeth's duties as your office assistant, and receptionist, I believe they call them these days, could be to mark interesting passages——"

"*Miss Olive!*"

Jonas, trying to make the bewildering jump from the newspaper incident to goiter to Elizabeth Darrell as his office assistant and receptionist, looked over at her. For once her poise had deserted her completely. She was sitting forward on the edge of the love seat, staring at Miss Olive with appalled embarrassment, scarlet-faced.

"Why, Miss Olive!" she gasped.

Miss Olive looked blankly around at everybody, and back at Elizabeth.

"Didn't Dr. Smith want you in the position? You said you were going to apply for it. I'm very sure you said it to me right here in this room, Elizabeth. I was sitting where Miss Van Holt——"

"Oh, Miss Olive, please! That was before——"

"Before you saw he was so young and handsome, dear?"

Philippa Van Holt raised her eyebrows, uncrossed one shapely leg and crossed it with the other.

"And unmarried? I should think that would be the chief reason——"

"I'd be delighted to have Miss Darrell for my assistant,"

Jonas said. He grinned cheerfully over at her. "I think it's a wonderful idea. If your grandfather can spare you . . ."

"If she wants a job she can have it, and I don't see it's anybody's business but her own."

"It's all set, then." Jonas grinned at Elizabeth again. "Tomorrow at nine, Miss Darrell."

"You know she was one of the best nurse's aides. Dr. French signalled her out for——"

"Miss Olive—please be quiet!"

"Oh, let her go on, Elizabeth," Philippa Van Holt said. It seemed to Jonas to be little short of refined malice. "I think it's fascinating and if Dr. Smith's going to hire you, he certainly has a right to know your qualifications—if any."

Elizabeth Darrell had got to her feet. She was looking past Philippa Van Holt, through the long window behind her into the Court. The scarlet was gone from her face. Jonas saw her lips part a little, the pulse throb in her throat. Philippa Van Holt turned her head to look too.

"Oh, midshipmen," she said indifferently. She brightened at once. "Or is it Tom? Most midshipmen are so young, but I adore Tom."

Jonas took out his pipe and began to fill it carefully.—Midshipmen? Tom Darrell was a midshipman, yet he had worn the uniform of a commissioned officer the night before. He had been out long after midshipman hours. No wonder his sister had said he was already in trouble . . . if he got caught.

"Tom's a fine boy."

Professor Darrell glared about him. Then his old eyes brightened. He looked like a man who had been travelling a month in the desert and come at last upon an oasis that was no mirage.

"Ha! Here we are. Where in hell have you been, Wetherby?"

The white-haired old Negro crossed the room to him, bearing his silver tray and its handsome burden of white-frosted silver julep cups.

"Ain' been nowhere, Professor, sir," he said serenely.

Professor Darrell sniffed, tasted, and approved. He waved the old man around to the others.

"Wetherby makes the best damned julep in Maryland," he said. "And get some cokes and milk out for the boys. Never give a midshipman a drink in this house. Against regulations. Not my own son when he was at the Academy, nor my own grandson. Let 'em wait till they graduate. I began drinking when

34

I was fourteen. 'S too early."

"They don't want no milk, Professor, sir," the old man said patiently. "They talkin' to Miss Jenny. They ain' comin' in."

"What do you mean, they're not coming in?" Professor Darrell set his julep down on the mantel. "Jennifer!"

"I'm coming, sir."

The girl appeared in the doorway, as bloodless as a small ghost.

"Where's Tom?"

"He's . . . not coming out today."

Her blue-grey eyes were fixed on him unwaveringly, as if in some fascination of despair. "That was George. He came to tell us . . . to tell us Tom won't be out today. He's going to come back later. George, I mean. Tom . . . Tom has the duty."

Professor Darrell stared at her coldly. "That's a falsehood. He had the duty yesterday."

He picked up his julep and drained it down. "And come in, or go away somewhere. Quit standing there shaking."

"Yes, sir."

She crossed the room quickly to her sister and sat down by her. Jonas, intent on his own julep, glanced over. The girl was shaking, as if chilled to the marrow of her bones or badly shocked. Elizabeth had taken her hand and was holding it tightly, as deeply alarmed, Jonas thought, as she was.

"And it's too bad we can't get poor Gordon Darcy any more," Miss Olive said cheerfully. "He was such a handsome and attractive young man."

She paused to sip her drink.

"This is very nice, Tinsley, although my father always thought it indelicate for ladies to drink anything but an occasional glass of sherry, or a little port. He allowed my mother a glass of port on Sunday evening. My father was famous for his juleps, Dr. Smith."

Jonas nodded politely. He kept his eyes carefully fixed on her. She was prattling on happily, like a child unconscious that it has left its playmates far behind and is alone in a deep and all-encompassing forest of silence.

"Your father's juleps weren't fit to drink, Olive." Professor Darrell's fey eyes gleamed at her savagely. "And what the hell do you mean about Gordon Darcy? Why can't we get him any more? Go phone him, Elizabeth, and tell him we want him over here right away. Do you hear——"

"There's no earthly use of phoning Mr. Darcy," Miss Olive

said. "None whatsoever." A brief cloud obscured the bright happy candor of her china blue eyes. "Mr. Darcy committed suicide last night. I would have mentioned it earlier, but my father——"

Philippa Van Holt's silver cup crashed to the bare pine floor at her feet.

5

Whatever further item of paternal wisdom Miss Olive was about to impart died unborn in the silent room. Her voice faded away. The cup rolled on the floor until it hit a chair leg and stopped. Jonas could have put a foot out and stopped it. He was intent on the problem of keeping his own grip firm on the damask napkin around the bottom of his own cup. When he recovered enough to look at the woman on the sofa beside him, Philippa was staring across at Miss Olive, her eyes distended, her red mouth stupidly open. The brown stain of applejack and bourbon whisky was spreading rapidly over her lap. She opened her mouth to speak. The color was drained out of her face as she got slowly to her feet and stood there, swaying.

Her voice was a gasping whisper that rose to a hysterical cry. "Miss Olive . . . what are you saying!"

"For God's sake, Philippa!" Professor Darrell was not too steady on his own feet. "Smith—do something. For God's sake what's the matter with everybody?"

Jonas caught the girl's shaking arm firmly and pushed her back onto the sofa. "Take it easy. Here—drink this."

He put his julep to her lips. She gulped part of it down and pushed the cup away.

"Miss Olive—what *happened?*"

"Yes, for God's sake, Olive, you old fool, don't just sit there! What happened?"

Jonas glanced for an instant at the two girls across the room. They were motionless, their faces blank unrevealing masks, curiously isolated, as if they were not there at all.

"I can't see that I'm half as much of an old fool as you are, Tinsley." Miss Olive's placid childlike voice was only mildly reproving. "I can't understand why you're all acting this way.

36

I haven't said anything you all wouldn't have known if you'd listened to our little radio station this morning as I did. Perhaps I shouldn't have brought it up at all. Papa always said good conversation is impersonal, you ought never to mention death and politics in society when there are strangers present. I'm sorry I brought it up."

"Perhaps you'd better go on, now, Miss Oliphant," Jonas said. "What was the rest of it?"

He didn't need to look at Elizabeth or Jenny. He could feel them coming to some kind of life again.

"Well, that was all there was to it, Dr. Smith. It said that Gordon Darcy's body was found dead out in the cottage that belongs to those new people that everybody thinks are so attractive, that came here five years ago and bought the Lacy place on Charles Street before they bought the place out in the country. And it must be very embarrassing for them. Though the man on the radio said they were away, and that just makes it worse in my opinion. And it didn't say he committed suicide, but for his own sake and theirs I hope nobody thinks he didn't, because it's not very attractive to think anybody else did it. I've lived in Annapolis all my life, and I've never heard of anyone we know setting out to murder any one else."

Miss Olive paused and looked at Philippa Van Holt.

"And of course I had no way of knowing you were going to be so upset about it. I knew he was a friend of yours, but I didn't know he was a close friend."

Philippa Van Holt's eyes were closed for a moment. She opened them then, staring down at the floor. When she looked at Miss Olive the expression on her face was a mixture of bitterness and pity, slowly rising anger and contempt.

"He was more than a close friend, Miss Olive." She spoke slowly and with deliberate emphasis. "It's something you wouldn't understand. I loved the guy. In fact, Miss Olive, I was married to him."

"Oh dear . . . oh dear me!" Miss Olive said hastily. "I . . . I had no idea——"

"No, you wouldn't have. You don't have any idea of anything. I'm telling you I was married to him. We both had our jobs to do. In a place like this you get along better if you look glamorous and unmarried. People do more for you. If you're just another couple you can shift for yourself, or go to hell—nobody cares. And we didn't lie about it. In New York or Hollywood anybody who knows anything knows about us. All

37

you had to do was look in any writers' Who's Who."

She bent her head, took her handkerchief out of her bag and raised it to her eyes. When she looked up again the mascara from her wet lashes was in dark smudges.

"I had a job to do. I had to get material for my story. None of the men around here would have taken me out if they knew I was married and Gordon was just around the corner."

She put her head down in her hands. After a moment she pulled herself forward and got to her feet.

"Where is he, does anybody know? Where can I find him?"

"Well, I imagine the police would know." Miss Olive was happy again, and helpful. "And I imagine Dr. Smith would be glad to go along with you. I don't think it's quite suitable for a young woman, even if she is a widow, to go by herself. My——"

"Oh, stop it!" Philippa turned on her angrily, and caught herself. "I'm sorry.—Go with me, will you? Please."

"Of course." Jonas was aware of the quick movement of Elizabeth's head as she turned it toward him, and the sound of her breath as she drew it in sharply.

"Let's go then."

Philippa went blindly to the door. She stopped there and turned back.

"But listen to me, all of you. You too, Miss Olive. You listen to me." Her voice rose sharply. "Gordon did not commit suicide. It's the last thing in the world he'd ever have even thought of doing. Somebody did kill him—here in Annapolis, Miss Olive —and somebody's going to pay for it. And just because you think suicide is nicer than murder, Miss Olive, is no sign anybody's going to write this off. Come on, Dr. Smith."

As Jonas followed her across the hall Miss Olive's voice floated like childish thistledown after them. "Dear goodness, Tinsley. It just goes to show——"

"Olive, will you shut your fool mouth? Wetherby! Where's that black scoundrel?"

Jonas looked back to see the old Negro crossing the hall, with another silver cup on another silver tray.

"Here I am, Professor, sir, an' here's your las' drink. An' you best mind yourself, black as your heart is, you best mind yourself what you're doin' an' what you're sayin'."

As Jonas opened the door for Philippa Van Holt he was glad there was another person in the Blanton-Darrell House who was not afraid of its owner.

"You drive, will you?"

She spoke with an apathetic bitterness that he thought was more disturbing than if she'd broken down and wept. She sat hunched forward, her mouth set, one hand rubbing her ankle, her eyes narrowed, staring moodily at the instrument panel, a determined and bitter young woman. He didn't doubt that she meant somebody was going to pay and that she'd be ruthless in seeing that somebody did.

He got in under the wheel. Coming around the curve up the center of the cobblestone drive were the two midshipmen he'd seen come earlier and leave. They were two troubled and unhappy young men, obviously on a mission that was hard for both of them.

He switched on the ignition. "Tell me about Tom," he said.

"Tom? You mean Tom Darrell?"

She came slowly back from the dark place her mind had been in. In the mirror over the windshield Jonas saw the midshipmen slow down, waiting for him to move along before they came on to the house.

"Where to?" he asked. "Do you know where we go? Is Eastport the nearest headquarters?"

She didn't answer at once. She was staring down at her lap and the dark wet stain that had spread over her knees and almost to the hem of her flared skirt.

"Home, so I can change, I guess. I'd better not go over there reeking of whisky. They'll think I'm drunk."

"All right. Where's that?"

She glanced at him with a faintly ironical lift of her brows.

"I forget you're a stranger here. I live with that screwy dame, in her father's house, over on St. John's Street across College Avenue. Miss Olive's ancestral mansion. Papa's been dead a thousand years but he still lives there. Or his ghost does. You know, it's crazy, but sometimes I think if she quotes the old gentleman again I'll scream. And her facts. I've learned more unrelated and inconsequential nonsense from her than I ever knew existed. Birds don't have any red or blue pigment in their feathers. I'll bet you didn't know that. It's just the light."

She closed her eyes and took a long deep breath.

"You go up Prince George Street to College Avenue. It's the little yellow brick house behind the State Archives Building."

Moving the long car around the curve and past the brick walk leading to his own front door in the wing, Jonas saw the midshipmen reflected in the mirror go up the steps, their white

39

caps off, and go on in. They looked like a pair of reluctant Job's comforters, one holding back for the other.

"You asked me about Tom. He's okay. Midshipman First Class, a three-striper if you know what that means. It means he's what they call high grease, a good all-around guy, academics and aptitude, one of the top midshipmen of the Brigade. He graduates this June."

She stopped a moment. Then she said less apathetically, "I hope to God *he's* not in trouble."

"What makes you think he is?"

Jonas asked it as casually as he could. He had been thinking about it more seriously than he would like Miss Van Holt to know.

"I've got eyes. Haven't you? Something's wrong. Usually that place swarms with midshipmen on liberty after Chapel Sunday noon. Tom's always home unless he has the duty, and you heard Professor Darrell tell Jenny she was lying because he had it yesterday. It didn't take microscopic powers of observation to see that both Jenny and Elizabeth were scared out of their wits. If you're a doctor, you ought to be able to see that as well as me. I'm just a writer, but it's my job to see things. Elizabeth was sitting on ground glass waiting for him to come. She forgot all about Miss Olive's making her look like a fool, springing the job business out in open meeting. Or didn't you notice that either?"

She gave him a mocking sidelong glance.

"Are you the strong silent type, Dr. Smith? Or is it just the extension of your bedside manner, acquired with long years of suffering and patience?"

"Meaning, Miss Van Holt . . . ?"

"Meaning you didn't open your mouth twice at the Darrells'. You just sat like a——"

"Bump on a log, is the usual——"

"I avoid the usual as much as possible, doctor. That doesn't apply, anyway. You're alive. I don't think you miss much. That's why I'd like you to be on my side in what I'm going to do."

"What are you going to do?"

She was silent for a moment. "I haven't figured that one out yet. When I do I'll let you know. Turn right. That's the house down there. Couldn't you guess it even if you didn't know?"

Jonas drew up in front of a small weatherbeaten yellow brick house half hidden in a snowy avalanche of silver moon roses, the white picket fence a misty cloud of blue and violet irises.

40

"I thought it and Miss Olive were enchantingly picturesque, when I perjured my soul to get her to rent me two rooms," Philippa said moodily. "I told her I was one of *the* Van Holts, whoever the hell they are. They must be okay, she even lets her maid get breakfast for me. And I'm allowed Papa's sanctum to receive my . . . my gentlemen guests in."

She caught her breath in a quick laugh that was more like a sob than laughter, and fumbled in her bag for her key. Before she got it in the lock the door opened. A colored maid with her hat and coat on stood aside for them to come in.

"There's somebody here to see you, Miss Van Holt," she said stolidly. "He's waiting in the library. I detained myself from a previous engagement to go to church. He wouldn't go, and Miss Olive don't want strangers messing around in her things when she's out."

"Thank you, Elsie."

Philippa took a dollar bill out of her bag. The girl took it, only partly mollified, and went on out, letting the screen door bang behind her.

"I think Elsie knows I'm not one of *the* Van Holts," Philippa remarked. "And about Gordon, too. It's funny how much they know, isn't it?"

Jonas opened the door. It was an idea that had crossed his own mind at the Darrells' as he'd watched the immaculate and aristocratic figure of old Wetherby.

"This is the library. It's where Papa's ghost——"

Philippa pushed open the small door at the left of the narrow hall next to the wrought-iron umbrella stand.

"Oh," she said. She stood poised, half-way across the worn threshold. "Oh," she said again.

Jonas Smith came to an abrupt stop behind her. He caught his breath. It took all the self-control he could muster not to do more. Before, he had merely looked over Philippa Van Holt's sleek perfumed shoulder. He stared over it now, at the man who was standing motionless behind the marble-topped table in the center of the room. It was a ghost standing there, but not the ghost of Miss Olive's father. The man was very tall and strikingly handsome, with a suntanned face and wavy blond hair. Jonas's eyes went mechanically down to his hand, to see if he still wore the green scarab ring and the gold bracelet. He had last seen this ghost lying in a pool of his own blood, quite dead, on the green-tiled floor of the Milnors' cottage on Arundel Creek. Gordon Darcy then wore expensive and perfectly tai-

41

lored evening clothes. His ghost had somehow changed to a blue chalk-stripe business suit, as expensive looking and as perfectly tailored.

"I thought buzzards only operated from a sense of sight," Philippa Van Holt said calmly. "It's one of Miss Olive's favorite cut-out facts."

She went on into the room. The brown eyes of the man behind the table moved with her until she said, "Dr. Jonas Smith . . . my brother-in-law Gordon—I mean Franklin—Grymes. And Grymes is their name, not Darcy. Dr. Smith, Mr. Grymes."

6

"How do you do?" Jonas said. He spoke as calmly as he could, hoping his recovery was quick and adequate. As he had never, so far as Philippa Van Holt knew, seen the dead man, a startled amazement at seeing his living replica could only seem strange to her to say the least. To his relief, Franklin Grymes gave him a look almost as startled as his own.

"I see you people have heard about each other," Philippa said easily. She put her bag and gloves on the table. "I didn't know people like Agatha Reed told their old beaux about their new ones and vice versa."

"Leave Miss Reed out of this, Philippa."

Jonas breathed an inward sigh of relief. If Franklin Grymes was engaged to Agatha Reed, if that fact explained his shocked surprise to Philippa's satisfaction, it was very good with him.

"Congratulations," he said, with no regrets at all.

"Thank you." Grymes turned back to his sister-in-law. "What's happened, Philippa? What are the police doing in Gordon's room?"

"You haven't heard? You were down at his hotel room and didn't ask anybody?"

"Damn it, Philippa, of course I asked." His face turned a slow brick-red. "I asked, but you know what hotels are like. They don't want anybody to know if there's been trouble. I didn't want to get mixed up with the police until I found out what the hell's going on."

"Affectionate brother and faithful friend," Philippa said deliberately. "It wouldn't be because . . ."

She looked at him in silent appraisal for a moment.

"You know one of Miss Olive's facts?"

"Who the hell is Miss Olive? What——"

"Keep your temper, darling. Miss Olive's my landlady. She knows a lot of facts. Not of life but about it. One of them might be interesting to you. Even to the police—who knows?"

She shrugged her shoulders lightly.

"It's about fingerprints. The right hand prints of identical twins resemble each other much more closely than the right and left hand prints of the same individual twin. That's interesting, isn't it? She read it in a book."

The Gothic walnut clock on the mantel, under the portrait of a forbidding and tight-lipped gentleman with a bald head and mutton-chop whiskers, ticked loudly and ominously in the silence there in the small room. Grymes was looking at his sister-in-law, his eyes narrowed. He looked steadily at her, the clock beating a deliberate tick, tock, once to every twice Jonas could count the pulse beat in the vein along his right temple. Philippa looked at him as steadily. The animosity between the two was as alive and as feline as the grey tiger cat who had been lying on the window seat in the sun and was now rising, arching its back, sharpening its claws on the linen cushion it had been lying on.

Franklin Grymes broke the silence.

"Just what in the hell do you think you mean by that, Philippa?"

He spoke slowly and distinctly. There was a dangerous quiet about his voice that was as ominous as the clock ticking in the silence had been before.

"I don't mean anything, dear." Philippa's voice was even. "Miss Olive's facts never mean anything. They're always unconnected with anything that's going on at the time she produces them. I'm keeping in the tradition. Any implication is in the mind of the hearer. However, if it should be of any interest to you—since you yourself are an identical twin—let me be the first to tell you that your brother's fingerprints are a matter of public record."

She paused for an instant. "—I don't suppose he mentioned that to you when you had dinner with him last night, did he?"

Franklin Grymes had not taken his burning eyes off her face.

"You devil," he said softly. "You she devil."

"All right! Call me a devil if you like!"

She turned on him as if he had lashed her into the proof of it.

"But my husband's dead! Somebody killed him! And if you cared anything about him you wouldn't be here now. You wouldn't have sneaked away from his hotel room and come here! If you'd cared about anybody but yourself you'd have gone straight to the police where I'm going now. You were down here last night and you're down here now. Where were you the rest of the time?"

"I was in Baltimore. I can prove it!"

"You needn't shout it at me."

Her tone was suddenly so matter-of-fact that it made him seem to be shouting much louder than he was.

"You don't have to prove anything to me. It's the police who'll want proof, not me. And Dr. Jonas Smith isn't interested in our little family quarrels. Unless he thinks he'd better warn Miss Agatha Reed what a . . . Oh well, the hell with it."

She broke off and went quickly to the door.

"I'm going to change my dress, and then I'm going to the police. Dr. Smith is going with me. You can go wherever you like. Back to the hotel room if you think it'll do you any good. But get out of my sight. I don't want ever to see you again. You look like him, but you're not like him. And I can't bear it. Do you hear? Get out! Get out of this house!"

Jonas heard her heels clicking madly up the steps, a door slam, a chair crash to the floor as she stumbled blindly over it. Then there was silence, and the clock ticking again. He looked back. Grymes had slumped down in the chair and put his head forward in his hands on the table. He was crying, his shoulders shaking with the dry sobs that racked his body.

He raised his face suddenly. There was something terrible in the hag-ridden despair that corroded it.

"It's a damned lie. I did care about him. I cared a lot about him. He was a . . . a so-and-so in lots of ways, but we got got along. He and I got along. We understood each other. But that she-devil up there . . . she's got me. She's got me, doctor. I tell you, she's got me. And she'll ruin me. That's what she's after. I know——"

He got up and went drunkenly to the door, remembered his hat on the chair by the table, came back and got it and went to the front door and out.

Jonas stood there. The tiger cat rubbed affectionately back

and forth against his legs, purring like a small successful witch. It was a hellish brew of some kind steaming in the Grymes-Van Holt cauldron. What, in the name of anything sensible or reasonable, he thought, was going on? It was bad about Grymes. He'd look back on the scene he'd put on with an intense and hideous embarrassment. And what was it all for? What did it mean?

He went over to the crowded mantel to look at the pictures on it. As Philippa had said, the Grymes' family quarrels were no business of his. There was a photograph of a midshipman inscribed "To Miss Olive from Tom." He picked it up, took it over to the window and looked at it in the light. That it was Midshipman Thomas Darrell there was not much doubt. The resemblance between him and his sister Elizabeth was as strong as the contrast between the two of them and the dark elf-cum-gypsy that was their younger sister. He was blond, clean-cut and serious-eyed, with a look of pride and dependability that was good to see.

Jonas looked at it, so absorbed in thinking about what this day's reaction to what had happened out at Arundel Creek would be to a young man with a face as open and straightforward as this that he did not hear Philippa Van Holt until she was there beside him.

"You think something's happened to him too, don't you?" she asked soberly. "I don't know what it could be that would be too serious. He wouldn't be unsat in academics, he's too bright and he works too hard. He wouldn't lie. That's serious, over the wall. He might have a girl and he might have married her and they found it out. But I've never heard of him having any particular girl. Or he could have frenched out and got caught. That's what they call being out at unauthorized hours. But that's sort of out of style, I'm told, since the new superintendent decided midshipmen should be treated like intelligent adults and relaxed a lot of the old rules. They have so much liberty now they don't have to play games with the Jimmylegs."

She put the photograph back on the mantel.

"I certainly hope that boy isn't in trouble. He really wants to be a naval officer. His father was a captain, killed in the Battle of Midway. Their mother died a long time ago. I don't know much about her. Of course Professor Darrell is sort of an anachronism—or he would be anywhere but Annapolis. He spends his mornings at the Annapolitan Club, his afternoons between the Yacht Club and the Alumni House and his evenings between the Yacht Club and the Annapolitan Club. He was a professor of mathematics two years in the last war at the Naval Academy and a year afterwards at St. John's College. Otherwise I don't suppose he's done a lick of work in his life. And he's a perfect stinker to poor little Jenny. Sometimes I want to cry when he bellows at her, and when I see her watching him like the adoration of the magi."

She broke off, drew her breath in sharply, put her foot up on the chair and scratched her slim and elegant leg.

"And very nice too," Jonas remarked.

"Man speaking or doctor?" She laughed. "Don't get me wrong. Just take a look out back. If I'm ever drowned you'll know where. This fantastic female I live with has a fish pond that breeds mosquitoes the size of jaguars. The fish are why you'll see her—and me, for God's sake—out walking this damned cat on a string. I walk it when Miss Olive baby-sits and cuts out facts. And let's get out before she flits in."

Jonas looked out the back window at the border of iris and peonies along the uneven brick walk. At the end of the garden he could see the pond under lilac and syringa bushes.

"Or if Miss Olive and the cat are drowned . . ."

The telephone rang in the hall.

"I'd better answer it. It might be the police, if Franklin got up nerve enough . . ."

He heard her say, "Hello. Why yes, he *is* here. Would you like to speak to him?" Her voice changed to instant concern. "Oh, no!"

Jonas went toward her. She shook her head at him, listening.

"Oh my dear, I'm terribly sorry. I know he'll come. He'll be there in about three minutes."

She put the phone down and snatched up her bag. "Quickly. Professor Darrell's had a stroke or something. Dr. Pardee's out in the country having a baby. She wants you, if you'll come. I'll drive you."

The screen door slammed behind them as they ran down the steps. She started the car, backed it and brought it around with a skill and efficiency that Jonas noticed admiringly in spite of his concern.

"It was bound to happen sooner or later, wasn't it?"

They shot out into College Avenue, turned down Prince George Street, and were at Blanton-Darrell Court in less than the three minutes.

"I'll stop at the gate, it'll save time," Philippa said. "I'll go on alone. Don't worry about me. The living are more important than the dead. But may I come over and see you later? I can't bear the idea of Miss Olive this evening."

"Sure, come ahead," Jonas said. "And thanks."

He slammed the car door shut, dashed into the Court and into his own house to get his bag. Miss Van Holt was right, of course. It was bound to happen sooner or later. The bulbous nose, the swelling vein in the old man's temple when he flared up about Jenny and the Sunday paper, the glaring old eyes, were all signs, to say nothing of Wetherby's "black as your heart is, you best watch yourself." More gravely concerning, to Jonas's mind, was what might have brought this on.

"Oh, thanks for coming!"

Elizabeth met him in the hall. She was almost as pale as the white sharkskin dress she wore.

"He's in here. We haven't tried to move him."

Jonas had already heard the thick stertorous breathing. Professor Darrell was lying unconscious in the middle of the floor in the room Jonas had been in. As he went quickly to him he was aware of the shocked and frightened faces of the two midshipmen standing helplessly in the background, and Jenny hunched into a small paralyzed knot of terror in a corner of the love seat. Wetherby was kneeling on the floor. "—It's all right, Professor, sir. The doctor here now. He young, but he here, sir, that's one consolation. You ain' goin' to die. God ain' got no use for you, not yet he ain', nor the devil ain'."

As Jonas looked at the suffused apoplectic face, purple membranes and the cyanotic stain darkening the finger nails he was not so sure.

"Let's get him to bed," he said. He motioned to the midshipmen.

"In his own room, if you can make it," Elizabeth said quickly. "It's ready." She took Jonas's bag. "Stay down here, Jenny, and wait for Tom."

The midshipmen and Jonas carried him up the broad stairway.

"I guess it's my fault," one of them mumbled unhappily. "All I did was tell him Tom was in a jam and confined to his room. I guess I should have waited. It's my——"

"No it isn't, George," Elizabeth said. "He had to be told."

In a corner room overlooking the back garden they lifted him onto the fourposter bed. Wetherby got the old man out of his seersucker suit.

"Have you left word for Dr. Pardee?"

Elizabeth nodded. "I talked to him. He said he wouldn't come. He's always said it was going to happen, and he wouldn't come when it did. But he'll be here. He and Grandfather quarrel, but they're old friends really. He's tried for years to make Grandfather behave himself."

She watched the needle of the dial of the blood pressure apparatus as Jonas listened to the pumping heart. Her hands were tightly clenched at her sides. The pale light from the darkened window behind her transformed her hair into a smooth softly golden cap.

"How old is he, Miss Darrell?"

"Seventy-three his last birthday."

"Is this the first——"

"He's never been sick a day in his life. That's why he thinks all doctors are fools. They always said this would happen and it never has, before."

Her eyes followed him, poignantly questioning, as he put his stethoscope back in his bag. Even in the darkened room her fragile lovely face stood out with startling purity above the grotesque and terrible figure of the old man on the bed, his powerful chest heaving, his purple lips emitting their drunken snores. It was at that moment that Jonas Smith knew he was deeply, and with no possibility of turning back from it, truly in love with her. His hands trembled as he closed his bag. It was a different thing from what had happened to him the night before, as different as the reflected image of her in the mirror was to her real and actual presence there across the width of the bed from him now. It was an intense and acutely physical awareness of her that quivered and burned in every nerve and pulse of his body and surged up in a blinding tenderness, a desire to go to her and take her in his arms, to comfort her and give her hope. Or what hope he could give her of the kind she needed then with the shadow of death there between them.

"Is he . . . Dr. Smith, will my grandfather . . . ?"

He steadied himself at the desperate appeal in her voice.

"I can't tell you." He was surprised to find his own voice as normal and professionally matter-of-fact as if nothing had happened to him at all. "We'll have to wait until he's conscious to see. He may not regain consciousness. You've got to prepare yourself for that. It may be a cerebral apoplexy, though as far as I can tell now there isn't any extensive paralysis at this point. It may come from an oedema in the brain—if you want the

48

technical language—or a cerebral angiospasm he may or may not get over. It has happened that people do come out of it. We just have to wait, Miss Darrell. There's nothing to do but keep him quiet and get fluids into him. Give him expectant care. Keep him from biting his tongue or choking on it. We ought to get a nurse."

"I can take care of him, Wetherby and I together. It'd be much worse if he woke up and found a stranger here. He'd fly into another rage."

"Was that what——"

She nodded as Jonas hesitated.

"He got infuriated when——"

She broke off, her eyes widening in sudden alarm. Jonas heard steps hurrying up the stairs, a man's voice.

"Jenny! What are you doing here?"

"I'm just waiting for you. Oh, Tom, it's all my fault. I've killed him too. I have! And oh, Tom, what I've done to you! Oh, Tom, Tom!"

Elizabeth was around the end of the bed like a flashing gold-tipped arrow, her face white, her eyes drained as grey as a rain-washed hyacinth.

Jonas took a quick step and caught her arm. "Elizabeth!" She had thrown the door open. In the hall just outside Jenny was held in her brother's arms, her dark head buried against his shoulder, sobbing wildly, her whole small body shaking and tormented.

"—I've killed Grandfather too. I've killed him too! First Gordon——"

"Stop her, Tom—make her stop! She doesn't know what she's saying!"

The midshipman's face was white as he stared over the girl's dark head at Jonas Smith and beyond him at the bed. He was as tall as Jonas, older looking than in the photograph on Miss Olive's mantel, and he was the man Jonas had seen at the cottage. There was no possible mistake. He was the man out there in the ensign's uniform.

Tom Darrell put his hand gently over Jenny's mouth, picked her up and carried her a few steps down the hall and into her room. Elizabeth turned back to Jonas, her breath coming in frightened gasps.

"It . . . she doesn't know what she's saying . . ."

The midshipman appeared in the doorway, strode past them to the bed, looked down at his grandfather for an instant, went to the window and stood there, his back to them. He turned in a moment and looked at Jonas. His jaw was set, his eyes steady.

"Who is this, Elizabeth?"

"Dr. Smith. Dr. Jonas Smith. My brother, Tom Darrell."

The men's eyes met in an unwavering scrutiny. The midshipman was broad-shouldered, erect in the blue uniform with the insignia of the First Class. The stripes that should have marked his rank of honor were no longer on his sleeve.

Elizabeth took an uncertain step toward him. "Tom . . . what happened?"

His eyes moved from Jonas to her, and back again.

"I frenched out last night. There was a girl I wanted to see. I was Midshipman Officer of the Watch. I left as soon as I secured Bancroft Hall. I saw her and came back. I'd have got away with it, but a fellow on a visiting team went out on a party and got drunk. He kicked up such a row when he got in that the Officer of the Day sent for me. I wasn't in my room. I came back through the gate and the Jimmylegs were waiting for me. I'd put on my ensign's uniform to get out, I was impersonating an officer. I was on duty and deserted my post. I'm through, Elizabeth. The Commandant let me out for two hours to see Grandfather. I've got to go back to my room and report to the Main Office every hour. They may let me come and see him tomorrow. But I'm out."

As Elizabeth turned away Jonas saw the tears in her eyes.

"—If you told the Commandant the truth, Darrell . . ." he said.

"I've told the truth, Dr. Smith. I went out to see a girl. I saw her. I got caught. That's the truth. It wouldn't be healthy even for a doctor to make any mistake about it. If you'll excuse me, I want to see Jenny before I go back to Bancroft Hall."

He started to the door. Jonas stepped in front of it.

"I meant the whole truth," he said. "Don't you people think all this is a pretty steep price to pay for one late date?"

7

"—Wickedly and damnably steep," Jonas Smith said deliberately.

He looked from one of them to the other. He couldn't tell which was the more staggered—the young midshipman totally unprepared for the blow, or his sister, in spite of everything not prepared for the crushing completeness of it. How she could have allowed herself to cling to any hope or deluded herself into believing there could be any, after the incident of the beach bag and what had gone on for the last hour and a half in her grandfather's living room, Jonas had no idea. That she had done it was poignantly clear as she reached out unsteadily for the mahogany bedpost to steady herself, in her parted lips and the look of shocked dismay she fixed on him.

The midshipman caught himself quickly after one speechless instant. His shoulders stiffened.

"We don't know what you're talking about, Dr. Smith." He spoke with a surprising composure that would have been more convincing if it had not been for the warning glance he shot his sister. "I think you must have got all mixed up somewhere, doctor."

"That . . . is right," Jonas said. He wondered what either of them would do, knowing how mixed up he really had got. "Not the way you think. If you don't know what I'm talking about I'll be glad to explain. The sooner the better." He turned to Elizabeth Darrell. "If you'll get Wetherby back here to stay with your grandfather I'll do it right now. Is there some place we can go where there won't be people listening in?"

He saw an evanescent spark of hope spring up in her eyes and die a small cold death as she caught another of her brother's swift warning glances. For an instant she'd been ready to trust him. The instant was gone, with little hope of its returning. Jonas was aware of it even more sharply a moment later as he went through a narrow passage off the old man's room into a small crowded study and heard Tom Darrell's quick whisper behind him:

"Watch it. Could be a trap. What do you know about him?"

Nothing, of course. They knew nothing about him—Tom less than Elizabeth if her brief impulse toward faith in him had been what Jonas wanted to believe it was, an instinctive if as yet unconscious response to his own emotion about her. So profoundly was he moved by it himself that he didn't see how there could help be some communication of it, no matter how tenuous, between them. But as Tom closed the door and Elizabeth went over to the window and turned to face him again, there was nothing left to indicate it. All there was between them was a blank defensive wall, invisible but as tangibly real as if it had had both substance and shadow of its own.

"I mean this," he said quietly. "I was at the Fergusons' cottage when Jenny came there to phone for you last night, or this morning rather."

He kept his eyes on Tom Darrell, standing with his shoulders back against the mahogany door, his hand still behind him holding the knob. He was acutely aware of Elizabeth without having to look at her.

Neither of them moved.

"I was out on the pier when they first came. What she told you, about the car keys and the telephone, is true. When she rowed over, I saw her change her dress and leave her own in Natalie Ferguson's beach bag. I didn't speak to her because I didn't want to frighten her any worse than she was frightened already. I followed her back to the Milnors'. I didn't know who Jenny was or who Gordon Darcy was, and I didn't know he was dead. I thought there'd been trouble—he'd passed out or something—and I'd stick around until you showed up . . . just in case. I was there when you two came. I didn't know who you were either, but I heard your first names. I saw what you did, Darrell, and I heard what all of you said. I saw you leave.

"As your sister can tell you, I brought the beach bag in town. She saw it in my place and took Jenny's dress and slippers out of it when she came to get something to get Jenny to sleep. Which is how I found out you're my next door neighbors."

The midshipman's eyes left him for the first time. He felt rather than saw the imperceptible nod Elizabeth gave him.

"Before I walked out with the beach bag, I called up the operator. She called the police. I haven't seen them yet. I'm as much an accessory after the fact of murder as the two of you are."

"It was not murder! She——"

"Shut up, Elizabeth."

Tom Darrell cut her off without moving his eyes from Jonas's. There was a stubborn determined light in them that was not so disquieting as something else there that Jonas was aware of but could not give a precise name to. It was in his voice as he said, "Go ahead, doctor. You wanted to talk. We're listening."

"I'm going ahead."

Jonas resisted the temptation that rose with a slight flush of adrenalin to add ". . . you damned young fool." Tom Darrell spoke with a controlled but determined hostility that seemed misplaced.

"I'm telling you all this is too steep a price to pay for one late date. If Solomon had one with the Queen of Sheba it would be too steep. Gordon Darcy Grymes has paid it one way. Your grandfather another. Now you. They've taken your star and your extra stripes off. You're going to sit tight and let them take your uniform off and kick you out of the Academy two weeks before you graduate. You're going to let your whole career be wrecked before you start it. What for?"

He would have been glad if one or the other of them had said what for, so he would sound less like a sententious ass. But neither did. The silence in the room was stony and uncompromising. He had a second temptation to say "Oh, what the hell" and skip the whole thing. If it was the sort of thing that could be skipped and done with . . . It seemed clear already that he was going to get the cooperation and gratitude he'd get trying to help untrap a trapped porcupine.

"I'll tell you then.—For a concept that went out with crinolines."

He saw the hot flush that stained Elizabeth's cheek and the quick tightening in Tom Darrell's already hard tight jaw.

"You may think it's a concept that's gone out, Dr. Smith. We happen not to. Gordon——"

"Look," Jonas said patiently. "We're not talking about the same thing, Miss Darrell. I'm not talking about Gordon Darcy Grymes. He's dead. He was a heel, he had it coming to him. That's that. What I'm talking about is what happens now. I'm trying to get both of you to use a little common sense. Your brother's trying to bull it through and wreck his career. I'm telling you Jenny was right last night. Everything she told you was true. And I don't know who the State's Attorney is, but he's a Marylander, either by birth or adoption, and he feels the way Marylanders do or he wouldn't be in the job. Call him up.

Take Jenny to see him, let her tell him the whole story. Even if it does have to go to the Grand Jury and get out in the papers, it's not going to hurt her as much as it's already hurt your grandfather. And not half as much as it's going to hurt your brother here if he's kicked out of the Naval Academy two weeks before he graduates. It won't hurt Jenny herself as much as what you're trying to do will, in the long run."

He was angry and getting angrier. He knew it was stupid. He was being as irrational in his way as they were in theirs. And at least they were keeping their mouths shut while he was going on sounding off with no visible effect except to increase the tension and make the defensive wall between them and him higher and more solidly opaque. It also convinced him more firmly of the truth of what he was saying. That he wasn't convincing them was very apparent. All he was doing was driving them, more stubbornly unyielding than ever, closer together behind the invisible wall. The stormy protest darkening Elizabeth's eyes blue sooty-black was evidence of that. Where he had ever got the idea of hyacinth tranquillity and lovely repose in connection with her was beyond him at the moment. She was exactly like the rest of them. They were all hot-tempered, stiff-necked and stubborn, putty in nobody's hands— even the youngest, as Gordon Darcy Grymes had found out to his surprise.

To his great surprise, in fact. The look on the dead man's face flashed across Jonas's mind again, as perplexing and disquieting then as it had been in the early hours of the morning. It didn't change any of the known facts, or make what he was saying less sensible, or Elizabeth or Tom Darrell any the more sweetly reasonable.

"—That's what I'm talking about," he said more quietly. "That's the concept I mean that went out with crinolines—that a gal couldn't defend herself without a lot of Grundys pointing their finger at her all the rest of her life. And if you hush this up now, all of you'll go on living in fear that some day it's going to crop up—just when it can really hurt her. It's a hell of a lot better to let her go through with it now and get it over and done with, and forget it, than it is to keep it a secret and let it turn into some kind of a guilt complex, and maybe make a first-rate neuropsychotic out of her.—If you can get away with it, that is."

He looked steadily at them for an instant. "You've forgotten Philippa Van Holt. She's out for blood, and she's plenty smart.

54

You might as well try playing around with a load of hot isotopes as fool yourself you're covering anything up when she's around."

He took his pipe out of his pocket and stuck it between his teeth in a gesture of finality. "Well, that's my say and I've said it."

"—And for a minute in there I thought you might be going to help us."

The tinge of ironic contempt in Elizabeth's voice made him flush with sudden anger.

"And you're both too pig-headed," he said deliberately, "to see that's what I'm doing. What's done can't be helped. It's too late to help your grandfather. It's not too late to keep your brother from wrecking his career as a naval officer just because a cockeyed sense of chivalry——"

"—Went out with crinolines," Elizabeth interrupted coolly. "Go on."

"I'm going on. In the first place, you haven't got a China-man's chance of getting away with it. Your brother's on the point of being kicked out of the Naval Academy for deserting his post on duty, frenching out, impersonating an officer, and a whole flock of Class A offences. What do you think'll happen to him when they find out he's an accessory after the fact of murder?"

"It wasn't murder. If anybody tosses you a gun and says shoot me or else and you shoot to protect yourself, it certainly is not murder! And I know he . . . Gordon did that same thing to me—one night on the road coming back from Washington. Only I'm older than Jenny and I tossed it back to him and told him not to be a fool. I was sure it wasn't loaded anyway. It was one of those fancy mother-of-pearl and silver jobs. This time it was a real one and it was loaded. That's the——"

"—Will you shut up, Elizabeth?"

Tom Darrell looked at Jonas with tight-lipped hostility.

"Listen, doctor. I told you we don't know what you're talking about. That's the way it still is. The minute we get out of this room we've never heard of what you're talking about. Get that, doctor. If you saw a murder and walked out of it that's some-thing for you to explain—not us. You say this guy had it com-ing to him. How do you know, doctor? What were you doing hanging around? Why did you duck out so fast? Who are you trying to cover up for? Not us. You don't know us. You never heard of us before. You talk about cockeyed notions of chiv-

55

alry, so that's not the reason you're pretending you want to help us, is it? It doesn't matter a damn to you whether I'm a naval officer or a garbage collector. Maybe there's some other reason you're so interested in what you call getting it over and done with? You seem mighty anxious to have somebody else whip up to the State's attorney and take the rap. Maybe it's you trying to get us to help you, doctor, not——"

"——Oh, Tom!"

Jonas heard the shocked protest in the girl's voice as her brother's meaning became too clear for her any longer to be blind to it. It had been clear to Jonas from the first words. He could neither mistake it nor, he thought with a certain amount of sardonic amusement, particularly object to it. It had been the known and no doubt well deserved fate of the Good Samaritan since the beginning of time. Furthermore, on the face of it, and from anybody else's point of view, it was a perfectly sound hypothesis. The reason that he could regard it, with a dispassionate if wry detachment, as of no real importance to himself, was simple. He had so completely forgotten Agatha Reed that it never crossed his mind that anyone would through her make any further connection between him and one of a pair of identical twins. At the moment he could stand there objectively and listen to the case being presented against him with what Mark Twain called the calm confidence of a Christian with four aces.

And more than that. The fact that Elizabeth Darrell's quick volatile anger, directed against him a few seconds earlier, was now after her first shocked protest directed at her brother Tom in defence of himself, was altogether satisfactory to Jonas Smith.

"Tom—stop it!" She flashed across the worn turkey rug and took hold of his arm. "You're being a complete fool, Tom! You're practically accusing Dr. Smith——"

"So what? And why not?" He ignored her hand on his arm, and looked coolly at Jonas. "What do we know about him? How do we know that what Jenny said is true? How do we know she wasn't too scared to know what really happened? I don't see any reason to trust somebody we never saw before—especially a guy that's so anxious to have a seventeen-year old kid dragged through the courts and her name on the front page of every newspaper in the country."

He turned back to his sister.

"Don't call me a fool until you think it over a minute, Sis.

Maybe I have a cockeyed sense of chivalry, but it's not as cockeyed as all that."

Jonas saw Elizabeth's fingers relax and slowly release their grip. She let her hand drop to her side. As her eyes met his he saw the confidence in them change into a bewildered and questioning incredulity. The small seed of doubt her brother had planted was still dormant, but he knew enough to know that no faster growing or hardier perennial is cultivated in the female mind.

"You don't believe that, do you, Miss Darrell?" he asked quietly.

"No. I don't believe it . . . not really. I . . . I don't believe it at all."

He saw her swallow and moisten her lips slightly as she looked away from him. If the small seed could sprout that quickly in his own presence . . . He felt a small sinking sensation in the middle of his stomach as he thought what it would do when he was gone and she had a lot more time to spend on it.

"It's absurd," she said slowly.

The necessity she felt to go on saying it was the most convincing proof she could have offered that she was no longer sure.

"It doesn't matter whether she believes it or not," Tom Darrell said deliberately. "It's what a smart lawyer's going to be able to make of it if you drag my sister into court."

"Oh, for the love of God," Jonas said. He turned in exasperated weariness to him. "Look, you dope——"

"Listen!" Elizabeth cut him off quickly, ran across the room to the other door and stood a moment. "It's Dr. Pardee." She opened the door and ran out into the hall. "Oh, I'm so glad you're here!"

Jonas shrugged. "She doesn't even trust me as a doctor, now," he thought. He started to follow her. As he moved, Tom Darrell spoke again.

"Let's get this straight, Dr. Smith."

"I've got it straight. Don't worry," Jonas said patiently. "As soon as you get it that way, let me know. I answer both day and night calls. And I think maybe if we could get together on this, we might be able to figure something out. Like why the gun was loaded this time, for instance. If that was the guy's routine in his love making."

"That's just what I've been thinking about myself, Dr. Smith."

Jonas turned, startled, and stared at Tom Darrell. His mouth widened suddenly into a broad grin.

"Okay—if that's the way you feel about it. But it would save wear and tear if you'd just get it through your thick skull that my interest in this is the same as yours . . . even if my reasons are different."

"Reasons?"

"Yes—reasons."

"If you've got any, let's have them."

Jonas looked at him for a moment.

"Arrogance is not a virtue in dealing with civilians, Mr. Darrell," he said imperturbably. "Nor is impertinence. Which I'm sure they teach you on the other side of the wall. If they teach you any good books, maybe you've heard of an old bird named Falstaff. He wouldn't give his reasons under compulsion—not if they were thick as blackberries. I'm the same way. What's more, mine are strictly my own business. Though if you'll come down off your high horse they oughtn't to be too hard even for you to figure out. So, if you'll get out of the way, I'll go in and see Dr. Pardee."

He said "Thanks," as Tom Darrell stepped silently aside, and opened the door. Through the passage he heard the heavy labored snoring of the old man on the four poster bed. His conscience suddenly bothered him. Maybe he'd been too rough on the young devil. After all, he was a first classman. Everybody knew a midshipman would never again be as important, even when he was a five-star admiral, as he was in his last year at the Naval Academy. It wasn't his fault, maybe, if he seemed stiff-necked and arrogant to the eye of a lowly reserve officer back in civilian life. And he was in trouble.

Jonas turned and looked back. Midshipman Darrell was still standing by the door, but there was nothing any longer arrogant or stiff-necked about him. His younger sister had crept noiselessly in from the hall. His arms were around her, his chin on the top of her small dark head, his eyes closed . . . a boy whose private universe was shattered, falling about him, trying to be a man when breaking down and being a boy would have been more natural—and more therapeutic, thought Jonas Smith, M.D.

"—It's okay, Jenny—don't worry, kid. It's going to work out. Just leave it to me, baby."

Jonas went into the old man's room and pulled the passage door softly to behind him. Elizabeth and Dr. Pardee were beside the bed. They both turned. Dr. Pardee gave him a searching diagnostic survey over the silver rim of his glasses.

"Don't take it so hard, doctor."

He was small, brisk and immaculate, with white hair and a white tuft of hair under his lower lip. He snapped his words out as if the race of mankind was a personal irritant to him and the sicker they were the more irritating.

"There's nothing you could have done. If he hadn't been such a pig-headed sot he would have died in his bed like a Christian ten years ago. I've no doubt his liver is pink as a baby's. There's no justice in nature, and you'll never be as good a doctor as nature is. So let her take care of him. She always has, the old scoundrel. Elizabeth, give me another pillow. I think we can make him more comfortable. And you, young woman—what's the matter with you? If you don't take care of yourself you'll die before he does. You get out of here. I'll get you a nurse."

"No, I'll——"

"You'll do nothing of the kind." Dr. Pardee's goatee snapped out like a Christmas cracker. "You'll do exactly what I tell you to do."

"Yes, sir."

"—You have to bully the Darrells," Jonas thought. He made a note for future reference as he went over and picked up his bag. It was clear that neither Elizabeth or Dr. Pardee had any use either for him or his opinion.

"Well, I'll go along, sir." He started for the door.

Dr. Pardee shot him a shrewd critical glance.

"Go," he said. "But come back. He's all yours. I'm too old to waste my time taking care of people who won't take care of themselves. You're welcome to half a dozen more I've got just like him. And come and see me when you have time. I'll call you up when I get home. I want to talk to these young people now. Good-bye."

"And thank you, Dr. Smith."

Elizabeth's dismissal was not quite as peremptory as Dr. Pardee's, but it still left a great deal to be desired in terms of any warmth or enthusiasm. Jonas went down the stairs and out the front door strongly suspecting it was for the last time.

"Okay, and the hell with it," he thought irritably.

8

He went along the uneven brick walk under the living room windows that was a short cut to the wing. He was irritated at the Darrells, at Dr. Pardee, and also at himself. There was no use in even trying to pretend he'd made an imposing impression, either professionally or as self-appointed friend and advisor . . . or to pretend either that his ego was not slightly tattered as a result. Or, furthermore, that he could get Elizabeth Darrell out of his mind. She was all around him, in the violet haze that tinted the shafts of sunlight through the wisteria as he walked through the narrow arbor to his door, and in the squirming wound his pride was suffering that it wouldn't be suffering if he hadn't been trying to show her how wise and good he was. She was probably putting him down as a pompous self-righteous ass.

He came out from under the wisteria where the corner of the wing made an angle with his front door, and stopped abruptly. A man was sitting on the steps. How long he had been there Jonas had no way of telling, but he gave the impression of being prepared to remain indefinitely if necessary. He had an air of ease and competent authority.

"Dr. Jonas Smith?"

He rose without haste. Between thirty-five and forty, stockily built, with a ruddy complexion, searching hazel eyes and a determined chin, he looked intelligent, level-headed and capable.

"I'm Sergeant Digges of the Anne Arundel County Police. I'd like to ask you a few questions."

There it was, Jonas thought—as inevitable as it was simple and entirely matter-of-fact.

"All right, Sergeant. Come in, will you?"

He opened the door.

"You're new here, Dr. Smith?"

"That's right."

Sergeant Digges followed Jonas across the vestibule into the reception room. He looked around him.

"Mighty nice place you've got." He glanced at the wild fowl

60

pictures on the wall. "Nice prints. Do much shooting yourself, doctor?"

"Duck, and an occasional deer," Jonas said. "Not people, Sergeant, if that's what you could be getting at. I've patched up a good many, but I've never shot one."

Sergeant Digges moved through the door into the consulting room. He was ignoring what seemed to Jonas a very good opening if it was brass tacks he wanted to get down to. Time was apparently not of the essence in Sergeant Digges' method of interrogation. As he moved from a casual examination of the portrait of Jonas's father in his academic robes over the mantel to the bookcase along the wall, Jonas went to the french window behind his desk, opened it and let Roddy in.

"Mind if I feed my dog?"

"Go right ahead." Sergeant Digges was more than amiable. "Nice dog," he said. He followed Jonas through what had been the connecting pantry and was now the office wash room and utility closet into the kitchen.

"One of the colored watermen out at Arundel Creek said a long lean young fellow with a spotted hunting dog and a blue cross on his car had been staying at the Fergusons' place out there the last few days," he remarked.

"The last six," Jonas said.

He got a can of dog food off the shelf, opened it and put it in Roddy's dish under the sink. It occurred to him suddenly that he was hungry enough to eat it himself.

"Miss Van Holt said the description sort of fitted you. She said she didn't know about the dog, except you looked like you'd have one, and being a doctor you'd have the medical cross on. And you'd just moved into here. She said she didn't think you knew anything about the shooting, though."

Sergeant Digges strolled back into the consulting room. Jonas followed. He was looking again at the portrait over the mantel, and around the room.

"I like to see the places people live in. You get a sort of different slant on people when you do."

He looked at Jonas.

"Take you, for example. I'd put you down for a pretty square shooter, meeting you and seeing you in this kind of place. It's hard to figure why you'd let yourself get off on the wrong foot when you're just starting out down here. I've been trying to figure what you had in mind. Maybe you can tell me. Why didn't you stick around till we got out there last night,

61

doctor? After you called up. That's a fair question, isn't it?"

"Sure. It's a fair question," Jonas agreed. "I guess I figured I didn't want to start out all mixed up in a lot of police stuff. The guy was dead, and——"

"How well did you know him, Dr. Smith?"

"I didn't know him at all."

"You sure about that, doctor?"

"I certainly am."

Sergeant Digges sat down.

"That's one thing I wanted to find out about. In our business it's practically a rule that people who don't have any connection with the people who get in trouble are always the ones that want to help us out. Our problem's mostly how to get rid of them. Curiosity, plain or morbid, I guess you'd call it. Or they want excitement, or to feel important. It's one way we have of narrowing things down. It's the ones that clam up or just plain beat it that we figure must have some personal reason—or they'd be curious like everybody else. You see what I mean, doctor?"

"Sure," Jonas said. "I see all right. Except that you forget a dead body's no treat to me."

"Nor me either. But we've got our duty, doctor. Or don't you look at things that way?"

Jonas nodded. "I do. But——"

"Then why don't you come on out there with me now, and——"

Sergeant Digges broke off. "Looks like you've got company, doctor."

Jonas swung his chair abruptly around. Then he got quickly to his feet. It was Jenny Darrell, and it was too late to stop her. She had slipped through the wicket in the privet hedge that divided his small private garden from the larger grounds behind the Blanton-Darrell House and was already halfway to the brick terrace, her head turned, glancing back the way she had come with every possible outward sign that her visit was surreptitious in the extreme. She had something in her hand, covered up with a white napkin, and as she turned her head and saw Jonas standing in the long window she quickened her step. Her small face was pinched and all but lost, so that it looked nothing but pale eyes and scarlet mouth.

"I've brought you some sandwiches, Dr. Smith."

The words came out breathlessly, pell-mell.

"I hope they're all right. I made them myself. But you don't have to eat them. It's just an excuse, really, because I want to talk to you. I want to ask you——"

"I'm sorry, I've got company now." Jonas spoke brusquely, but he put his hand out for the plate. "But gee, thanks. That's darned sweet of you. I'm half starved."

Her startled glance had darted past him into the room. He saw her hands sink down at her sides and the tip of her tongue creep out to moisten her lips as she swallowed and blinked her long lashes, one foot moving back as she tried to edge away off the terrace.

"Hi there, Jenny."

Sergeant Digges had come to the corner of the desk.

"Hello, Mr. Digges."

She swallowed again and edged a step further away.

"I . . . I just brought Dr. Smith some sandwiches. I thought he . . . he probably didn't have any food in the house. And I wanted to ask him about Grandfather."

She looked up at Jonas, the corners of her mouth trembling. "—Help me out of this. Please help me . . ."

Her eyes appealed desperately as she hurried on.

"Nobody will tell me anything. Nobody'll let me help . . ."

"There's no way you can help, Jenny," Jonas said. "There's nothing any of us can do but wait."

"What's all this? What's the trouble?" Sergeant Digges took a step forward.

"Professor Darrell had a stroke this noon," Jonas said. "He's still unconscious. Dr. Pardee was with him when I left."

He turned back to Jenny.

"There's one thing you can do. Go home and stand by, and help keep the place quiet. So run along like a good girl and I'll see you later."

He lifted the edge of the napkin, took a sandwich and smiled down at her. "And thanks for these."

Then for a grim and awful moment his smile froze, and the bite of bread and cold roast chicken he'd taken froze, a dry lump, half-way down his throat. The girl in front of him was not leaving. She was staying. A subtle but determined change had come over her. As clearly as if it were written in neon lights above her head Jonas Smith read what was happening to her. She was making up her mind, slowly, stubbornly, and in open and outright defiance of her sister and her brother.

"Oh my Lord God," he thought, "—she's going to blurt out the whole thing . . ."

He groaned inwardly and with a sudden panicky sinking in the pit of his stomach. And he had to stop her. In spite of everything, including the fact that he had just barely got through advising her brother and sister it was the only intelligent and rational thing to do, he knew he had to find some way to stop her. Drawing herself up into a taut slender arrow of determined honesty, she was turning from him to Sergeant Digges, about to speak. His own impulse, blind and unreasoning compared to the straightforward simplicity of hers, was nevertheless immediate and compelling.

He saw her chin go up. "I think I'm just going to——"

"—to go home." He finished abruptly for her. "So scoot along, honey child." He thrust the plate of sandwiches aside into Sergeant Digges's unexpectant hand and took a firm but outwardly casual grip on her shoulder. He felt the tense quiver of protest that shot through her small rigid body as he turned her around and propelled her off the terrace and across the garden to the wicket in the hedge.

"Now shut up and go on," he said savagely under his breath as he opened the wicket and pushed her through. "—Scoot along, baby," he added cheerfully.

He closed the gate and fastened the latch. Sergeant Digges was in the open window, the plate still in his hand, watching him with a detached and he thought somewhat skeptical air. As Jonas reached the terrace he turned and set the plate down on the desk.

"Pretty young, isn't she?" he remarked dryly as Jonas came inside. "I thought it was middle-aged women that went all out for doctors."

Jonas stifled the hot impulse of anger that flared up in him. He shrugged and took another sandwich. Sergeant Digges was watching him impassively. Whether he seriously thought Jenny's visit had any personal or emotional significance Jonas couldn't tell. He knew it was better to ignore such a suggestion than give it possible credibility by making an issue of it.

"Or could it be there's something on her mind, Dr. Smith?"

"Plenty, would be my guess. It's touch and go whether her grandfather wakes up or not. That seems to me to be enough on anybody's mind."

"Maybe so. Only I've never heard about there being much love lost between Jenny and her grandpa."

"I guess you know them both better than I do, Sergeant," Jonas said. "I'm a stranger here myself."

"I expect I know 'em pretty well," Sergeant Digges remarked thoughtfully. "Well enough, I'd say, to make me sort of wonder if there could be some kind of connection between the old fellow having a stroke right after this fellow Darcy Grymes gets his. I'm not saying there is a connection, mind you. All I'm saying is it seems sort of funny it happened right now, after all these years he's been hell-raising around town and everybody saying it was going to happen and it never did. It's what you'd call a *re*-markable coincidence, doctor. Because the Professor he thinks Elizabeth's white with a blue rim around her . . . so I guess it could be quite a shock after the big rush this fellow Darcy Grymes's been giving her and all.—Elizabeth Darrell."

It wasn't until he repeated her first name and added her last that Jonas realized how abruptly he had halted his sandwich half-way to his mouth, or how blankly transparent the stare on his face must have been.

"But I see you know her too, doctor," Sergeant Digges remarked. "For a stranger it sure looks like you know how to get around places. In fact I wonder if you ought to *call* yourself a stranger, come to think of it. For a young fellow that's just been in town one night—or the part of one night that was left after there's been a pretty serious shooting—you sure know quite a few of the Three Hundred. Not that I'm saying any of you are *personally* mixed up. I'm not trying to do any of this psychological stuff. I don't have any use for it myself. I'm just an ordinary country policeman, doctor—working for a pretty hard-headed community that likes facts and doesn't like any of this fancy whoop-de-do they get by with in the movies and all. So, what do you say, doctor?"

Sergeant Digges picked up his hat from the floor beside his chair.

"What do you say we take a run out to the country now? And then maybe you'd like to make a statement. We figure it's always the best thing to get our facts down straight in black and white, so the State's Attorney knows what he's got to go on. The wheat from the chaff, like the preacher says."

He got to his feet. Roddy, alert to any move toward the outdoor world, bounded forward.

"Sure, you can come, boy."

Sergeant Digges reached down and patted his shoulder. "Never did like to see a field dog cooped up in the house all day, myself," he said. "Let's go, shall we?"

9

"Okay," Jonas said. "Come on, Roddy."

He had a momentary twinge of doubt about Sergeant Digges's beguiling pretense at being a friend and lover of all God's creatures whatsoever. His original impression of a shrewd and hard-bitten intelligence was only slightly clouded by all the meandering amiability that cloaked it. Brother to prince and fellow to beggar could be a dangerous technique. At the moment, however, and as applied to himself, it seemed so entirely reasonable that Jonas accepted it and in fact liked it. It was only when they had crossed College Creek leaving Annapolis on their way out to the country that it began to worry him again, although not for himself at all.

They were going down the hill to the Severn River Bridge, between the Naval Academy Hospital and Perry Circle on the old golf course.

"You know, people are funny, doctor," remarked Sergeant Digges. "I suppose you find that out in your business too. Window curtains, for instance. People see out through window curtains. They never seem to figure anybody else can see in through them. Then again you might say, well, why shouldn't they look out to see what's going on if they want to? You might say it's natural people'd be curious seeing a neighbor walk off with a policeman. I expect maybe you'd say it's just natural even young people'd be interested."

Up to then Jonas Smith had sincerely hoped Sergeant Digges had not spotted the two shadowy figures behind the white muslin curtains in the front bedroom of the Blanton-Darrell House as they left the wing to get in the police car. If he had spotted them he could hardly have failed to recognize Tom Darrell's navy blue uniform or Elizabeth Darrell's softly shining gold hair. Whether, having seen them and recognized them, he had gone beyond that and got the impression of watchful waiting and intense anxiety that Jonas had got, still was not clear.

"I guess it's natural," Jonas said. He kept his eyes straight

66

ahead of him on the narrow paved road. In the brilliant atmosphere the shadows of the trees and telephone poles along the rim of the old golf course stood out black and so physically well defined that they looked like solid obstructions thrown across the road. Perhaps the same thing was true of Sergeant Digges, and much of the seeming substance behind his casual comments was not substance but shadow without substance, the substance being only in Jonas's mind because he had special knowledge that made the shadows seem real when they were not. If he made the mistake of assuming that innuendo was fact, he would find himself walking neatly and directly into the psychological trap that Sergeant Digges, pretending he had no use for it as a plain ordinary country cop, had been assiduously baiting from the moment he walked into Jonas's house.

"It's certainly a mighty pretty day," Sergeant Digges said. "I'd figured on going fishing myself this morning."

He spoke with the air of a wistful ruminant as they crossed the Bridge. Men and women, young and old, fat and thin, were leaning over the parapet, their lines in the blue water below.

"I could have, if people had stuck around last night. Stuck around and told the truth. Now I've got to take it step by step. I'm counting on you to help me, doctor. I guess we'll start at the Ferguson place if that's okay with you."

He turned off the Ferry Road in a few minutes onto the dirt road leading to the creek. As they bounced over the corduroy that brought them closer and closer to the physical scene of the death of Gordon Darcy Grymes, Jonas realized with an abrupt mental start just how far his precipitate flight early that morning had removed him from it. His concern with the people involved in it had blinded him completely to the practical details that concerned Sergeant Digges. He'd thought of the Milnors' cottage. He'd forgotten the Fergusons' house. He had completely and totally forgotten, until that instant, what Sergeant Digges would see the exact minute he crossed the threshold there. He'd forgotten that mud and silt dries, and dries in the form it is deposited in.

A vivid image of Jenny Darrell splashing up from her beached boat, stumbling, terrified and hysterical, across the terrace, into the living room, flashed into his mind, and in his mind he followed her from the telephone across the grass rug and bare polished floor of the passage into Natalie Ferguson's bedroom, saw her by the closet door, her sodden evening shoes in her hand, her torn mud-stained net dress dripping, her wet

67

stockinged feet depositing their outlines on the bare waxed boards.

"Good Lord . . . why didn't I mop up?"

He thought it with a sudden desperation that was staggering in terms of his own stupidity. Elizabeth Darrell had mopped up at the Milnors'. All he'd done was grab the beach bag, and leave the whole story written in mud and silt for anyone to read.

It was too late to think about it now. What he had to think about was some story that would hold water and wash . . . some plausible explanation of a lady in her stocking feet . . . And suddenly, as Sergeant Digges swung the car off the gravelled corduroy across an iron culvert into the white oyster-shell lane that branched left down over the marsh to the Milnors' and right up the slope into the Fergusons' circular driveway, Jonas Smith M.D. came to his proper senses.

The story to tell was right there in his mouth, as glaringly matter-of-fact and obvious as the oyster-shell lane, a white and brilliant ribbon in the sun. The story was the Truth. The Simple Truth, without deceit or evasion. Jenny wanted to tell it, he had advised the Darrells to tell it. There was no doubt in his mind that all Sergeant Digges's roundabout psychological technique of indirection was his advice to Jonas, in a different form but to the same end: when you're in doubt, come clean. And he was caught. Only a fool would try to blunder on in face of the palpable and overwhelming physical evidence that it wouldn't take a bright child to read.

"Well, here we are, Sergeant," he said. They drew up at the entry door. Jonas got out. The Simple Truth, he was thinking . . . but how to tell it? How to tell it so Sergeant Digges would get the picture of the kid trapped in a lonely house on the deserted creek with a guy who'd been drinking and knew what he wanted. How could he give the right meaning to the muddy prints by the phone where Jenny Darrell had called her brother for help, the stains in Natalie's bedroom where she'd ripped off her torn dance dress . . .

He threw open the door into the living room and stopped short, so unexpectedly that Sergeant Digges bumped into him from behind. The front door onto the terrace was open. Just outside it, as surprised to see him as he was to see her, was Myrtle, the Fergusons' colored maid. And the floor was spotless. There was no sign of dried mud or silt, no visible print of the small slender foot of a frantic and terrified young girl.

68

"Doctor? 'Deed, doctor, I wasn' 'specting you today. It was my understanding you was gone into town and was planning to stay there. That was the wrong information I received. That's what I been telling this woman who been callin' you up ever five-ten minutes the las' hour and one half."

Her eyes moved past Jonas to Sergeant Digges in the door behind him. The friendly ebony shine on her broad cheerful face dimmed as if it had been a bright mirror someone had blown his breath on. Its lightness and gaiety congealed to a stolid and resentful defenciveness.

Nor was Sergeant Digges's approach, Jonas thought, in his best manner.

"What are *you* doing here?"

"I'm doing my job, that's what I'm doing. You jus' ask th' doctor if you don't believe me."

Myrtle Hawkins's defence was spirited and equally tactless.

"I been on my vacation while he been here, and I'm cleanin' up th' mess he left. Because I got to go in town and help my uncle until Miz' Ferguson get home when she get home."

"Your uncle?"

"Yes, my uncle. My uncle's Mr. Wetherby work for Professor Darrell. Everybody who is anybody knows my uncle an' Professor Darrell. The Professor he sick. That's why I'm going in help out. You can ask my uncle if you don't believe me."

"Did he tell you to clean——"

"He didn't tell me nothin.' Nobody have to tell me what I got to do. I know my own self. I been around here all my life. I know my job. An' I know how a man an' a dog eatin' an' sleepin' an' in an' out's goin' to leave things. An' Miz Ferguson tol' me to have the place ready when she get back."

"And thanks a lot, Myrtle." Jonas went on into the room. "I'm afraid we did leave it a mess. You can finish up and go along. I'll see you at the Darrells', and we'll settle up then if that's okay with you."

"That's okay with me, doctor." She glowered at Sergeant Digges. "I jus' don' like people make pretence I'm somewhere I ain' got no business to be doin' somethin' I ain' ought to be doin'."

She marched across the room to the kitchen door.

"I know one thing. I ain't goin' round *murderin'* people. Nobody ain' goin' to accuse me of it. I was home in the bed *asleep* when it happened. I don' know nothin' at all about it."

She banged the door behind her. Jonas looked at the Sergeant.

"Okay. So I lost my temper," Sergeant Digges said. "It was my mistake. I never got any place getting mad yet, and I expect I'm a little old to start. Now where was it you said you were, doctor?"

"I was in bed asleep. Like Myrtle. Back here."

Jonas went to the passage door and opened it. The pine floor was shining clean.

"I woke up at eighteen past one by the clock on the table there."

He pushed open the door of the end bedroom and pointed across the bed to the pine table beside it.

"I went out on the porch and saw a light at the Milnors'. I thought I'd better go over and have a look. They asked me to keep an eye on the place. I went across the marsh and through the orchard——"

"The dog go with you?"

"No. I left him here."

"What gun did you take?"

"None. I didn't happen to have one here in the first place. I'm a peace-loving guy in the second, Sergeant. I never pack a gun unless I plan to shoot something with it."

"I see," Sergeant Digges said. He went deliberately back along the passage into the living room, and stopped in front of the gun cupboard next to the fireplace. He tried the locked door.

"The key's under the clock on the mantel," Jonas said. "But be careful. Ferguson doesn't like people monkeying around with his private property."

Sergeant Digges turned and gave him a wry and skeptical half-smile.

"You seem mighty cheerful to me, all of a sudden, doctor," he said. "If there's some joke I dare say I could use it too."

Jonas sobered his face abruptly. There was no denying it. The reprieve from the Simple Truth given him by Myrtle's devotion to her duty and respect for her uncle Mr. Wetherby had buoyed him up immensely. Nevertheless he had not meant to be so obviously transparent as all that.

"I don't know any jokes, Sergeant." He shrugged his shoulders. "Except——"

The sudden jangling of the telephone cut him off.

"Three rings?"

70

Sergeant Digges took a quick step and glanced at the dial.

"That's you. Better answer it."

Jonas had planned to let it ring. There was only one woman he could think of whose voice he would like to hear, and that not with Sergeant Digges around. But Elizabeth Darrell would not be likely to call him there. Maybe her grandfather . . . He went quickly to the phone and picked it up.

"Hello," he said.

"Jonas! Angel . . . you poor lamb! What have I done!"

It was Philippa Van Holt. Her voice was high-pitched, urgent in spite of the exaggerated persiflage that veiled it, and it resounded from the country instrument through the room. Sergeant Digges could have been on the porch and not have missed a word.

"Look, Jonas! Believe me, I had no idea the gendarmes were going to haul you in when I said I thought the description the fisherman was giving sounded like you! I'd never have said it if I'd thought! And I never mentioned Agatha. I left her and that beautiful character my brother-in-law entirely out of it. And I'm appalled! I'm stricken! I was just on my way to see you when I ran into Tom Darrell on his way back to the Academy. He told me that grim creature had taken you off somewhere. My God, you can't believe I think you knew anything about it! It never crossed my mind, I swear it didn't.—I haven't made it awkward for you, darling, have I? *Tell* me I haven't!"

—Not as awkward as you're making it now, Jonas thought dismally. He pressed the ear piece closer to his head to try to cut off the metallic reverberations of her voice.

"Not at all, Philippa," he said. "Not in——"

"Oh, thank the Lord! I'd never forgive myself." She was breathlessly off again. "I tried to back water the minute I'd said it, and I thought I'd got away with it. But he's——"

"Look," Jonas put in firmly. "He's right here. Better be careful what you say about him. It might be awkward——"

"Oh, dear! I'm so sorry! Well, good-bye. Give him my love, and I'll see you tonight. 'Bye!"

Jonas put the phone down. His eyes were fastened out of the window on the end of the pier. The Milnors' rowboat that he had left tied there the night before was gone. He hadn't noticed it till then. He turned away from the window, perplexed and not without a vague sense of misgiving, waiting for Sergeant Digges to make some comment on Philippa Van Holt's airy lack of discretion.

71

But Sergeant Digges apparently had no comment to make.

"You and I were talking about some joke," he said instead, going back to where Philippa's unfortunate interruption had come in. "I was just afraid maybe you were making some mistake. I thought I'd like to set you straight, in case you were."

"Mistake?" Jonas asked.

"Yeah. We all make 'em, doctor." Sergeant Digges went on deliberately. "I thought maybe you might be making one. I thought maybe you were thinking I hadn't been around here early this morning, and not being in the big time hadn't bothered to make pictures, and get a cast of the lady's foot. So I just wanted to set you right. Who was she, doctor?"

10

"—Who was she, doctor?"

There was no surface change in the deliberation and apparent friendliness of Sergeant Digges's manner, but the change was there. Jonas sensed it with a subtle quickening of all his perceptive faculties. The time had come, and seriously, for him to fish or cut bait. If he was going to tell the Simple Truth, now was the time to tell it. But he hesitated, not because of any fundamental confusion but because, in some curious and involved way, he suddenly had the impression that something was going on in Sergeant Digges's mind, in spite of all his canniness and insight, that was going to make the Simple Truth as Jonas had it to tell come as a hell of a shock to him.

"Maybe I'd better say right here and now, doctor, that we don't believe in killing people in Anne Arundel County," Sergeant Digges said evenly. "And nobody's getting away with it—not even if it was my own mother. I thought I'd just better make that clear, doctor. So I think we'd better quit all this horsing around. There was a woman here last night. She either shot this Darcy Grymes and came over to use the telephone, or she came here before he was shot. It was either one way or the other, I figure. And if I was in your place, doctor, and had anything to say, I'd say it. It doesn't look to me like you're in a very good spot right now. In fact, I wouldn't be surprised if I wasn't going to have to ask you to come along with me for a few days, until we find out just which way it was."

"You mean you think I had a hand in shooting Darcy Grymes, Sergeant?" Jonas inquired coolly.

"I'm asking you who the woman was who came here last night, used your telephone and got clothes out of Mrs. Ferguson's closet. Clothes maybe but shoes for certain. She was in her stocking feet when she went in there, and there's no sign of her staying or coming back, and there's a pair of those sandals in there that don't have any heels, just a strap, and one of them's black suede and the other's dark blue. So it looks like in a hurry she made a mistake and grabbed two that weren't mates, standing next to each other on the rack by the baseboard. That's just what we call routine investigation, doctor. So what I'm asking you is, who was she?"

"Who was she . . . or else. Is that it, Sergeant?" Jonas went on quickly. "Assuming that I know her and that I was here and not already on my way across the marsh, if I don't tell you you'll throw me in the can? In that case, Sergeant, the answer's easy. Nuts to you, my friend. I've never been in jail, and it might be an interesting experience."

"Not if you figure on practicing medicine around here, doctor."

"I don't know. Doctors aren't allowed to advertise. I'm not sure this wouldn't do the trick." Jonas grinned easily. "There are a lot of angles to things, Sergeant."

Sergeant Digges regarded him calmly for a moment. Then he said, "Miss Van Holt's a very attractive young woman, isn't she?"

"She's a knock-out," Jonas agreed. "Of course I don't know her well. I just met her this noon."

"So you told me, I believe. Or she did, one. I always figured comforting the widows and orphans was the preacher's job, not the doctor's. Maybe things have changed. Do most women call you angel and darling three hours after they first meet you, doctor?"

"And bring me sandwiches?" Jonas added tranquilly. "It looks like it, doesn't it, Sergeant. But as you said, we all make mistakes. If you think Miss Van Holt, or Mrs. Darcy Grymes, is an old friend of mine, you're making one. It's just my sympathetic manner, Sergeant."

"I'm glad to hear it."

Sergeant Digges turned toward the door. "And you say you never knew her husband."

"Never."

"Okay. Then let's go. You say you went over the marsh and through the orchard? And didn't take either your dog or a gun?"

"That's right."

"You didn't happen to go by car?"

"I walked in," Jonas said. He paused an instant. "But I came back by boat, in case you're interested. I see you've taken it away from the end of the pier. Or is that just routine investigation too?"

"That's right," said Sergeant Digges. "Along with sending fingerprints over to Washington to the FBI. In case you're interested."

It was the second time a warning signal clicked on and off in the back of Jonas Smith's mind.

"I don't know why I should be, particularly, Sergeant. Do you?"

"In that case there's no use your worrying. Come on, doctor. I'd like to see just how it was you got over to the Milnors'."

They did not, to Jonas's relief, cross the marsh. After one trial it was apparent that in ordinary shoes neither of them could have kept his footing on the cross-sections of the row of creosoted pilings that formed the barrier for the Ferguson-Milnor terrapin venture.

"We'll play it safe and take the car, doctor," Sergeant Digges said.

Jonas said nothing. It was as clear as daylight that if the Sergeant believed him at all, it was with so many reservations that anything he could say would sound as if he did too much protest. In the broad light of day he wondered himself how he had managed the crossing, in the moonlight, without slipping off into the mud and mallows and moccasins. And it was not until they had gone back and gone in the long way that Sergeant Digges referred to it again.

"I don't say anybody couldn't go over there that way, doctor —in the dark and all. A lot of people do things under what you might call emotional strain they couldn't do in a lifetime of their right senses."

"I don't get you," Jonas said coolly. "If it's me you're talking about I wasn't under any emotional strain."

"That's just what I'm saying." Sergeant Digges could not have been more placid. "I never did like to go on circumstantial evidence. I like to have facts to back it up, myself."

He had brought the car to a stop in the Milnors' lane at the end of the old wagon track through the woods and was opening the door to get out. Jonas glanced at him abruptly, started to speak and decided to shut up, wondering how many times Digges was going to have to hit him over the head with it before he finally got the word. He had it now. For some strange and to Jonas unknown but not unstaggering reason, Sergeant Digges appeared to think he was accessory before as well as after Gordon Darcy Grymes's sudden and violent departure from this life. He not only seemed seriously to think it, but apparently he had every intention of acting upon it. Incredible as it seemed to Jonas himself, it suddenly occurred to him that nobody but a fool and a dolt could go on overlooking the fact as if it did not exist.

"Look here, Sergeant," he said curtly. He'd got out of the car and was standing in the lane waiting for Digges to come around on his side. But Sergeant Digges was waiting for Roddy bounding up the road to join them.

"Come on, boy—come on!" he called. He turned and came over to Jonas.

"What were you saying, doctor?"

—What was he saying? Jonas thought. His momentary indignation had obscured the fact that what he had intended to say was pointless unless he said the whole thing. If he said the whole thing now, having not said it before, he would be in the not very admirable position of having stuck by Elizabeth's little sister Jenny up to the point where he was on the spot himself . . . So far and no farther. He looked at the Sergeant, his jaw tightening. It was probably precisely and exactly what he was counting on. More of his damned pseudo-psychology . . . and it had come damned close to working.

"Nothing," he said shortly.

It was clear, he decided, that he had better move more warily, or he would find himself behind a camouflaged eight-ball, if he didn't in fact find it attached to one ankle by a short heavy chain.

"Nothing at all," he said. "This is the way we go, if you still want to know how I came over last night."

"That's what we're here for, doctor."

"I came out right along here, beyond the Milnors' jalopy by the big woodpile."

Sergeant Digges's face was expressionless. "Okay. You show me."

Jonas strode forward briskly. He was still irritated, at himself for a bungling fool and at Sergeant Digges for his air of tacit unbelief whether genuine or assumed, and his kind of galling patience that seemed to imply he had all the rope in the world and time to play it out until Jonas Smith chose the proper moment to hang himself with it. He was coming along behind him now, throwing an occasional stick off into the woods for Roddy to retrieve, as if they were on an outing of the Crabtown Wildlife, Debating, Chowder, and Marching Society. And as the wagon road curved around a clump of holly and dogwood trees, Jonas took a final step over a lush glossy cluster of poison ivy entwined with honeysuckle in the middle of the road, and came to an abrupt halt.

In front of him, at the right hand side of the road, was the woodpile. The woodpile was where it had been the night before. The old broken-down jalopy that had been parked beside it was not there.

"This it?"

Sergeant Digges was just behind him.

"Yes," Jonas said. He looked around him, perplexed, and down the road. "This is it. Did you people move the Milnors' old car? It was here last night. Right here by this woodpile."

"You're sure of that?"

"Of course I am. What the——"

"Just don't get excited, doctor. I'm asking you a civil question, that's all."

"I'm not excited," Jonas said. "I'm just telling you. The Milnors' car was here last night when I came up through there."

He pointed to the right of the road farther along the lane.

"That's interesting, now, doctor. Not the Milnors' car. It's over in the garage at the end of the road—where it was last night, with the rear end propped up on a couple of old orange crates. The wheels off, and the engine out."

Jonas listened silently.

"I expect if there was a car here, it didn't belong to the Milnors. And it wasn't here when we came out last night. I was down along here myself and I didn't see it."

Sergeant Digges paused and looked at Jonas.

"You're sure it wasn't your own car you saw, doctor? The colored people over the way say they heard three cars come in and only two go out. Of course they don't have any way of knowing who they belonged to . . ."

"I forgot to tell you," Jonas said equably. "I walked over."

He moved along a few steps and looked around. The poison

76

ivy and honeysuckle along the grass strip between the bare wheel tracks was flourishing and apparently undisturbed. He kept in the tracks and went forward to where he had come up from the shore through the woods, Sergeant Digges following after him.

"I came up this way," he said. "If you want to go down and look, maybe you'll see my tracks. I doubt it, though—I jumped from the last pile to the dry bank."

He looked back along the wagon road to the woodpile. The car had been there, a solid fact, no illusory trick of moonlight and shadow. Furthermore, he had heard it when it left. It came back to him now. It was when he'd got the beach bag and was leaving Natalie Ferguson's room. He remembered going out on the porch, listening, and looking across the marsh, waiting to see the headlights shine through the trees, thinking it might be the police, wondering if someone else had called before he had, and then dismissing the whole thing because he saw no lights.

What he had heard must have been the jalopy. Thinking of that, Jonas Smith scowled. It was a new factor in the situation, and a disturbing one. Whoever had driven that car in and hidden it off the lane in an unused wagon road might have done it for their own purposes . . . but they had not left without headlights for fun. Nobody would risk driving the narrow lane through the trees and over the marsh—even a white oyster-shell lane in the moonlight—without headlights except for some compelling reason; and the wagon track to the main lane had no oyster-shell and was ticklish at best. Jonas felt a sudden chill at his heart, thinking what might have happened. There could be another person around, an actual eyewitness perhaps, some one—maybe some two—who had been there and who knew enough to have felt the urge to get out as quietly and unobtrusively as possible before anyone caught them there.

He listened to Sergeant Digges and Roddy crashing through the woods down to the marsh shore and back again. So far, whoever it had been had laid low and said nothing. That was a dangerous thing to count on. If whoever had been there did know something, had perhaps seen what he had seen or any part of it, they might keep still for a time, out of fear, perhaps, in case they themselves had no right to be there . . . and consciences might start to work just when Jenny, and Tom and Elizabeth, thought she was safe with no more worries. Or, at the other end of the scale, there was a thing called blackmail.

77

Sergeant Digges was coming out of the woods back to the wagon road.

"What time would you say it was you came through here, doctor?"

"Half-past one or so," Jonas said shortly. "I didn't keep a stop watch on myself. It was twenty minutes past one when I waked up. Eighteen if you want it to the dot. Half-past would be pretty close."

"And you say you saw a car here in the road?"

"That's right. I took it for granted it was the Milnors' old bus."

"And no one in it."

Jonas thought a moment. "I didn't see anyone in it."

"And then you went through the orchard?"

Jonas nodded. "That's right. Like this." He went along the road, as he had done in the early hours of the morning, until it came to an end at the Milnors' clearing among the neat rows of young peach trees set out in the sunny slope to the creek. They went through the orchard and came to the oyster-shell road leading down to the cottage on the point.

Gordon Darcy Grymes' car was still where he had left it. Two blue-uniformed officers were sitting on the fenders, talking to a khaki-clad State trooper balanced on his motorcycle beside the county police car. A colored boy of about sixteen was sitting on the front bumper.

Sergeant Digges nodded to them. He followed Jonas across the road and into the woods. They came up to the three-pronged tulip tree.

"I stood right here," Jonas said.

He pointed down. There was no doubting someone had stood there. A pink lady-slipper was trampled into the ground and the branches of a small huckleberry at the base of the big tree were bruised and broken.

"I didn't want to go barging in if it was some friend of the Milnors who knew it was all right to come out when they were away. The car was just there, with the lights off. There was a light in the house, but everything was perfectly quiet. I stood here a while. Then I went over to the kitchen window to look in."

He went through the clump of dogwood and holly and across the cleared space under the pines to the cottage. He pointed down again.

"I sure wrecked their mint patch."

The mint growing under the window and around the outdoor icebox against the whitewashed wall was crushed into the earth. One large flat foot with a ridged sole marking was firmly imprinted in the moist ground.

"That's mine. I looked in here. The door of the kitchen was open and the guy was stretched out on the floor. He looked dead to me, with blood all over the place. When I went inside and looked at him he had a gun by his hand—in it, as far as I could see. There wasn't any question in my mind—he'd died instantly."

He was thinking as coolly and quickly as he could. By leaving out the three Darrells and telescoping events he could stick to the truth, even if it was not the whole truth. He could have done it with more inward assurance if he had not been haunted by the new knowledge that somewhere in the shadows, and no telling how near to him, someone else may have been watching too . . . that Jonas Smith may have been not only the observer but the observed.

"And what time would you say that was, doctor?"

"How the hell would I know, Sergeant?" He spoke irritably, and checked himself. "I keep telling you I didn't have a stop watch with me. You could figure it out. It couldn't have been very long."

"I'm just asking you."

Sergeant Digges turned to the group in the road. "Roy—come here."

As the colored lad got up from the bumper and started over, a car came through the wooded lane and braked to a dramatic stop half-way down to the cottage. The policemen straightened up, including Sergeant Digges. Dr. Jonas Smith straightened up too. Except for the car, and the stylish foot and elegant leg that first came out of it, he would not at the moment have recognized Phillippa Van Holt. She had changed her clothes and taken off her makeup. She wore a black dress, unrelieved except for a short string of pearls around her throat, but it was one of those black dresses that did not need relief, especially on Philippa Van Holt. As a modern version of a widow's weeds it was extremely effective, and with much of its suntan washed off her lovely face had a new pallor that was equally so. The violet shadows under her luminous brown eyes made them larger and appealingly sad.

11

"You shouldn't have come out here, Miss Van Holt."

Sergeant Digges had left Jonas and the colored boy and was helping her the rest of the way out of her car.

"I had to come some time, Captain. When Dr. Smith said you were out here, now seemed the best time. After all, you know, I'm not what you call the . . . the shattered type. I can take it."

"Where the hell does she get the brave little woman stuff?" Jonas thought. He had to admit it was effective. Even the colored boy was giving her a gloomy wall-eyed tribute. The two uniformed policemen had slid off the fender to their feet and the State trooper was standing beside his motorcycle. Jonas shook his head. Perhaps he was the one who was out of step. Just because he had seen her as sophisticate and she-devil was no reason for him to mistrust her present role, now that enough time had elapsed, very likely, for her to have an honest reaction from shock and bitterness to genuine grief and unhappiness. And she seemed anxious about him too. She smiled wanly. Then she came over to him and said softly under her breath, "I'm sorry as hell if I've got you mixed up with red tape. I didn't mean to—*believe* me."

She turned quickly away from him, her eyes widening.

"That's . . . his car, isn't it?"

She looked at Sergeant Digges. "He must have driven out himself. Was somebody with him? Or did he meet someone out here? I don't understand. He told me he was going to bed early because he wanted to be in Baltimore the first thing this morning."

"We're not sure, Miss." Sergeant Digges was grave. "What time did you see him last?"

"At five o'clock. I went down and had a cocktail with him in his room. I didn't stay long, because his brother was coming to have dinner with him at the Yacht Club, and his brother and I aren't awfully good friends. Anyway they had some business to talk about and I had a dinner engagement of my own. But I talked to him again around ten. He said he was practically in

80

bed then, and he certainly didn't sound as if he had any idea of going out. I'm sure he would have told me, because we have sort of a . . . well, I don't know what you call it, and it must sound odd to anybody who lives in a sweet place like Annapolis. What I mean is, we always told each other what we were doing. You see, Captin Digges, we *understood* each other."

She turned away quickly for an instant.

"But I guess that doesn't make sense to anybody but me. You see, in our jobs each of us *had* to be free to live his own life."

Jonas glanced at Sergeant Digges. His face had the same slightly wistful expression it had had when they were crossing the Severn Bridge, with everybody having Sunday off to go fishing except Sergeant Digges.

"I just can't imagine him coming out here to meet anybody."

Philippa looked at his car again.

"And he must have. Or they'd have taken his car and ditched it somewhere, wouldn't they?"

"—Except that we can't find his car keys," Sergeant Digges said. "And unless whoever shot him was in walking distance, or got a lift from somebody who was . . . You didn't give anybody a lift into town, did you, doctor? You see I'm still trying to figure out what made you leave so quick."

"I told you why I left," Jonas said patiently. "And I didn't give anybody a lift. I went in alone—me and Roddy. And I don't particularly get your logic, Sergeant."

He had to raise his voice a little. Roddy, having left the rabbit he had been tracing through the orchard, was down on the pier, running back and forth along it, barking excitedly at something in the water, stopping and bracing himself to dive, changing his mind, whining and barking again.

"You say two cars went out of here. I don't see you need to bring mine in at all.—Shut up, Roddy! Quiet!"

"What's he after, do you suppose?"

Sergeant Digges started across the lawn toward the pier. Roddy, silenced, was still trying to make up his mind to jump.

"Go get it, boy! Get it, Roddy!"

The dog dived off into the creek. His tail was a feathered black-and-white spotted sword of Excalibur waving up over the muddy churning water. Jonas's heart sank to a new and dismal low.

"Well, I'll be damned," Sergeant Digges said. "—Excuse me, miss. He's got something. Come on, boy. Bring it. That's a boy."

Roddy, wading up out of the shallow mud-bottomed creek to the shore, stopped to shake himself, bounded happily up the bank and across the grass to his master, and laid Gordon Darcy Grymes' sodden pigskin key case at his master's feet.

"Good boy," Jonas said cordially. He could gladly have strangled him. "Go away. You're wet. Go away, boy."

Roddy was shaking himself all over Philippa Van Holt's gossamer-sheathed legs. She did not appear to notice it. She was staring fixedly down at the mud-soaked key case with stamped gold letters that spelled out "Gordon Darcy" plainly visible through the silt that blackened it. She stood motionless, her lips parted a little. Sergeant Digges looked from her to Jonas before he bent down and picked the case up.

"Is this your husband's, miss?"

Philippa nodded, her eyes still fixed on the ground where it had been. She nodded again without speaking.

"And you didn't seem particularly surprised at what your dog brought up, doctor. You didn't throw it there yourself, by any chance, did you?"

"I didn't throw it there, Sergeant," Jonas said calmly. "And I'm as surprised as you are. I'm just not the demonstrative type."

The Sergeant had opened the case and was scraping the silt off the keys.

"Sergeant Digges," Philippa said slowly. Jonas noted she had given up the "Captain." Her voice was flat and colorless, and she was still looking down at the ground. "Was . . . had my husband been drinking?"

Sergeant Digges spoke reluctantly. "He had an empty flask in his pocket. There's a glass on the table. I guess he'd been drinking some."

"Then I can tell you what happened."

Her voice was still quiet and even.

"He threw his own keys in the Creek. And he was with some girl. It's . . . it's an old routine of his. I know it very well. You'll find another set of keys under the hood. And I think I'd like to go now. I'm——"

"—There wasn't no girl with him when I saw him, miss." The colored boy spoke up, bright-eyed and alert. "There wasn't no girl any place around."

Philippa turned and looked at him with expressionless eyes. "What time was that, Roy?"

It was evident from the way Sergeant Digges asked it that he

82

knew the answer he was going to get. Jonas waited warily, sensing some sort of tightening in the devious net the Sergeant had been patiently weaving.

"It was fifteen minutes before one o'clock," Roy answered promptly. "I was looking at the clock, because some people was late supposed to come from New York, and I was off at one o'clock, and if they didn't come I wouldn't take up their bags and I wouldn't get no tip and I was looking for half a dollar. That's how I know the time it was, because that's when they came and that's when I saw Mr. Darcy come a hurryin' out of his room ain't looking to the right nor to the left."

"Sure it was Mr. Darcy, Roy?"

"Sure's I'm born to die. I know Mr. Darcy. I'm always takin' him ice and soda and cigarettes. He knows how to tip the boys. He don't throw you no nickels and dimes. He don't know nothin' less'n a quarter. I ain't likely to make no mistake about Mr. Darcy."

"You saw him come out of his room alone. How do you know there wasn't somebody in his car?"

"Because he didn't get in his car. His car's always parked behind the hotel, and he went out front, he didn't go out back. I saw him go down the front steps when I was raisin' the window for the people from New York. I saw him plain as I'm seein' you."

Sergeant Digges was looking steadily at Jonas. "—So that if Dr. Smith says he heard a shot at eighteen minutes past one, and saw Mr. Darcy in on the floor there ten or fifteen minutes later, it means he must have got out here mighty fast."

"He was goin' mighty fast," the colored boy said. "He was goin' down them front steps like a streak of greased lightning."

Jonas Smith saw and deliberately avoided Philippa Van Holt's sherry-brown eyes as she moved them unobtrusively his way. There was no use revealing either to her or to Sergeant Digges that Roy had made a mistake. It was not Gordon Darcy Grymes he had seen. Gordon Darcy Grymes was out at Arundel Creek with Jenny Darrell at quarter to one.

"You're sure it was Mr. Darcy, Roy?" Philippa asked slowly, glancing away from Jonas. "You're sure it wasn't his brother? They're very much alike."

"Franklin Grymes?" Sergeant Digges said. "No. He was in Baltimore. He called me up this morning. He left right after they had dinner and got back to his apartment at ten-twenty. I checked with the girl at the switchboard there. But he's presi-

83

den of the Grymes Old Foundry Corporation. He's a prominent and respected citizen . . ."

"Oh, I'm sure of it. But so is Dr. Smith."

A faint smile lighted Philippa's eyes.

"The only reason I asked is it's so hard to tell the two of them apart. I couldn't always do it myself, not at a distance. You know they were identical twins. But I'm not insisting. Except that if it happened by any chance that my husband's brother *was* in his room while he was away, I'd certainly like to know it. Especially——"

She broke off abruptly. "Sorry. It sounds as if I thought he wasn't telling the truth."

Sergeant Digges was watching her, intent and alert.

"It's just the keys," she said quietly. "They confused me. You see, I knew my husband very well. It's just that old technique of his, pretending to throw his keys away when he was a little tight and on the wolf prowl that confused me. I'm sorry. I shouldn't be unjust to him . . . not now."

She moved uncertainly a few steps toward her car, stopped and turned back to the cottage where death had come to Gordon Darcy Grymes, her eyes filled with indecision. It was as if she wanted to go but couldn't bear to leave. She looked again at Sergeant Digges.

"You asked me if he had any enemies. I said no. I've been trying to think if there's anybody, but I can't. I can't think of anybody who wasn't charmed by him—even the men he knew, except a few who were jealous. Because all he had to do was look at a woman once. But there was no one around here he was interested in particularly, anyone married or engaged, with a husband or fiancé to get upset. But of course this is the South. It may be different here."

Jonas waited. If she brought brothers in, he was thinking, that would tear it. The sharp image of Tom Darrell and Elizabeth watching him and Sergeant Digges from behind the window curtains flashed into his mind. But she left it at that. She stopped talking and moved slowly away.

"You wouldn't say there was any real hard feeling between him and Mr. Franklin Grymes, would you, Miss Van Holt?" Sergeant Digges asked.

"No, Sergeant. Not really. But you know how close identical twins are. I suppose if something sours between them it's bound to go deeper than it would in an ordinary brother relationship. But I'm sure they patched things up at dinner last night. When

84

my husband talked to me before he went to bed—or said he was going to bed, I mean—he sounded very cheerful. He said they'd had the best time they'd had together for a long time. I'm sure things were all right between them. I think they particularly wanted to get things settled now because Franklin's engaged to marry a perfectly charming girl—as Dr. Smith here can tell you."

Sergeant Digges's glance at Jonas indicated doubt if Dr. Smith could even tell him when to take an aspirin tablet. He turned back to Philippa.

"What had been the trouble between your husband and his brother?"

"It wouldn't be fair for me to say anything until you've talked to Franklin. He can tell you much more about it than I can. I've never got it very straight. My husband had an intense sort of loyalty to his brother."

She spoke quietly and with dignity. Remembering the scene between her and Franklin Grymes in Miss Olive Oliphant's study, Jonas wondered for an instant whether he had dreamed that up, or was now dreaming this. Still, it could be that the earlier flare-up was an emotional reaction at seeing him just after she had heard of her husband's death. Her tone had changed even from her first mention of him as they were talking now, as if she was trying to undo any injustice her first impulsive statement about him could have done him in Sergeant Digges's mind.

She moved slowly away. Sergeant Digges watched her with a compassionate look on his rugged face until she reached her car and got inside. When he turned to Jonas there was nothing remotely compassionate about his expression.

"You heard what she said, doctor. We know there was a girl here. Here and over at your place. So come on, doctor. You and I'll go inside with Edgerton here, and he'll take down any statement you want to make."

He motioned to one of the uniformed officers. "Come on, Bob. Come on, doctor."

"Okay," Jonas said. "But it's going to be a tough job to get it all in, Sergeant. According to you I must have been pretty busy between eighteen past one and twenty past two when I put in my call to you people . . . getting dressed and over here, and on friendly enough terms with a guy I never saw before to shoot him—*and* take his girl. You may think I'm a fast worker, Sergeant, but I'm not that fast."

"I'm figuring you could have been here already when he got here, doctor. You say eighteen minutes past one is when you were waked up by a shot. Maybe so. Something brought him steaming out there mighty fast. It's a funny thing about a guy that's in the habit of taking other fellows' women. They're the kind get maddest when another fellow takes theirs."

"Oh, for God's sake, Sergeant."

"Okay. All I'm saying is there's a girl mixed up in this some place, and somebody's going to tell me who the hell she is, doctor. It's not likely she's somebody nobody ever saw before. She wouldn't be a perfect stranger now, would she? A fellow doesn't go out on a limb and do his damndest to saw it off on account of some dame he isn't pretty far gone on."

Sergeant Digges started leisurely around the end of the cottage toward the door.

"And who's this Miss Van Holt was talking about? This girl friend of her brother-in-law's?"

He glanced back sharply. Jonas Smith's reaction-time was slow enough, at that question, to allow him to read anything he liked in it, from perfectly ordinary stupidity to fear and guilt. Actually it was a simple matter of semantics. Calling Agatha Reed anybody's girl friend was a shock that it took a little time to absorb. Even lady friend, so applied, would have startled Jonas.

"You mean Miss Reed. Miss Agatha Reed."

"You know her?"

"She's an old friend of mine."

"I see."

"And through a glass darkly, Sergeant, if you think there's any tie-up around here with Miss Reed."

Jonas realized he was speaking with more warmth than the facts called for, but there was something in Sergeant Digges's eyes that was a mote to be yanked out before it obscured the whole landscape.

"We were engaged once. It's all called off, so don't let it worry you, my friend."

"Who called it off, doctor? You or the lady?"

"The lady, Sergeant."

"Why?"

"That is her business."

Jonas grinned suddenly. "As Mr. Franklin Grymes said this morning, please leave Miss Reed out of this." It was a feeble joke, so feeble that Sergeant Digges failed to recognize it. It

86

was also a mistake, as Jonas realized instantly.

"So you've been talking to him about the lady this morning, have you, doctor?"

Jonas groaned again. "No, Sergeant. No. And skip it, will you? I just haven't got the strength to go into it now. Miss Reed was home in bed. I swear it. Miss Reed is always at home, and always in bed, at the correct hour. So leave us not get all hot and bothered about Miss Reed."

"Okay. You're the doctor."

Sergeant Digges chuckled at his own joke, as feeble as Jonas's.

"We'll skip Miss Agatha Reed . . . for the time being. Now let's see. You wanted to make a statement, I believe. Do you want to go inside, or stay out?"

"Either one, Sergeant. It's your show. I'm cooperating. The scene of the crime has no terrors for me."

"I'm glad to hear you call it a crime." Sergeant Digge's' eyes rested thoughtfully on his. "I've been wondering why, if you just saw a guy on the floor with a gun in his hand and nothing else, you didn't just take it for granted he'd done it himself. That'd seem a sort of logical conclusion, wouldn't it?"

Jonas would have liked a moment in which to think. Having none, and with the Sergeant's level gaze fixed on him, he said coolly, "Not the way you've been talking about it. Also the expression on his face. I doubt if he would have looked quite so surprised if it was his own idea."

Something almost imperceptibly like a smile twitched one corner of Sergeant Digges's mouth.

"I'm interested to hear you say that, doctor. Now if you'll just step right over to where you say you saw him."

Jonas went across the room to where the dark stain was viscid-dried on the green-tiled floor and the white string rug was dyed a dirty brown.

"—About there, you'd say?"

"Right."

"So you could see him through the kitchen window?"

Jonas turned and looked through the open door at the window over the sink. He turned back, nodding.

Sergeant Digges's eyes rested steadily on him. He said, "Looking straight at you, wasn't he, doctor? That's how you got him . . . straight through the heart, the second he turned around. Come on, doctor—quit stalling. You're licked, doctor. You shot him. What did you shoot him for?"

87

12

For a dazed instant Jonas Smith heard not believing he had heard, staggered by the direct assault out of the blue and by the impact of what he saw, with a flash of mental clarity, was the most extraordinary and implacable logic. He was facing the window. The ledge was on a direct level with his heart. A gun there, aimed easily at him as he stood now, would do to him precisely what it had done to Gordon Darcy Grymes held in the hands of an hysterical girl facing him from the other direction, across the wide room from the porch door. The angle would be the same, the difference in her height and his made up by the foundation of the cottage. The distance even, between killer and killed, was not greatly different, across the room where Jenny Darrell would have been standing, and from the window in the kitchen where he himself had stood, to where Gordon Darcy Grymes had stood. It was logic. All it didn't have was the truth.

Jonas looked from the window to Sergeant Digges.

"No," he said calmly. "He wasn't looking at me. I didn't see him standing up. He was lying on the floor. That stuff was all bright red and still wet. I see what you mean, Sergeant . . . but it just happens I wasn't the guy that did it."

"Then why don't you tell me the truth, doctor?"

"I've told you the truth."

"Not all of it. Not the whole truth."

Jonas shook his head. "Sergeant, I don't know the whole truth—about anything. In my profession that's the first thing they try to teach you. Now if you want that statement you've been talking about, I'll be glad to make it. Or is it the local can? Make up your mind, will you?"

Thinking it over, some minutes later, he was wondering why Sergeant Digges had made up his mind the way he had. He was still not in jail. Or not yet. Up to the last minute, there in the Milnors' cottage, he hadn't been sure the Sergeant wasn't going to spring it on him in good earnest, as a means if not an end in itself. Behind his hardly veiled exasperation and annoyance Jonas could see him weighing the obvious advantages of locking him up against the whole flock of imponderables that made up the less obvious disadvantages of it. It had been touch and go, and Jonas had guarded his tongue for fear he might say something that could be construed as a wise crack sufficient to tilt the balance and land him behind the bars. Even when he set out with Roddy to walk back over to the Fergusons' house, he was not entirely sure the offered lift into town wasn't actually intended as one leg up in the direction of the jail.

However, he was at the Fergusons', not the jail, and as he called a taxi and put down the phone his hand lingered on it, the impulse to pick it up again and call Elizabeth Darrell so strong that he tore himself away by force and went barging out onto the terrace, to get away from the temptation and try to examine himself with some degree of ordinary sanity. He wanted to talk to her. He wanted to hear her voice, to be sure again she was real and not a dream. The excuse of calling to ask about her grandfather that kept popping back into his mind every couple of seconds was plausible, but not really valid. Until Dr. Pardee formally invited him back he had no standing in the case.

"Gee, I want to see her! I've got to see her!"

He flopped down in the Gibson Island chair on the terrace, took out his pipe and knocked it out on the arms of the chair. He was acting like a damned fool, and he knew it. Everything that had happened since he had looked at her, standing on the other side of her grandfather's bed in the darkened room, was driven out of his mind. The creek, its shining waters girdled with young green and gold with the reflection of the trees on the banks around it, and serenely blue from the cloudless sky above, the creek and the white herons wading the marsh, the rustling leaves of the oaks, the croaking of the frogs, all of it mingled into something warm and lovely, making him forget Sergeant Digges, and Gordon Darcy Grymes, and remember only a smooth golden head and fringed wisteria eyes and a moving velvety voice.

He moved abruptly. "I keep forgetting she doesn't think I'm so hot." He got up and put his pipe back in his pocket. "Oh well, the hell with it." There was an old poem about What care I how fair she be if she is not fair to me. At his age, with his experience, he ought to start making some kind of emotional sense, not going around having mystical visions and practically landing in the jail-house through his own unaided efforts.

He whistled to the dog, busy at a snake hole on the bank, and sat down again. He couldn't go until his taxi came, and it didn't hurt him to think about her . . . expecially when he couldn't help it. He looked down at Roddy, obediently there beside him, gazing up into his eyes. He reached down and rubbed the drooping damp ears.

"It's the first time I've really been in love, boy." He grinned. "Don't look so bloody doleful. It's not you it hurts."

He straightened abruptly. The phone was ringing. He sprang to his feet. It was Her. You couldn't want anybody so intensely without communicating it some way. He dashed to the door, yanked it open, and stopped half-way to the table. It wasn't her. He was crazy. It was Van Holt, or somebody . . . somebody he didn't care whether he ever talked to again or not. He went the rest of the way soberly, picked the instrument up and said "Hello" so brusquely it surprised him.

Then he held his breath, his heart beating so fast it almost choked him. He sat down in the chair by the table, smiling happily like a love-sick zany.

"Excuse me for calling you, Dr. Smith, but I was . . . worried," Elizabeth Darrell was saying. "Philippa Van Holt was just here. She said she was afraid the police were . . . were . . ."

"They haven't yet," Jonas said cheerfully. "But thanks for worrying. How is your grandfather? Is the nurse there?"

"Yes. There's no change."

"I'm on my way in town. If you want me for anything——"

"Thank you."

Her voice cooled abruptly.

"I don't see anything to be so cheerful about. Anyway, Dr. Pardee's coming back. I think we'll do very nicely. That wasn't why I called. I just didn't want you to be in any trouble on our account. Good-bye."

Jonas held the phone for a moment, still smiling. Her rebuke was no doubt deserved. He didn't mind. She was worried about him, she'd called him up . . . those were twin baskets of rubies and fine pearls tossed into the empty hands of a beggar in the streets. He bounded up, whistling, treading the golden mountain top, reprieved from the slough of dismal despond. The taxi's honking in the drive was the song of the morning lark in his ears.

"Come on, Roddy! Let's go!"

His delirium was brief. Its first set-back was the last words coming from the radio in the taxi before the boy switched it

90

off to hear where Jonas wanted to go.

"—mystery woman believed to have been with the dead man at that time. Keep tuned to this station for late developments. It is now five-fifteen Eastern Daylight Time."

The second was in town when he was eating a thick steak at Gregory's on Maryland Avenue. In the bright blue-and-red leather booth in front of him were four young St. John's students talking about Aristotle. Three girls in the booth behind him were talking about Gordon Darcy Grymes and Elizabeth Darrell.

"—Hubris is the pride and arrogance that leads the gods to strike you down," said one booth. "It's Nemesis that pursues you and does the——"

"—make any difference to Liz if Gordon was married," the other booth was saying. "She can't ever marry anybody while that horrid old man's alive. Especially if he's going to be paralyzed. He's always managed to get rid of every boy Liz ever even started to like. She'll end up just like poor old Cousin Olive. The Commodore told me once she had all kinds of beaux but she couldn't leave Papa. At least he left her a little money to live on. All Liz'll get's that white elephant of a house and she'll end up renting rooms and taking boarders. I just don't get it."

"Liz is super," one of the other girls said.

The third one giggled. "You know what Miss Olive said? She said she didn't see why we thought her generation was so repressed. She said they didn't have cars to park in but she couldn't see what could happen in a car that didn't use to happen at coon hunts when she was a girl. Papa never did approve of coon hunts."

"I guess they didn't have ticks with spotted fever in the woods in those days," the first girl said. "Anyway, I'd like to know who the mystery woman is somebody saw in Gordon's car. Mother and Dad were coming home from a party around one. Gordon was just getting in his car, but he didn't recognize them, he was in such a hurry, and Mother didn't recognize the girl. But she was so busy holding Dad up I guess she didn't have a chance. I don't know why people drink so much."

Jonas drained his beer glass, got up and paid his bill. He glanced back from the counter. The three girls had their bright little heads together. He couldn't see their faces. But it didn't matter. He'd heard enough. The mystery woman was not Jenny Darrell, as he'd assumed hearing the tail end of the radio broadcast. It was whoever was waiting for Franklin Grymes when he came whipping out of his brother's hotel room at a quarter to one o'clock.

He left the restaurant and hurried down toward Prince George Street to Blanton-Darrell Court. Just so it didn't turn out to be Agatha Reed, he thought. It was one of those grim and preposterous ideas that he wished devoutly had never occurred to him, and that stuck like a tack in the heel of his shoe, more uncomfortable with every step he took. Having assured Sergeant Digges that Miss Agatha Reed was home and in bed, it would be funny as hell if Miss Reed had turned over a new leaf and taken to tearing around the country-side in the middle of the night. It would be so funny, in fact, that Jonas Smith groaned inwardly. The old eight-ball in front of him was looming to planetary proportions.

He entered the Court through the iron gate marked "Private, Keep Out, No Dogs Allowed" that was at the opposite end of the place from his, and out across the Darrells' back garden to go in through his back door. Roddy sprang on ahead of him, and made a sharp detour, wagging his friendly tail.

"Oh, hello!"

Less than forty-five minutes before, his heart would have leaped a mile at the sight of Elizabeth Darrell sitting on the stone bench in front of the myrtle tree. Now it only gave a jolt upward to become a sudden lump in his throat as he saw her there, Jenny beside her, both of them startled at his barging in, disturbing what had obviously been a troubled private conference.

"Hello."

Elizabeth got up, not stiffly, but so nearly that it could reasonably be called that. Jenny Darrell drew back a little, her eyes larger and more haunted than ever. Then she managed to get up too, her small brown hand creeping like a child's into her sister's.

She moistened her lips. "Hello, Dr. Smith."

Jonas went across to them. He wished they wouldn't act as if he were an ogre of some kind, and throw up a hedge of thorns and a wall of glass every time he came near them. It was irritating, considering the spot he was in on account of both of them. And then he was ashamed of himself. They were scared. They were badly scared, and pathetically on the defensive, waiting for their whole world to crash down around their heads.

"I want to talk to you two," Jonas said soberly. He looked around the garden.

"We came out here so we could talk, without the nurse or Wetherby hearing us," Elizabeth said quietly. "We had the radio on. They're hunting a girl . . ."

Jonas nodded. "They're hunting a girl," he repeated, "—but not the right one. They still don't know what time Gordon went out to the Milnors'. They think it wasn't till after one, because the bellhop saw him in the hotel. But don't get your hopes up on that one. Digges hasn't seen Franklin Grymes yet. He's just talked to him. The minute he sees him it's going to bust wide open. They're identical twins, and even Philippa says she couldn't tell them apart. She probably could, but I sure couldn't. When it breaks, Digges is going to start back at the beginning. And there's one thing I think I've got to tell you. You might as well know the worst.—Somebody else was out there last night. There was a car over on the old wagon-road. I saw it, and I heard it go out after you all left. It went without any lights, and it looks as if somebody wants . . ."

He stopped, aware of the tightening of Jenny's grip on Elizabeth's hand, and some imperceptible but definite communication between them. He looked from one of them to the other.

"Look. There's no use leaving me in the dark, if you know something I don't. I'm the guy they've got on the griddle at this point. I can make fewer errors and more runs if I know what the score is."

"Tell him, Jenny."

The younger girl moistened her lips again. "I don't know. Dr. Pardee gave me something and made me lie down. I guess I was dreaming. I was out there, and Gordon was there . . . but there was somebody else. I just sort of . . . sort of *knew* it. I was just standing in the room, and I *knew* it. I don't know how, but it was so . . . so plain I woke up——"

"She woke up screaming at the top of her lungs," Elizabeth said quietly. "I thought it was just a dream. But I don't know . . ."

"I don't either," Jonas said.

He looked intently at Jenny. It could be. It could be something she'd heard in a moment of shock and buried deep in her unconscious mind that had come up in a dream state. But that in itself was terribly important at the moment.

"You haven't heard from anybody?"

"No."

A tremor shivered through Elizabeth's slim body.

"But it's a ghastly sort of feeling," she whispered. "What if somebody starts ringing up . . ."

Jenny pulled her hand away from Elizabeth's and looked desperately up at Jonas.

"I'm going to go and tell them. Please make her see it isn't right for me not to! Please! I don't want you to be in trouble, or anybody else. It's my fault, it's me that ought to suffer. I did it. And it can't hurt anybody, now. It won't hurt Grandfather, he'll never know. Elizabeth was just afraid he'd throw me out of the house, and there'd be no place for me to go without her having to leave him here alone, and something dreadful happen to him . . . but it's happened anyway. Please, Dr. Smith, *make* her see!"

It could have been the Hubris that leads the gods to strike at pride and arrogance, or Nemesis pursuing the whole lot of them. Whatever it was, it chose its moment, Jonas thought, with pathetic irony.

"Miss Darrell! Miss Darrell!"

The shade in the window of the corner bedroom snapped up, the white figure of a frantic nurse leaned out.

"Miss Darrell! Come quickly! Your grandfather!"

"Oh, no!"

Elizabeth's clenched fist went up to her mouth, her eyes blinded with tears.

"Oh, no, no!"

She started forward. Jonas was already half-way across the garden to the back door. He took one more step, and came to an irresistible halt. Through the upstairs window, hoarse and weak and full of the authority of life, not death, he heard a familiar bellow:

"Wetherby! Where's that black scoundrel? I want a drink!"

13

"You must go in, Jenny. You'll catch cold, sitting out here."

It was a vapid thing to say when his heart was moved with so much compassion, finding her still out there on the stone garden bench, a frail small ghost in the deepening shadows, so

94

pitifully alone and secluded while inside the lighted house everything was robust excitement and lusty tumult.

Jonas Smith wiped the cold sweat off his brow. He was glad to be out of it and let Dr. Pardee try to beat some sense into the old devil's head. With Wetherby and Elizabeth and himself all worn out trying to make Professor Darrell stay in bed, the nurse dudgeoning off, Dr. Pardee dudgeoning in, Jonas wondered why the hell they just didn't let him get up, go to his blasted poker game, drink a hogshead of Maryland rye if he wanted to and be done with everything permanently. And Miss Olive Oliphant's appearance with her cat and her overnight bag and a startling bit of information to the effect that jimson weed was used in ancient Mexico to discover thieves was not what Jonas would have prescribed as a soporific.

In the welter of cross-purposes and passions he had forgotten Jenny until Professor Darrell had ordered him out of the house and coming back he saw her still huddled on the stone bench.

"You'll just make yourself sick, Jenny," he said gently. He sat down beside her and took her limp cold hand in his.

"I don't know what to do," she whispered. "I wish he didn't hate me so. It's because I look like my mother, and he hated her worse than he does me. Her father was just a workman over in the Academy Yard, and my father was the regimental commander when he was a midshipman, and it nearly killed Grandfather when he married a Yard workman's daughter. He wouldn't ever let her come in the house here. She died out in China when I was born, and my father had to bring us back here, and Grandfather liked Elizabeth and Tom because they looked like my father, but I was dark like my mother. And her name was Jennifer, so everything he does to me he's sort of taking his revenge out on her. And if I ruin everybody's life— Tom's, and Elizabeth's—he'll never forgive me . . . or her. So I don't know what to do. I don't know any place to go. That's . . . that's why I liked him . . . Gordon, I mean. He was so nice to me . . ."

"There, there . . ." Jonas patted her hand awkwardly. He would have liked to put his arms around her as he would a small miserable child, but if he had done so Sergeant Digges would have been certain to turn up. On the other hand it was a good thing for her to talk and get some of it out of her system so she could sleep and rest.

"He sort of . . . fascinated me," she went on wretchedly. "I was a terrible fool. At first I just thought it was accidental when he'd come by places I was and pick me and the kids up, because he was taking my sister out. Then . . . I don't know. She got mad, and he said it was just because she was jealous, and I guess . . . I guess it sort of went to my head. And I started . . . meeting him places. Then I got scared. I had a date with him Saturday, and I called him up and said I couldn't come because I had to go to the hop with my brother, and he was just as nice about it as anything. It didn't seem to make any difference to him, and I was sort of ashamed and thought I'd been imagining things. So when he was outside the Number Three gate, I thought it would look crazy if I didn't let him take me home. Because Tom had the duty and got his roommate to drag me, but he hadn't signed out to drag, so he could come and get me but he couldn't take me home past the gate. I had to walk home by myself when everybody else was with somebody, and I felt silly on the street all by myself, so I was really glad when I saw him.

"He said what about dropping in at the St. John's dance, he thought Elizabeth was going to be there. I said I had to come home, but nobody was here, and it seemed sort of easier to go than sit on the porch and wait, because he said he didn't want me to go in the big house all by myself, and when he said the Milnors were expecting him to pick them up I thought it would be all right. I didn't want to be silly, and . . . act like I didn't have *experience,* and couldn't take care of myself, or anything. Don't you know?"

"I know," Jonas said.

"And you know Philippa."

"Philippa?"

"Philippa Van Holt. Of course I didn't know he was married to her. She's always been terribly nice to me, but she made me mad too. She saw him drop me up on the Circle about a week ago, and she waylaid me the next morning, just pretending she was up that early, and she said she wanted to give me some good advice. I said I didn't want any, and she said if she saw me with him again she'd tell my brother, and if that didn't help she'd tell my grandfather and that would fix me. She said it was for my own good. I got real mad, and she said Okay, I could be a damned fool if I wanted to. Then she said, 'Look, kid—you just haven't got the stuff to bat in his league,' and . . . I don't know, I guess I just wanted to show her. People are always telling me what I should do and shouldn't do . . .

everybody. Anyway, that's what happened. And out there . . . when he wouldn't let me go, and threw the gun over at me . . ."

"Did you get mad then, Jenny?"

She didn't answer for so long that he turned and looked at her. She was shaking her head back and forth slowly, tears glistening in her great dark eyes.

"No," she whispered. "I was . . . I was too scared to get mad. I've never had a gun in my hands before. Grandfather taught Tom and Elizabeth how to shoot but he'd never let me touch a gun. He said I was such a fool that I'd kill somebody. And I wouldn't do anything he didn't want me to. He doesn't like me, but maybe he will some day. I love him very much. And I guess he was right—only I didn't mean to kill anybody. I just had the gun in my hand, holding it out. I was almost as scared of it as I was of him. And then it went off. There was a horrible crack, and he did like they do in the movies, sort of went double, and he . . . he was lying on the floor, and I just stood there. And then I threw it down and ran. I didn't know what to do till I saw the boat down on the shore and I remembered the Fergusons' phone. And . . . that's the way it happened . . ."

He gripped her hand harder to keep it from shaking.

"But you see," she said quickly, "—but no, you can't see. You can't because you don't really know. Grandfather won't ever believe me. He'll say I'm a . . . a slut, just like my mother. He calls her dreadful things, just as if she weren't Tom and Elizabeth's mother just as much as she is mine. And he knows they aren't true. My father told me it took him ever so long to make my mother marry him, on account of Grandfather. And I'd rather die than have him say everything I know he'll say. I just can't stand it, having him think I'd do anything horrible. I don't know what I'm going to do. I'm such a coward. I'm such a horrible little coward, or I'd have . . . I'd have done something to myself a long time ago, to keep from being so much trouble to . . . Elizabeth and Tom and . . . everybody."

"Look, Jenny," Jonas said quietly. "Up to now you've made sense. Now you're not making any sense at all. I don't like it. In the first place, you're not a coward. But you'd be a coward if you even thought of doing anything to yourself. You're a wonderful little girl . . . and how do you think Elizabeth and Tom and Wetherby would feel if you threw in the sponge at this point? Don't you know, Jenny, we're all proud as hell of you, just for having guts enough to put up a fight——"

"But it was my fault. Grandfather says it was Mother's fault she married my father. He says she led him on. That's what I did to Gordon. I led him on.—What's the matter?"

"The night air . . . it chokes me," Jonas said. He knew that laughing at her would be as near fatal as anything he could do. He coughed again and composed himself soberly.

"You didn't lead him on. He didn't need any leading on, honey. Get that firmly out of your little head. Try to think of it the other way. Think of the number of girls you've kept from doing what you did . . . or what you didn't do. Let's be philosophical about it. Let's just forget it ever happened."

"That's all right to say, but——"

"I know. But let's sit tight. Sergeant Digges thinks I did it, and I'm damned if I'm not going to let him go ahead thinking so. The more I hear of Mr. Gordon Darcy the more I'm in favor of what happened to the skunk. You just leave it to me, will you? We'll fox the whole lot of them."

"Sergeant Digges is my mother's second cousin," Jenny said. "What?"

"Sergeant Digges is my mother's second cousin."

"That's what I thought you said. Well . . ."

"—Well?"

"Well, I'll be darned. I guess that's what I was going to say." Jonas grinned down at her. "How does he get along with your grandfather?"

"Oh, dear," Jenny said. "Grandfather would probably horsewhip him if he ever came near the house."

"Oh, well, then." He got to his feet. "What are we worrying about?"

He pulled her up, tucked her arm into his and marched her toward the big house.

"You're going in, and you're going to sneak quietly up to your room and go to bed and to sleep. No pills, no nothing. You're going to go fast asleep. And tomorrow——"

"Should I go to school?"

"School?"

"High school. I'm a senior in high school."

"Oh."

For some reason, Jonas had never thought of what she did on week days. Gordon Darcy Grymes's stock, already subterranean, took a new and lower nose-dive.—A kid, a school kid

98

at that, he thought, with complete and final contempt.

"Sure, I'd go to school. I'd act just as if nothing had happened. Avoid Grandpa. If he's going to have another stroke, let's let Sergeant Digges give it to him."

"Oh, you shouldn't say that."

Nevertheless Jenny giggled. Jonas steered her across the porch and into the house considerably relieved in his mind. If she could giggle, she was in no immediate danger of doing anything to hurt herself.

"Now scoot along. I'll see you in the morning. You're going to sleep like a log. Good-night."

He bolted back across the porch and down the steps. The plump figure of little Miss Olive had emerged out of the living room into the front hall. At the moment Jonas was in no mood for abstract knowledge. Nor did he wish to hear again how Miss Olive had been present, with and without Papa, at every birth and death in the Blanton-Darrell House since the affecting demise of the Professor's grandfather, who had imbibed even more freely than the Professor, nor would she under any circumstances fail them now. The fact that the current Tinsley Darrell apparently had no intention whatsoever of dying now or in the foreseeable future deterred her not at all. Miss Olive was set for the night.

Jonas cleared the steps in one jump, glanced up, and ducked.

"—Wetherby! For the love of God, give me just one drink! This stuff is poison!"

The tumbler of water hurled through the sick-room window crashed and splintered on the brick at his feet.

"You're killing me, you black devil! You *want* to see me die! Where's Miss Elizabeth? *Elizabeth!* Where's my granddaughter?"

"There, there, now, Professor, sir. Just ca'm yourself. Ca'm yourself down, sir, an' drink this. You going drink it if'n you bus' every glass in this here house. It ain' nothin' but water, Mr. Tinsley, an' it ain' never hurt anybody yet."

"You're killing me! Ugh, the nasty stuff! It'll rot my liver! It'll rust my kidneys! It's not fit to drink! Get out of here! *Elizabeth!*"

"See now—you ain' hurt none. Now you just set back an' rest yourself. Rest yourself to your content. Miss Elizabeth, she tired. She lyin' down."

As Jonas stepped over the broken glass, the Professor's shuddering groan sounded in his ears.

"Horrible! Horrible! Ugh!"

If recovery was not complete, the prognosis, Jonas thought, was distinctly and highly favorable. He went on a little way across the grass.

"—Dr. Smith . . . where's Jenny?"

Elizabeth Darrell came running from the kitchen wing. Her hair had come loose from the black ribbon that held it moulded to her head and was falling in a long pale gold bob around her shoulders, making her look almost like a child herself except for the sheer panic in her drawn white face.

"—I've looked all over the house . . . I can't find her any——"

"She's okay. She stayed out here. I've just sent her in to bed."

"Oh, thank goodness!" She stopped, reached out for the corner of the porch to steady herself, and drew a quick relaxing breath. She pushed her hair back from her face. "I forgot all about her until just now, and I get so scared . . . I'm afraid she'd do something crazy, like running away . . . or something."

In the fan of soft yellow light from the open door Jonas saw haunting anxiety in her eyes, and knew the desperate fear in what she meant.

"I don't think you need to worry about that," he said gently. "I've just talked to her like a Dutch uncle. I think she's got a lot of stuff out of her system. So——"

"Did she talk to you?" Elizabeth interruped him quickly, and turned away for an instant as he nodded. "Oh, dear. But maybe it's a good thing. She's always chattered and gabbled about everything, until . . . until *he* came along."

"Well, it was her first love affair. I guess she was pretty tangled up. She knew everybody disapproved of it. And she's not very proud of herself right now."

"I know. And I guess I didn't use much tact—when I found out he was meeting her after school and taking her all over the countryside. I could have killed him myself. And he was so darned attractive when he wanted to be."

"Were you in love with him too?"

It was a form of personal torture he was inflicting on himself, but it seemed terribly important for him to know. He tried to suppress the acute pang of jealousy that made his stomach feel as if it were being put through a rock crusher just then.

"No—don't be silly," Elizabeth said curtly. "I've got a little sense and I'm not seventeen years old. And I'm not sure he didn't go after Jenny just to get even with me . . . at first, anyway. He was terribly vain and frightfully spoiled. I like men who're men, and don't stand around like peacocks. Gordon missed his calling. He ought to have been in the movies instead of writing about the people who are."

She stopped and looked up at him searchingly, trying to find in his face some answer for the questioning perplexity in her mind.

"I wish I could understand you. I just don't. I really don't."

"Isn't it pretty obvious?" Jonas asked gently. "I'm very simple. Philippa says I'm just plain transparent."

At the mention of her name he saw Elizabeth stiffen, withdrawing from him as if she had actually walked away, her defences up, regretting her momentary lapse from them.

"That's what I don't understand about you, Dr. Smith," she said evenly. "And it rather frightens me. I don't see why you're doing what you seem to be doing, unless . . . well, I just don't know. One minute you seem to be . . . to be on our side. And then you aren't. You seem to be letting yourself in for a lot of trouble, but I don't see why. It seems sort of crazy, to me."

"I suppose it does," Jonas said soberly. Her hand was still resting on the corner of the porch. He had to put his own in his pocket to keep from reaching out and taking hers. A moment before he could have done it, but not now when she was remote and withdrawn, being very cool and practical in summing him up. "But it really isn't crazy at all. It has a sort of super-sanity, in fact. It's one of those things I never believed in, much, until it walloped me. It's a . . . a sort of *coup de foudre*. I never really believed you could see a girl just once and from then on not care how much trouble you got yourself into if it was going to make anything a little easier for her. That's what happened to me. I've just fallen in love, that's all."

Her face was turned up to his. In the suffused light from the windows on the porch it had a pale luminous radiance as she listened to him, her lips parted a little, her eyes wide like a child's making a faltering approach to a meaning that was not wholly clear and waiting . . . just to be entirely sure.

Jonas took his hands out of his pockets.

"Elizabeth!"

Her name was on his lips, but it was Miss Olive's childlike voice that gave it sound and totally different substance, and tore to shreds the gossamer web the magic moment had woven between them. Elizabeth took a quick step backward.

"Elizabeth! Come and get something around you. You'll catch your death of cold. Papa was always very particular about a young girl being out after dark without something around her."

Jonas's arms, for once in complete agreement with one of Papa's dicta, fell to his sides.

"I'm coming right in, Miss Olive."

"Oh dear, I don't want to take you away from Dr. Smith. I wouldn't do that for the world. You just wait . . . I'll hand you a wrap. I wouldn't think of——"

"Please, Miss Olive.—Good night, Dr. Smith."

She ran up the porch steps.

14

Jonas could still hear Miss Olive, protesting and plaintive, and Elizabeth patiently trying to reassure her, as he crossed the grass toward the wing. Disappointed and sore, he could have throttled Miss Olive. He kicked open the wicket in the hedge, banged it shut and crossed the small enclosure to the french window into his consulting room. And stopped. The window was open. From inside he could hear the bony crack-crack of Roddy's tail on the floor welcoming him home. The glow of a lighted cigarette shone briefly in the dark. His mind did a quick flash-back, wondering how long his guest had been there, as he glanced over through the hedge, doing some rapid calculation of the distance to the bench where he and Jenny had sat. Sergeant Digges would have to have the ears of a lynx to have heard anything she'd said, but the mere fact of the two of them sitting there together in the dark, if he had seen them, would certainly have suggested something to his eager mousetrap of a mind.

"Good evening," he said. He stepped through the window, reached for the light on the desk and pressed down the switch.

"Oh," he said.

"It's me. Remember me, doctor? I'm the woman you said could come and see you this evening."

Philippa Van Holt uncurled her slim legs and sat up in the big red leather chair by the fireplace. She tossed her cigarette

102

into the grate, stretched her arms and yawned, an amused smile on her lips.

"I've had a very pleasant time, and Roddy's been telling me the story of his life. The only thing he wouldn't do was break out your Scotch. I could do with a drink. Can I help get the ice or something?"

"Thanks, I'll get it."

Jonas went out into the kitchen. She followed him and took down a pair of glasses from the cupboard.

"I hope you don't mind my being here," she said seriously. "I thought I couldn't take Miss Olive tonight, but when I got home and found she was going out for the night, I decided I could take the place better with her in it than I could alone . . . just me and Papa's ghost. I guess I must be cracking up. I simply couldn't bear being over there alone. So I hope you don't mind."

"Not at all. Glad you came."

He handed her a Scotch and soda. She was the last person in the whole blue creation he felt like spending the rest of the evening with, but she was there, and she did not look very happy. He reminded himself that after all Darcy Grymes had been her husband, and she'd said she loved the guy.

"I'm a mess," she said all of a sudden. She was back on the red leather chair, her legs curled up under her again, her head on one hand, her drink in the other resting on the arm of the chair. In the black dress, her face pale and drawn, all the glamor and glitter that shone around her when he saw her get out of her car for the after-church julep was so gone that it took an effort for him to remember what she had been like then.

"I just wonder," she said after another long moment of silence. "I wonder if it's worth all the stress and strain. He's dead, and nothing'll bring him back. I don't think Sergeant Digges is getting very far very fast. And if I sort of give up, I wouldn't be surprised if maybe they won't decide it was suicide after all. That's one of the reasons I haven't told him about the date Gordon had last night—for dinner and what not. It was with Jenny Darrell."

"I thought he had dinner with his brother," Jonas said deliberately.

"Because she broke it. I guess Elizabeth and Tom got after her. You know—or I guess you don't know—my husband was a curious melange of noble and ignoble characteristics. He was spoiled. Everything was too easy. He liked to eat his cake and have it still intact with the frosting on it and the candles lit at

103

the end of the party. He was never really handicapped by what you'd call a moral sense. Maybe it was part of his charm, and he certainly had it. He didn't have any sense of responsibility, which I guess is why he married me . . . a sort of wife-mother-guardian-business manager arrangement. I'm going to miss him a lot more than you'd think to hear me talk, because he was terribly good for me. I'd still be a fourth-rate acress if he hadn't got me interested in writing publicity, and he was always swell to me. I don't quite know what I'm going to do without him."

She sipped her drink slowly, staring over the rim of the glass at something visible only to herself.

"Jonas," she said finally. "Jonas . . . this is a crazy, cock-eyed notion—but do you suppose by any chance he could have picked her up after the hop? He had a gal out there at the creek. There's no use pretending he didn't, with those keys in the water. He had even more behavior patterns than most of us. I could always tell when he'd lost money at the races, or was getting ready to do something fabulously extravagant. You can't live with a person and work with him without knowing him."

She stopped a moment, still staring in front of her.

"I just wonder. I've been thinking about it ever since I got home. She went to the hop. I know that. She and her date came by for Miss Olive to see her dress that Miss Olive had fixed up out of an old one of Elizabeth's for her. The hop isn't over till twelve, and her date was a first classman who doesn't have to be in till one."

She frowned and set her glass on the floor. "You know, I've been wondering if that was what happened. If she called him up, or they'd worked it so he met her after her midshipman went back to the Yard. That would explain him leaving the hotel at a quarter to one."

"But you thought that was his brother . . . not him."

"I did, but I'm beginning to wonder," she answered slowly. "If he was whipping out to meet Jenny—or any late date—it explains the time and the big rush. And I haven't any real *reason* to think it was his brother. I was down in his room this evening and none of his papers are gone."

"And they would be if it was brother Franklin?"

Jonas gave her a sardonic grin that faded promptly as she shrugged her shoulders and lifted her arched brows.

"Quien sabe?"

She picked up her glass again. "I'm not making any

more judgments in re. my honorable brother-in-law until some-body produces a few facts. I can be so wrong about people . . . especially when I dislike them as intensely as I do him."

"Why do you?"

"Well, for several reasons that are neither here nor there. But let's skip it. It's all water under the bridge, now that I won't ever have to have dear Franklin in my hair any more. And it goes double, of course. Anyway, let's not talk about it. I've got to forget, so the quicker I begin the better off I'll be. Let's have one more drink, and you tell me about you. What on earth did you come to this latent burial ground to practice medicine for?"

"—Because Elizabeth Darrell was here," Jonas thought. He wondered what she was doing then . . . if she was thinking about him, his head swimming around in the rosy glow of the stratosphere.

"I thought I'd like it here," he said. "There's really not much to tell . . ."

"Well, it's all completely fascinating."

Philippa Van Holt drained her second Scotch and soda at last and got to her feet. "I've got to go. You have to work in the morning, don't you? I've stayed too late as it is."

She went through the reception room to the front door.

"I sort of hate to stay in that house by myself tonight. Miss Olive even took the cat with her. And it's absurd of course, be-cause she's certainly no protection. Miss Olive, not the cat. She's one of these people that never sleep a wink, you know, and you could knock the house down two minutes after they've gone to bed and it wouldn't make them turn over. And it's re-volting, the way she snores."

She shivered a little.

"I don't know why I should be so jittery. I'm sure nobody would want to . . ."

She broke off. Then she said. "But I don't suppose he thought anybody would want to . . . to kill him. I wish I knew who it was out there with him. But I wasn't going to think about it any more, was I? Good night."

"I'll walk over with you," Jonas said, "and see you lock your-self in. I don't think you need to worry."

"You needn't come. I'm a big strong girl."

Philippa stopped. "Or come as far as the street. All this nur-sery stock around here makes me feel the redskins are lurking."

She went ahead of him a little way along the path, stopped

again and turned around.

"You know you've been terribly sweet to let me bore you with my memories. I never knew I could be so lonely. I'd have died tonight, without you." She looked up at him. "Would you . . ." Her voice had sunk to a whisper. "Would you mind kissing me, just once?"

"I might even like it," Jonas said with a grin. He bent his head down to kiss her cheek. She moved so that her lips met his and clung softly a moment.

"Good night, dear," she said. "Don't come any further. I have my car. I'll see you tomorrow."

And how it happened Jonas did not quite know, but he jerked his head around just in time to see Elizabeth Darrell slip up the steps and into the Blanton-Darrell House. He heard Philippa Van Holt's sudden ripple of lilting laughter.

"You . . . stinker," he said.

She laughed again. "It's for your own good, doctor. She'd have been a rotten secretary. And it'll teach her a lesson not to go lurking about at night in bushes."

She started to laugh again, stopped and turned abruptly, looking over at the big house.

"—Was she listening to what I was saying to you in there?"

Her voice was sharply edged.

"I shouldn't think so. I guess she came out to get a little peace and quiet from her grandfather. He's pulled through, you know."

"I didn't know. I thought Miss Olive was going over to be in at the death."

"It was after she got there."

"I see."

Philippa was still looking at the Blanton-Darrell House. Even in the darkness Jonas could see her eyes narrowed. She turned back to him.

"Jonas—what did Tom french out of the Academy for, last night?"

"To meet a gal."

There was no use trying to lie to her, pretend he didn't know, and send her off to find out for herself.

"I thought he didn't have a girl?"

"He must have, if he frenched out to see her."

She looked up at him for a moment, shrugged and turned away.

"Well, I'm going. So long. I've had a very interesting evening.

106

I think I'm beginning to see a lot of things I didn't see before. It's wonderful, isn't it? And you know I'm really quite fond of Jenny. Good night."

Jonas heard her car door slam, outside the gate, and the whirr of her motor. He stood there in the path. She hadn't said "But I don't like her sister," not in so many words. The implication was too distinct for him to fail to get it. He turned slowly and looked across the grass. The windows of the big house were dark. The light over the front door was a frail yellow fan behing the glossy blackness of the two magnolias. He looked up at the windows a long time, and moved slowly back to his own door. They didn't have a prayer, or a feeble hope of one, against the hard and shrewd tenacity of Miss Philippa Van Holt.

He went inside and through to his consulting room, sat down at his desk, reached for the phone and sat for a moment with his hand on it. He wanted to call her and tell her he wasn't really kissing Miss Van Holt, but he gave the idea up. It didn't seem so important, now that they were faced with really serious trouble. He settled deeper down in his chair, a heavy scowl on his face, his mind a dismal kaleidoscope in which no picture was complete in all its parts and nothing rang with any high fine decisive truth that he could grab hold of and say This I know, This I can depend on. He seemed to himself to be caught out in some fantastic and shifting game of Which is Appearance, Which is Reality that didn't make sense. The grimly troubling realities were all too clear. Nothing but wishful thinking taken to a schizophrenic degree could pretend they were otherwise. There was only one source of satisfaction that he could see in any of it. That was that he hadn't allowed himself the luxury of counting on Elizabeth Darrell's hiring herself out as his secretary. The hex Philippa Van Holt thought she was putting on that wasn't causing any disappointment he had to swallow and take much time to get over.

He stopped thinking suddenly and held his breath, every nerve in his body alert and wary. The window behind him was still open. He listened intently, hardly breathing, not moving a muscle of his body. He relaxed for an instant, thinking it was Roddy pursuing the rabbit of his dreams, and saw that Roddy was across the room in front of him, stretched out flat on the tiled hearth. What he had heard, or thought he heard, was behind him.

He tightened himself together, a sharp thin streak of plain primitive fear shooting down his spinal column. Somebody

107

was out there. He was being watched. He could feel it in every nerve. He tensed again, figuring what he should do. He could make the open window in about one jump . . .

Then Jonas Smith relaxed suddenly, and grinned. Who was he afraid of? Jenny Darrell was hardly likely to decide to shoot him, Tom Darrell, who conceivably might, was safely confined to his room in Bancroft Hall behind the wall of the United States Naval Academy. There was only one person who would be interested in spying on him. Now that he thought of it, it seemed a little strange that Sergeant Digges, after all his threats and accusations, had left him so peacefully alone, without surveillance, from the time he'd walked off from the Milnors' cottage at five o'clock. Why it had not occurred to him that it was just more of the old line that Fisherman Digges was playing out for his final catch, he was at that moment at a loss to see, except that he had been too involved with the various women in his life to be using his head properly.

Jenny, Elizabeth, Philippa . . . Sergeant Digges' watcher in the shrubbery must be slightly confused by this time. Jonas's face brightened suddenly. Maybe Philippa's parting gesture was going to be funnier than she thought. It was hardly likely Sergeant Digges or any of his men would overlook the possibilities involved in a tender scene between the dead man's widow and their chief suspect. That, Jonas thought, should fox them up completely. He sat quietly at his desk. The idea that his shadow had been out there while Philippa was talking about Jenny's date with Gordon Darcy Grymes he could dismiss without alarm. Roddy had been in and out too many times.

An idea came to him, and he gave a low whistle. Roddy flashed back from the insubstantial fields and streams of his buried life.

"Go find him, boy."

Jonas jerked his thumb toward the window behind him. Roddy lit out. In a second Jonas heard him paw open the gate in the hedge. He sat there with a pleased grin on his face, listening, waiting for Roddy's excited bark at the sight or sound of the intruder. There was nothing. After a moment Jonas got up and strolled through the window across to the swinging gate. The moon was up but dimmed by a wreath of clouds. It took him several minutes to make out the dog's loping figure coming back across the gardens from the direction of the entrance gate. He was coming happily, his tail wagging.

"—Oh, oh," Jonas thought. Roddy had met a friend, and

108

Roddy's friends among the Anne Arundel County Police were limited. Jonas went slowly back into the house. If Sergeant Digges was interested enough to take up the watch himself, maybe it was not as amusing as he had thought it was. As he locked the window and turned off the lights to go up to bed, he wondered whether it was wise to take anything for granted. He was trying to think back to Roddy's sorties in and out while Philippa was talking. It would be pretty funny if all he was doing was going out occasionally to speak to his friend the Sergeant.

15

"I don't know whether you expected me this morning or not, Dr. Smith. Miss Olive says it was firmly understood that I wanted a job and you'd given me one. I'll be glad to go home in case she's wrong."

It was the second time Jonas Smith had opened the front door to find Elizabeth Darrell on his steps. If he had been staggered the first time, when she came for a sleeping tablet for her younger sister, he was, this time, five minutes to nine o'clock Monday morning, more than staggered. He was reduced to a lump of inarticulate red-faced clay. She stood there cool and poised, her gold hair drawn in an efficient-looking bun at the back of her head, her crisp grey-and-white striped cotton dress precisely what the well-dressed office assistant should wear. The only thing that was missing was a smile to indicate that the intra-office relationship between doctor and assistant, employer and employee, would be on a reasonably cordial and friendly level. While he couldn't exactly blame her, he didn't know any way of explaining the episode of Miss Van Holt the night before, especially as the cook his sisters had got him was busily dusting the reception room at that moment, and more especially as he had a pretty definite idea Elizabeth Darrell was not at all interested, in who he kissed or why. And why she was there was confusing enough to Jonas Smith. She couldn't want a job that badly. But there she was.

He stepped aside from the door. "Come in," he said. "I hoped you'd show up, but I wasn't sure on account of your grandfather. How is he this morning?"

"He's fine. He's up, but Wetherby's playing gin rummy with him, so I hope he'll stay reasonably quiet. Miss Olive's gone home, which ought to help, and Jenny's gone to school."

For a moment he wondered if she was there because she wanted an excuse to get out of the big house too, but it didn't seem reasonable.

"In here, Miss Darrell," he said.

"Good morning, Martha." Elizabeth greeted the old colored woman, who stopped dusting promptly and looked at her with wide eyes.

"You ain' sick, is you, Miss Elizabeth? I thought it was the Professor was sick."

"No, I'm going to work here too, Martha."

She put her bag on the small desk between the windows and looked at Jonas. "Now if you'll explain how you want things done, Dr. Smith."

"Well," Jonas said, "I don't guess we'll be stampeded, exactly, this morning, Miss Darrell. In fact, I was going in to read the papers."

"Then go ahead. I probably know as much about this end of it as you do anyway—I worked in Dr. Pardee's office last summer. So why don't I just see what's here and what we need, and get Martha's cleaning schedule settled so she's through here by nine."

"Swell," Jonas said. As he sat down at his desk and opened the morning paper he listened to her low business-like voice coming through the closed door with a pleasantly radiating sensation of warmth and contentment all around him. He didn't know why she was there, but she was there. That was enough. He grinned. Maybe she'd decided to put up a fight for her man. It didn't hurt him to dream it, did it?

His face sobered abruptly as he turned to the back page of the paper, "Prominent Baltimorean Questioned in Shore Murder of Brother."

"Franklin Grymes, head of the Grymes Foundry and Construction Company, was being questioned last night in connection with the death of his brother Gordon Darcy, Hollywood publicity and public relations man, who was shot to death late Saturday night in a secluded shore retreat in Anne Arundel County near Annapolis.

"No explanation was given by the police. Interest was roused, however, when reporters learned that Mr. Grymes's car

110

was missing from the garage operated by the apartment house in which he lives. Mr. Grymes dined with his brother at the Annapolis Yacht Club and returned the car to the garage at approximately 10:30, when he is said to have retired for the night, leaving word he was not well and was to be called only if his brother, or his fiancée Miss Agatha Reed, prominent in Baltimore social circles, called him.

"George Browne, of the 1400 block East Eager Street, garage attendant, discovered the car was missing some time before midnight. As four cars have been stolen from the garage in recent weeks, he tried to call Mr. Grymes and failing notified the police. The matter was dropped when the car reappeared between 3:30 and 3:35 A.M. while Browne was absent picking up another car. It is understood Mr. Grymes has informed the Anne Arundel County Police that he returned to his apartment at 10:30 and did not leave it after that time.

"Special interest is attached to the case in the Baltimore area as Mr. Grymes is the fourth of that name in direct line from the Scotch-Irish indentured servant Isaiah Grymes, who established the foundry which has been a landmark in East Baltimore from 1785 until the present time. Its original form is now hardly recognizable, due to the enormous changes made before and during the War, when it became one of Baltimore's outstanding industries under the leadership of the present Franklin Grymes, to whom it passed at the death of his uncle Franklin Grymes III, a colorful figure in Baltimore life of the last quarter century.

"Franklin Grymes III is especially remembered by members of various civic and historical societies, whose efforts to purchase and preserve the Old Foundry he indignantly resisted. A delegation sent to interview him was confronted by a cannon made by the firm, used against the British in the War of 1812. It was set up in the courtyard of the Old Foundry, with Mr. Franklin Grymes at the business end. He gave the delegation to understand that if they insisted upon making a monument out of it, it would fittingly contain them and any further of their emissaries. His faith in the Old Foundry was more than justified during World War II, when the Army and Navy 'E' flew proudly from its flagstaff. The cannon is still in the courtyard.

"Gordon D. Grymes, who was shot and killed Saturday night in an abandoned summer cottage on the shore, is unknown in Baltimore. A spokesman for the firm told reporters last night

111

that he had never had any connection with it."

Jonas put the paper down. "Well, well," he thought. When little Jenny threw a stone into the pond the ripples spread out far and wide. He reached into his pocket for his pipe, and took his hand out hastily. There was some one in the reception room—an emergency case, from all the commotion.

"I've got to see the doctor immediately, do you hear?"

It was a woman, her voice high-pitched and hysterical.

The door opened. "There's a woman here—" Elizabeth began. "Jonas!"

The woman brushed her aside and was in the room. Jonas sat staring at her. It was Franklin Grymes's fiancée Miss Agatha Reed. But a different Agatha . . . never would Jonas have believed Agatha Reed could look so much like a maenad, hatless, her brown hair pushed wildly back, her perfect nose pinched and sharp, her eyes distended.

"Jonas! Send her out of here—I've got to talk to you!"

Jonas pulled himself together. "Would you mind, Miss Darrell . . ."

Elizabeth glanced at him, and drew the door shut behind her.

Agatha Reed's eyes had flown to the paper on his desk. "Jonas—you've seen it! You've——"

He interrupted her. "Take it easy, Agatha. Sit down. You'll——"

"I can't sit down, I'm out of my mind. It'll ruin him."

She threw her handbag on the desk, put both hands to her temples and pressed hard, her eyes closed, biting her lower lip. "It's *ghastly*. Everybody in Baltimore already thinks he did it. And he didn't, Jonas! He *didn't!* And you've got to help me. That policeman said you were out there. He said you were trying to protect some woman. He must think it was me. He kept asking all sorts of questions, over and over again till I thought I'd go mad! And then, this morning—*that*."

She thrust a finger at the paper on the desk, recoiling as if it were some noxious thing.

"—They didn't tell me they knew the car was gone!"

"It was gone, then?"

"Yes! But not the way they think."

She tried to steady herself, and came over to him. She took his arm and shook it urgently.

"Listen, Jonas. This is what happened. Gordon's been trying to make trouble for Franklin. Franklin's been trying to see him. He's been coming down here, calling him up—doing everything he could to get things settled."

Jonas took a deep breath. "What things?"

"I don't know. Something about the business. But that's not important. Saturday Franklin came down just on a chance, and he did see him. They had dinner together. Gordon wouldn't say one thing or the other, but he was friendly. Franklin came back to Baltimore. When he called me up he was tired and going to bed, but he sounded so depressed and low that I suggested he come and pick me up and we'd go somewhere and have a drink. He did come, and we went for a drive, and when he said how friendly Gordon was I suggested we come down here and see him—maybe if I met him too we could make some sort of arrangement. Because the firm *belongs* to Franklin."

Jonas blinked at her.

"Was Gordon saying it didn't?"

"Oh, I don't know the details." She brushed him off impatiently. "He parked out in front as near the hotel as he could. Franklin went up to his room to see if he'd come out with us. He wasn't there, but his door was unlocked and Franklin went in. The phone was ringing and he answered it. It was some girl. She wanted to know if somebody was there. Franklin didn't hear who it was, but this girl said, 'Are you sure, because I'm going to ask the manager to come up and see.' Before Franklin could say anything she'd hung up, and he decided he'd better leave as quick as he could. He didn't want to get mixed up in any of Gordon's kind of trouble. And they *look* so much alike."

"I . . . I know," Jonas said. "What happened then?"

"Nothing." There was a faint flush over her high cheekbones. "Nothing at all. We went back to Baltimore. But because the car wasn't in, the police don't believe us, and we don't want to . . . to have to——"

The flush in her cheeks deepened.

"——Agatha!" Jonas said. "You——"

"Oh, stop it!"

Agatha Reed stamped her foot, her eyes burning. "It's all your fault! You always made fun of me for being a prude . . . and all I did was to go to his apartment and have one creme de menthe—but if anybody finds out that I was there at three o'clock in the morning I'll be the laughing stock of all Baltimore!"

Jonas shook his head. "——Of that small part of it that your friends make up," he thought. But of course that was what Agatha meant by "all Baltimore," and anyway he felt a slight

113

twinge of pity for her.

"—But it's not that, Jonas! I'll tell if I have to, no matter who laughs at me or what anybody thinks. But that's not it. It's Franklin. He just can't get mixed up in this, he just can't! It'll ruin him! And you can help us. You know we weren't out there. The girl you were with can't matter that much, Jonas. If you tell the police who she was, maybe they'll let me and Franklin alone. You can't just sit and let them ruin us, Jonas—it wouldn't be fair!"

She was pleading with him suddenly, her face raised to his, tears streaming down her cheeks. "—You don't hate me *that* much, Jonas!"

"—Oh dear God," Jonas thought. He could only shake his head. He didn't hate her, and it wasn't fair. He took out his handkerchief and put it in her hand.

"Don't cry, Agatha."

And somehow Miss Agatha Reed was in his arms, sobbing bitterly, and he was comforting her the best he could.

For Elizabeth Darrell to open the door, at exactly that moment, was perhaps inevitable . . . but the squeak of the hinge as the wicket swung open and the shadow that preceded the solid substance of Sergeant Digges onto the terrace were no doubt what the young St. John's students at Gregory's would have put down to Aristotle's hubris, followed quickly by Nemesis in person.

"Excuse me, doctor," said Sergeant Digges. "I'll come back when you're not busy."

"Excuse me, Dr. Smith—you have another patient."

Elizabeth Darrell glanced at Sergeant Digges's retreating form. She pretended not to see Miss Reed at all.

"It's Miss Olive. Shall I tell her to come back, or will you see her now?"

"Ask her to come back, if she doesn't mind."

Jonas gently disengaged Miss Reed. "I'm going out for a few minutes. I'll be back in half an hour."

Elizabeth closed the door.

"Powder your nose, Agatha," Jonas said. "And get out of here and go back to Baltimore. Just sit tight for a couple of days and let's see what happens. Where's Franklin now?"

"In Baltimore."

Agatha dabbed at her nose with the feather puff she took out of her bag. "I drove down. My car's outside. He's . . . he's taking Philippa Van Holt to lunch. She's Gordon's wife. He

114

thinks maybe she'll be more reasonable."

She did not say more reasonable than what, and Jonas did not say what he was thinking, which was that Franklin Grymes could not be very bright. He said, "Come on, I'll take you out to your car." What he needed was more time to think. "We can go this way."

He led her through the window out on the terrace and through the wicket.

"Which gate did you come through?"

"The one over there."

They crossed the Darrells' garden to the entrance past the big house. On his way back he glanced up at the sick room of the Blanton-Darrell House. Through the open window he could see Professor Darrell's iron-grey head and his heavy shoulders in a striped dressing gown.

"Gin!" Professor Darrell roared, at that moment. For an instant Jonas thought he was crying out for sustenance, but he was wrong. "That's only two dollars and forty-six cents I owe you now, you thieving scoundrel! Tell me I'm going to die, will you!"

Professor Darrell leaned triumphantly back in his chair and Jonas crossed the grass quickly and quietly. He went through the wicket, across the terrace and inside and sat quietly down at his desk again. He wanted to think. In fact he had to think. And it was not easy. He sat there with his elbows on the desk and his head in his hands. Agatha said it wasn't fair, and it wasn't. He had got to that point and no farther when the telephone on the desk beside him buzzed. He reached out mechanically and picked it up.

"—Dr. Smith's office."

He had just opened his mouth to say "Hello" when he heard Elizabeth Darrell's voice. It was a nice voice, and the sound of it cleared the scowl off his face. He held on to the phone to hear it without the detached if not frosty note it had had each time it had been addressed to him that morning.

"Elizabeth? Tom. Can I talk to you now?"

"Yes. He's gone out. I'm here alone. Is it . . . is it . . . have you seen the Commandant?"

Her voice came quickly, breathlessly urgent.

"I just saw him. I just got out. He's okay, but it's no soap."

Tom Darrell's voice was subdued but firm.

"They've got to put me out. The papers are going to Washington, to the Secretary, and I've got to see the Supe this afternoon. They've got to throw the book at me. It's not their fault. I've——"

"Tom, listen to me! There's no use . . . I've got to see you, before you see the Admiral—before they send the papers to Washington. It's no use, Tom. We've got to do what Dr. Smith said. He's just giving us the chance before he does it himself. He's trying to be as decent as he can, Tom, but he can't help it. He told me about it last night. He's fallen in love with Philippa. He said it was a *coup de foudre*—that means a thunder-clap—so he's got to do whatever she wants him to. I'll tell you about it. I'll come over before noon lunch formation. I've just been waiting here till you called. I wouldn't have come except I told you I'd be here."

If Elizabeth Darrell said any more or if Tom said anything, Jonas did not hear it. He was holding the phone, conscious eventually of the dial tone singing in his ear. When it started, how long it had been going on, he could not have told. The whole thing was a *coup de foudre* of another sort that left him utterly dazed.

Suddenly he came back to his senses, jammed the phone down on the cradle and got to his feet. He strode across the room, threw the door open and came to a halt. Her chair was empty. As he started for the hall door Martha, the maid, came around the stair landing.

"You looking for Miss Elizabeth?" she asked. "She gone. She flew outa here. Maybe her grandpa's took worse again."

"Thanks," Jonas said. He reached the front door, pulled it open and stopped again.

Sergeant Digges was on the bottom step.

"Going some place, doctor?" he inquired pleasantly. "I'm afraid it'll have to wait. It's time you and me had a little talk. —it wasn't anybody sick you were rushing off to see, was it, doctor?"

"No," Jonas said.

Sergeant Digges followed him into his consulting room, pulled a chair up to the corner of the desk, sat down and put his hat on the floor.

"I didn't think so. You don't see doctors breaking their necks for sick people, these days, especially the young ones. Funny attitude they've——"

"Could we discuss the medical profession some other time, Sergeant?"

"We could, I expect." Sergeant Digges crossed his legs and

116

examined his shoe string with deliberation. "I'd like to do it now.—What I wanted to ask you was, how long would it take me to learn to take out somebody's appendix?"

Jonas had picked up the newspaper to drop it in the waste-basket. He let it fall back on the desk.

"—Take out somebody's . . . you . . . I don't get it, Sergeant." He did not try to keep the sharp edge of irritation out of his voice. "What's the——"

"Me," replied Sergeant Digges imperturbably. "Take out somebody's appendix. Sort of shocks you, doesn't it? Well, it sort of shocks me when some young squirt prances in and starts doing my job instead of leaving it to me. I sort of figure my job takes training too, and experience, and a certain amount of knowledge. And what you'd call technique, and equipment—like you've got in there."

He nodded toward Jonas's small laboratory and storage cupboard.

"Just for instance, now. That gun somebody stuck in Grymes's hand. I guess whoever did it didn't stop to figure the difference in the fingerprints a live and a dead man's hand makes. Or remembered that nobody ever handled a gun and left it all shined up except for one set of post-mortem prints. Even my kid knows you can't put a gun in a dead hand the way a live one would take hold of it."

Sergeant Digges regarded Jonas tranquilly a moment.

"Before you start cutting a person open, you find out what his history is, and try to get some kind of a background picture to go on, don't you, doctor?"

"Of course."

"Okay. How much did you find out about this fellow that was killed out there?"

Jonas smiled patiently. "I've told you, Sergeant. I never——"

"Okay. You never saw him before. Did you know he was thirty-four years old, a physical 4-F so the draft never got him? Or that he worked for a publicity firm, public relations specialist, they call themselves?"

Jonas shook his head.

"Not that that's important, except you're apt to wonder why a fellow that lived out in California had to come here to get somebody to kill him, in a place not many people know him. Now, take that gun again. When you got started figuring things out, doctor, what did you find out about it?"

"I . . . nothing," Jonas said curtly.

117

"Maybe we ought to pool our information, then, doctor." Sergeant Digges could not have been more dead-pan. He reached in his pocket and brought out a telegram. "When you don't have facilities to do your job, you go to a hospital. We go to the FBI or some other place that maybe has what we need and don't have. This is from the Los Angeles County Police. The Grymes boys were born and raised out there, and out there they register guns and issue permits to carry them. This one was registered in 1938 and a permit issued. It's the one that killed this fellow, all right."

Sergeant Digges looked steadily at Jonas.

"And would you know who registered it, and who the permit was issued to?"

"Gordon Darcy, I presume," Jonas said.

Sergeant Digges shook his head. "No, doctor. Not Gordon. It was Franklin, doctor. Franklin C. Grymes. Gordon Darcy Grymes's brother. In 1938."

Jonas thought quickly. He had a vision of Agatha Reed's pleading tear-stained face and her sudden passion in defence of the man she was engaged to marry.

"That doesn't necessarily mean Franklin Grymes still had it. He could have given it to his brother, or something. That's a long time ago."

Sergeant Digges nodded. "He could have, I expect. Only, he got into a little trouble, and spent one night as the guest of the Los Angeles County Police and his permit was revoked. That was in January, 1940. Franklin Grymes came to Baltimore to work for his uncle in the Old Foundry in August, 1940. Gordon Grymes stayed out there and got a job with these publicity people. According to Franklin's story, he hasn't seen his brother since then—not until Saturday night."

Jonas shook his head. "I give up, Sergeant. I don't know what you're talking about. I'm all balled up."

"No reason for being balled up, doctor. All I'm saying is that the gun we found out there on the floor of the Milnors' cottage was registered and owned by Franklin Grymes."

His eyes still rested steadily on Jonas's.

"And there's another little item of information I might as well give you, doctor. Except I was sort of thinking of keeping it to surprise you with some time."

"What's that?"

Jonas did not mean to speak as quickly as he did. A sudden alert gleam shone in the sergeant's eyes for an instant. He relaxed into his complacent amiability again.

"Well, if you're real anxious to hear, and in case you don't know already, I'll tell you."

He fished in his pocket for a second telegram.

"This is from the FBI in Washington. I expect you know they get fingerprints from police departments all over the country and keep 'em on file. Well, the night Franklin Grymes spent in the L. A. County Jail they took his—routine stuff if you get in trouble and go to jail. So, the FBI's got 'em. We sent 'em this gun Gordon Grymes was killed with, and the liquor glass on the table, and the silver flask out of his pocket. And just to do the job right, we sent 'em the dead man's fingerprints too. They're all the same, all identical. And the funny part of it is, they don't belong to Gordon Grymes. They belong to his brother Franklin."

Sergeant Digges paused a moment, regarding Jonas intently.

"If that gets you all balled up, doctor, I'll put it the other way. The fellow that was shot and killed out there at the Milnors' wasn't Gordon Darcy Grymes. He's Franklin Grymes— the guy that got arrested and got his permit to carry the gun revoked in 1940. And the fellow up at the Old Foundry in Baltimore is not Franklin Grymes . . . he's Gordon Darcy Grymes. —Surprises you, doctor. Leaves you all of a heap, doesn't it, doctor?"

16

"—That surprises you, doctor?"

For a long two minutes, Jonas Smith M.D. said nothing at all. He sat in a virtual state of suspended animation, staring stupidly across his desk, trying mechanically to make up his mind whether what he thought he had heard Sergeant Digges say was what Sergeant Digges had in fact said.

What he thought he had heard him say was that the body he had seen in the Milnors' cottage out at Ardundel Creek was the body of Franklin Grymes. That was so completely cock-eyed he must have made some mistake. But Sergeant Digges was sitting there, looking at him with a kind of triumphant glaze over his alert hard-bitten countenance. There seemed to be no doubt he had said it, and moreover that he meant it.

"I thought maybe it would surprise you," Sergeant Digges said quietly.

"*Surprise* me?"

The word was understatement to a comic degree. Jonas laughed mirthlessly.

"It really does, Sergeant. In fact it surprises the hell out of me—so much I don't believe a word of it. It . . . it can't be true, that's all. Are you . . . sure about it?"

Sergeant Digges nodded.

"Fingerprints don't lie, doctor. They're the one witness we ever get that doesn't—consciously or unconsciously, it doesn't matter. They're the only one I'd ever trust absolutely."

He sat there, looking steadily at Jonas across the desk. "Well, doctor?"

"Don't say well to me, for God's sake."

Jonas tried again to stagger out of the bewildered daze it had left him in.

"Don't ask me—tell me. It just doesn't make any sense that I can see. You really mean it wasn't Gordon Darcy Grymes that was out at the Milnors'? It was his brother Franklin. And it's Gordon, not Franklin, who's up in Baltimore right now?"

If he stated it himself, he was thinking, perhaps he could get it straightened out.

"That's it, doctor. That's exactly what I'm telling you. I thought maybe you'd be able to help me figure it out, you seem to be on such good terms with the widow and the fiancée, or the fiancée and the widow . . . one or the other. I thought maybe you might know which is which, and what various people are up to, and why."

Jonas shook his head, silently, and kept on shaking it.

"You're sure, doctor?"

"Absolutely."

Jonas took a deep breath. "Look, Sergeant. I tell you again I don't know any of these people. This just doesn't make any sense that I can see."

"It doesn't to me either—not right now. But it will."

Sergeant Digges reached for his hat and got to his feet.

"I'm going to take your word for it—for the time being, that is."

He put his hat on the back of his head and moved toward the door.

"I don't know where you fit in, in all this, doctor. Up until

120

I got these telegrams, I figured it was plain sailing. I was going to come here and put all the cards down. You could take it or leave it—quit all this stalling around or go to jail. I'm not say-saying that isn't where you'll wind up tomorrow morning. But right now I've got this on my mind, and until I get it off I'm not bothering with you any more."

Jonas nodded. "I know. All you're going to do is dog my tracks. Don't try to fool me, Sergeant. But be a little more careful, will you? I get nervous at night. I don't like people prowling around my back yard listening to my conversations. Next time come in and join us, will you? Miss Van Holt was here as a friend, not a patient. Nothing private or confidential. See what I mean?"

Sergeant Digges looked at him for a moment. He smiled faintly.

"Okay, doc. I'll remember that. I guess I must be slipping."

He put his hand on the door knob.

"One other thing," he said deliberately. "I'm not joking, doctor."

Jonas got to his feet. He had no doubt of it.

"What is it, Sergeant?" he asked soberly.

"What I've just told you about the Grymes brothers is strictly in the lodge. I want you to understand that. I thought I wasn't going to tell you. Then I decided I'd like to give you a break, if it happened you were getting tangled up with the wrong people . . . just to let you know there's no hard feel-ings as far as I'm personally concerned. If I don't hang you I might need you myself if I got real sick some night. Right now, I'm telling you to keep your trap shut. You understand?"

"I understand. You needn't worry."

"Okay. And that goes for all your lady friends whatsoever. Get it?"

"I get it," Jonas said.

"All right. Now get along wherever it was you were going. But stick around Annapolis, doc. I might want to see you later. So long."

"So long, Sergeant."

Jonas stood where he was for several minutes. He heard the Sergeant speak to Martha and Roddy in the front hall. The door closed as he left the house, Martha and Roddy went back to the kitchen. He registered it all automatically in the periph-ery of his mind, absorbed in trying mentally to arrange every-thing. He felt a little the way the atomic experts must have

felt when they set up their first chain reaction and saw where
it had landed them. The shot Jenny Darrell had fired had certainly set one up. Who else the final blast was going to sear was
a question that Jonas Smith could ask but not conceivably
answer. There were other questions . . . so many that it was
as if all the rats in Christendom had gathered and his mind
was precisely where they were staging the big race.

—What were the sweepstakes in the grand switcheroo,
Jonas Smith thought . . . when was it made, and how, and
why? Did Jenny think she was out with Gordon Grymes when
she was really with Franklin? And above all, where did this
leave Miss Philippa Van Holt? It was fantastic. The whole
thing was so utterly fantastic that every question he asked
himself instead of clearing anything up made it more of a jun-
gle growth of entanglement and utter confusion. He was
tangled up, he was confused, he was dizzy in the head. Whatever any of it was, whatever it could possibly mean, the only
point of contact he had out of which he felt he ought to be
able, somehow, to make a reasonable judgment of some sort
was the unhappy scene he'd been present at in Miss Olive's
Papa's sanctum in the little yellow brick house on St. John's
Street the day before. It was more bewildering now than it had
been then. He recalled Philippa's outburst of venomous animosity before she ran out of the room and up the stairs, and
Franklin Grymes's—or was it Gordon's—collapse into frenzied
despair. But it still didn't make sense. On the other hand . . .

Jonas straightened his shoulders and shook his head to clear
the snarled-up cobwebs out of it. He was getting the blast end
of the chain reaction mixed up with the initial step that set it
into being. The solid inexorable and irrevocable fact was that a
man was dead and Jennifer Darrell had killed him. It didn't
make any difference—except to him—whether his name was
Gordon, Franklin or George B. Patapsco. Whatever his name,
he was still dead. If the tangent Sergeant Digges was off on led
straight into the hornet's nest it seemed to be leading into, it
was only a question of time when it would lead back again.
Nothing had changed. Nothing except his own moral position.
And that, it was not easy to justify.

He thought about Agatha Reed. It wasn't right to let anyone who was innocent of murder get caught in the meshes of
the kind of publicity net Agatha was already being tripped
up with. He looked at his watch. It was thirteen minutes to
twelve. Elizabeth would be on her way to see Tom in Bancroft

122

Hall before noon meal formation. He didn't want to stop her from seeing him, because after all if she could make him tell the Superintendent the truth when he saw him that afternoon, they might take back the book he'd said they had to throw at him. They wouldn't kick a boy out of the United States Naval Academy for putting his sister's honor and safety above the rules and regulations. The rules and regulations had not been broken by Midshipman Tom Darrell for the first and only time in the history of the Academy. Plenty of flag officers, if not actually the one Tom would see that afternoon, had frenched out over the wall in their midshipman days without destroying either themselves or the United States Navy.

And now they—Elizabeth, Tom, Jenny, himself—were faced with a serious problem in moral values. No matter which Grymes brother was which or what they had done that the one remaining alive in Baltimore was so frantically anxious to conceal, the unalterable fact was that he had not killed the other one at the Milnors' cottage. If, in order to prove that, he had to face the ruin he and Agatha so desperately maintained he did, it seemed to Jonas that maybe he'd been right in the beginning, and Jenny had been right in wanting to make a clean breast of the whole thing. The chain reaction Jenny had set up so far killed one man, given another a stroke that miraculously hadn't killed him or paralyzed him for life. It was on the point of ruining her brother's career, getting him kicked out of the Service in disgrace two weeks before he graduated. It was ruining the other Grymes, wrecking Agatha Reed's life; it had made a widow out of Philippa Van Holt. It was a sobering thought to realize how a seventeen-year-old's inexperience and lack of emotional security could affect so many adult lives.

Including, Jonas reflected, his own. Which brought him back to Elizabeth Darrell. She could tell Tom anything she liked, and he could make his own decision, but there was one thing she had to know. She had to know that he was not in love with Philippa Van Holt. It was the one important thing in Jonas Smith's life just then, a driving impulse he had to fulfill.

"If I don't tell her, I'll go nuts," he thought. It was stupid, it could wait. Yet he knew very well it could not wait. He had to tell her before she saw Tom. He had to save all of them from that one error at any event—and because he was in love it seemed an error of the most overwhelming magnitude. And if he hurried, he could intercept her.

He did hurry, but he would have hurried more effectively if

he had left his car at home.

"Are you from in town, sir?" The guard at the Main Gate stopped him politely but firmly. "You'll have to park outside the Yard."

With neither a pass nor business that authorized him to enter without one (he did not know then that he was in the distinguished company of the wife of a President of the United States, sightseeing incognito, who had not been allowed in either), Jonas had to back into Maryland Avenue and turn down Hanover Street. It was across from St. John's, on College Avenue, that he finally found a place to park. As he strode along the uneven brick sidewalks back to Maryland Avenue and the gate, he was too preoccupied to notice the roots of the ancient maples until he stumbled over them, or the two most magnificent of Georgian town houses, Chase and Hammond-Harwood, facing each other in stately quietude across the sunlit street, until a couple of women, guidebook in hand, stopped him with some questions to which he could give only the most common of answers, "Sorry, I'm a stranger here myself," before he hurried on to the Academy gate.

It was too late by then. He knew it before he passed the guard. The Yard was alive with a thousand young men in blue fatigues and white caps, their books and papers under their arms, streaming in varying degrees of marching order from every direction; enthusiastically converging toward the great pile of Bancroft Hall and food. He cut across in front of the green-copper domed chapel where in the quiet crypt are enshrined all that physically remains of the First Commodore, and hastened down toward Tecumseh Court, already a solid mass of blue and white. There were midshipmen everywhere, streaming up the steps into the great rotunda, or left and right to the nearer entrances to their rooms.

He was much too late. Across the sea of young men he saw her, already down the steps and hurrying along the walk from the court toward the Santee Basin, bare-headed, the sun glistening on her hair, the midshipmen turning to look at her, some of them waving as she waved back and hurried quickly on.

Jonas was half-way to the road to the dock when he saw her car pull out and disappear around the sailboat shelter at the shore end of the great building. He turned back and hurried across the Yard to the Main Gate. It was too late to see her before she saw her brother Tom, but she was probably headed home and he could see her there. How he was going to say what he had to tell her was so far not entirely clear in his mind. To barge in and say "It isn't Philippa Van Holt I'm in love with you, it's you," wasn't as simple as it had seemed when he'd come out of his daze, sitting at his desk, and dashed out into the reception room. Furthermore, in the emotional state she would undoubtedly be in after seeing Tom in Bancroft Hall it was unlikely she'd be particularly interested in anything he had to say on any subject.

He hurried on, not even stopping to pick up his car. The gate at the Darrells' side of the court was nearer than his own, and the one she would probably go in, coming up King George Street. As he turned the corner he looked both ways, expecting to see her either already in the drive or close to it. And there was a car in the drive, headed out, however, not in. It was an ancient and dilapidated vehicle, painted red and black, with a racoon's tail tied to the radiator cap and both fenders badly in need of repair, and it was coughing, jumping forward and bolting back like an asthmatic and recalcitrant mule. None of which, however, was as startling to Jonas as its occupants.

"—Damn it all, Olive, can you drive or can't you drive?"

Professor Tinsley Darrell in the front seat, jamming his hat back from where the last buck had jolted it to the back of his head, was purple with rage. Miss Olive Oliphant at the wheel reached down and pulled on the brake. She sat back and folded her white gloved hands.

"Tinsley . . ." she began. They both saw Jonas. He came up to the window of the car.

"—Dr. Smith, Professor Darrell is just as provoking as he can be."

Miss Olive's mild china-blue child's eyes were a little resentful.

"Damn it all, Smith, she said she'd drive me to the Club. That blasted fool of a Wetherby won't do it. He's trying to make me stay in the house so he can clean me at gin rummy. Doctor's orders! No murderous pill-roller is going to tell me what to do. Can this woman drive or can't she drive? That's all I want to know."

"Tinsley, you've got to calm yourself," Miss Olive said. She turned to Jonas. "I can drive very well, Dr. Smith. Papa always said I drove as well as any young woman he knew. He didn't approve of young women driving an automobile, but after Innis died and Papa tried to learn himself, he allowed me to learn, and I drove our automobile until we sold it when Papa

125

got too nervous to let me drive him any more. And if Tinsely doesn't like the way I drive, I think he ought to drive himself. Or get a taxicab. I only agreed to drive him because I thought he'd work himself into another disorder if he stayed at home."

"Damn it all, Olive, I can't call a taxi. I gave Elizabeth my word I wouldn't call one."

"You gave her your word you'd stay in the house, Tinsley."

"That's a lie. That's a black lie. I said I wouldn't call a taxi."

"Tinsley, you——"

"Look . . . both of you," Jonas said. He put his hand through the window and patted Miss Olive's. "Professor Darrell, you oughtn't to be out. Miss Olive, you shouldn't have agreed to take him."

Professor Darrell's protruding bloodshot eyes glared at him like an angry horse's. "Doctor, you mind your business and I'll mind mine."

"Dr. Smith, I wouldn't have agreed to take him except he was going to drive himself or try to walk. And I think it would look very badly for him to collapse on the street, either driving or walking, and have people say he was intoxicated *before* he got to the Club. Papa always thought it very poor manners for a gentleman to *go* to his Club under the influence."

"What in the blue-shirted hell does it matter how he gets there, Olive? Your father, Olive——"

"I'll thank you to be very careful what you say about my father, Tinsley."

Miss Olive spoke with gentle spirit.

"Papa never minded a gentleman coming *home* from his Club slightly overcome. But Papa always felt there was a place for everything.—A place for everything, and everything in its place. It was one of my earliest lessons. And if you're going to speak unkindly to me, Tinsley, I'm not going to drive you anywhere. I'm going to leave you sitting right here in the road. In fact, that's just what I intend to do, Tinsley."

Miss Olive took hold of the door.

"Olive, if you leave me here . . ." Professor Darrell controlled himself with a dangerous effort. "Olive, I swear to God——"

"Papa never allowed blasphemy, Tinsley."

Miss Olive opened the door and got out. Her rose-colored lips were pressed firmly together and her fresh clear cheeks delicately flushed.

"Tinsley, *I'm* not sure you haven't already been indulging.

126

Good day, gentlemen."

She took a few steps along the drive, a plump little figure striving to maintain her gentle indignation.

"—Oh, Dr. Smith!" She turned and came back to Jonas, fishing down in her white crocheted bag. "There's a piece I was reading about urushiol that I cut out for you," she said brightly. "I thought it would interest you. They're manufacturing it—synthetically, I believe is the word they use. And some time, doctor, I'd like to come and see you. My insomnia is troubling me again. Perhaps you'll be able to give me something for it."

She found the clipping and handed it to Jonas.

"Thank you, Miss Olive," he said. Hoping she was not planning to take synthetic urushiol for her insomnia, he repressed his amusement, took the clipping and put it carefully in his pocket. "Any time you'd like to come around."

"Thank you, doctor." Miss Olive tripped off along the drive toward the street. Jonas turned to Professor Darrell, sitting bolt upright in the front seat of the old car, his stick between his knees, both hands clenched around it.

"Don't you think you'd better give up, Professor, and go back to the house? It isn't safe for you to drive, and you're just working yourself up to another crisis."

For a moment he thought he'd precipitated it himself. Professor Darrell's hackles were rising, the blood suffusing his full florid face. Then he let his breath out, like a jet of steam escaping from heavy pressure.

"I'm not going to walk back, damn it, doctor. Get Wetherby. Tell the worthless scoundrel to come here and get me. It's his car. I wouldn't touch the thing. I'll go back."

Jonas looked at him with a sudden curious small twinge of pity stirring inside him. The Professor was still trying to bluster, but the heart had gone out of it. He looked tired. He was tired.

He managed to glare at Jonas once more. "Damn it all, doctor—I'm not *anxious* to die."

"Why don't I drive you back?"

Jonas got in the car and started it up with only a few shuddering spits and jerks. They went around the drive to the front door of the Blanton-Darrell House and came to a stop. Professor Darrell got out.

"Thank you, sir," he said. He waited until Jonas got out, and shook hands with him formally and with impressive gravity before he went up the steps and into the house. Jonas stood for a moment, listening.

"—Wetherby! Get that junk heap out of the front yard! Do you hear what I say? And where is my granddaughter?"

It was what Jonas wanted to know too.

"I'll get it right away, Professor, sir." Wetherby's gentle voice came from just inside the door. "You jus' rest yourself. Miss Elizabeth ain' comin' home jus' yet. She lunchin' with some of her friends some place. She be home after you take a short rest."

"Damn it, Wetherby, I'm——"

Jonas went along the path to the wing. What a pair, he thought . . . what a place. If anyone had asked him then why he had come to Annapolis, Maryland, all he could have done was shake his head and say, "You tell me."

17

He put his hand out to open his own front door, dropped it back to his side and took a long breath to give himself a little moral preparedness for whatever was going to happen now. So far, every time he had gone in the place or come out of it he'd run into something he did not expect. Whether the jinx was naturally on it or whether he had brought it with him was hard to say. Considering his landlord the owner, it was quite possible it was included in the lease, in which case it would not have surprised him to find the devil himself waiting in the reception room.

Or Elizabeth, he thought. She wouldn't just walk out permanently. He opened the door and stepped in eagerly, the victim of hope and folly. She was not there. He swallowed his disappointment, cursing himself for being fool enough to give it a thought.

"Doctor?" Martha came out from the kitchen, Roddy at her heels. "Doctor, you supposed to call Dr. Pardee's office right away soon as you come in. Then I'll put your lunch out on a table outside. It's a pretty day."

"Thanks, Martha."

In the consulting room Dr. Pardee's number was written on a piece of brown paper torn off a bag from the grocery store.

He dialled it without enthusiasm.

"Dr. Pardee, please. Jonas Smith calling."

"Oh, Dr. Smith. Dr. Pardee isn't here He's had to go down in the County for an emergency O.B. I'm his secretary."

It was a pleasant efficient voice at the other end of the wire.

"He asked me to ask if you could go out to St. Margaret's and take his Maternal and Child Health Clinic for him this afternoon. He's due there at two o'clock and he can't possibly make it. He thought you might be able to take it. He'd certainly appreciate it."

"All right," Jonas said. He did not mean to sound ungracious, and as he put the phone down he had to remind himself that he'd come to Annapolis to practise medicine. Nevertheless, the idea of spending a whole afternoon out at St. Margaret's, away from where anything might happen at any moment, without any chance of seeing Elizabeth and getting rid of the unhappy lump that had settled in the pit of his stomach, was not the one he liked very much. Nor did he feel more cheerful about it when at the end of lunch Martha came out of the house with a telegram.

"They phoneded it in when you was out an' I said they had to bring it."

Jonas tore it open. It was from the Fergusons and the Milmors, in Cambridge, Massachusetts. For a moment he looked down at it without seeing it. Somehow he'd forgotten about the Fergusons and Milnors. It came as a slight shock to realize that of course they'd have a personal interest in a murder on their own premises. He should have called them himself.

The wire was from Joe Ferguson.

"Congratulations. Didn't know you knew him too. Have decided to go on to Quebec until all bodies removed and stink blows out and over. Personal alibis respectably established. Girls at Wellesley 75th Anniversary Fund Raising dinner stone sober. Milnor and Ferguson at Class Reunion Dinner also cone stober. Try to evade the Law till we get home to stay you with flagons. Natalie sends love.—Joe."

Jonas crumpled the message up and put it in his pocket. So they thought they were funny. On the other hand, it was better than having Mrs. Milnor rushing hysterically back and making a fuss about it. A little mollified at that thought, he fished back in his pocket to take the wire out and read it again. Another piece of paper came with it and fluttered to the terrace. It was Miss Olive's clipping. He reached down and picked it up with

129

a sudden smile. Cute little old Miss Olive. Her running battle with Professor Tinsley Darrell had probably been going on all their lives.

"Urushiol Imitated in Synthetic Compound."

He read the caption over the double column, and glanced through the rest of it before he put it back in his pocket and went on with his lunch. Up to that time he had barely noticed it was soft crab he was eating. By the time he got through a second serving of strawberry shortcake the prospect of conducting Dr. Pardee's clinic for the afternoon had even taken on a certain amount of anticipation. After all, the chance to learn from one of the best Public Health setups in the nation was one of the reasons he'd come to the quiet village on the banks of the Severn. He looked at his watch.—Quiet? he thought suddenly. Had he said quiet?

He thought of it again as he went down College Avenue to pick up his car where he'd left it to go into the Academy Yard. He put his bag on the front seat and waited with the door open. Sergeant Digges was coming down the St. John's College Hill from McDowell Hall. Under the tulip trees and horse chestnuts in full and glorious bloom, ambling along between the borders of boxwood on either side of the brick walk, a stone's throw from the six-hundred-year-old Liberty Tree on the Green, Sergeant Digges looked a little anachronistic.

He saw Jonas and crossed the street. "Hi, doc."

"Hi, sarge."

They grinned at each other.

"I'm not leaving town," Jonas said. "Thought I'd better tell you. I'm just going out to the St. Margaret's Health Center to pinch hit for Dr. Pardee. It's his day but he's down in the County."

He got in under the wheel. "What are you doing at St. John's? You haven't got time to read the Hundred Books."

"They gave me my degree when they still used football players," Sergeant Digges said amiably. "But I wasn't up there to read Plato. Just an old Annapolitan custom. If there's any devilment going on, first thing you do is blame it on the Johnnies. They don't have to be in bed with lights out at ten, like over the wall. So I was just making a routine visit. It payed off, though."

"What do you mean, payed off? Did you rubber-hose a confession out of the President of the Student Council? Or was it the President of the College?"

130

"It wasn't a confession," Sergeant Digges said imperturbably. "Just a car. And old jalopy, out there in back of Randall Hall. You saw an old jalopy out at the Milnors' that night, didn't you, doc?"

Jonas nodded. He was a little puzzled. "But there are all kinds of 'em around. I just met Miss Olive trying to drive the Professor up to the Annapolitan Club in Wetherby's. It's——"

He stopped abruptly. Sergeant Digges was looking at him with an odd gleam in his eye.

"Did you, now?" Sergeant Digges remarked. "I expect I ought to step around and have a look. All I meant about the one up at the College is that the boy that owns it couldn't find it Saturday night when he wanted to take his drag out for a little ride, after the dance. He figured one of the other fellows borrowed it. It was there all right Sunday morning."

He closed the car door. "Well, so long, doc. I'll be seeing you."

Jonas put his car automatically into motion, waited for the light at the corner of College Avenue and King George Street to change from red to green, and crossed the bridge over College Creek in a robot-like trance. His conscious brain centers were actively and acutely preoccupied with something of more immediate importance. After having spent two days and practically landed himself in the local hoosegow trying to keep Digges's nose off the trail leading to the Blanton-Darrell House, he had shot off his big mouth and fairly shoved him onto it. But he had done more than that. It was the obverse of the coin he himself was looking at, and the pattern stamped on it. What had made him come out so promptly with the information about Wetherby's car? There was little doubt in his own mind. It was an idea that had registered in his subconscious the instant he had seen Miss Olive Oliphant and Professor Darrell in the battered old vehicle there in the drive, registered and popped out, at an oblique angle, the first chance it got. He recognized it clearly now. It wasn't the old car itself. It was the knowledge that both Miss Olive and Professor Darrell could drive a car. His own oblique statement was his subconscious forcing him to recognize a fact, and its potential implications, that he had refused to look at because he didn't want to look at it.

It was acutely disturbing, and bewilderingly so, for after all neither Miss Olive nor the blustering wicked old inebriate in the Blanton-Darrell House meant anything to him except as they impinged on the lives of Elizabeth and the poor little kid whose life one of them had made such complete hell on earth. Nevertheless, he was disturbed. They could each drive. The St. John's back campus was less than a block from Miss Olive's, not more than two from Blanton-Darrell Court. Even then, it was not clear in Jonas's mind why he should be worried. It was as if some sort of black cloud had sifted in around him, obscuring the daylit windows of his mind.

Suddenly, and again without any logically arrived at reason for doing it, he took his foot off the gas and slowed to a stop on the tarred shoulder of the road. He reached into one pocket and took out his pipe, and into the other and took out the clipping Miss Olive had given him. He stuck his pipe between his teeth and unfolded the clipping. Through a glass darkly . . . He had said that to Sergeant Digges, out at the Milnors' cottage. He was saying it to himself now. It was only the frantic honking of a speeding car passing a truck on a last minute dash to the two o'clock ferry that roused him from a grimly concentrated and not entirely effectual revery, and sent him back on the road, going at top speed to keep his appointment at the Health Center a couple of miles ahead of him. There was something knocking insistently on a basement door of his mind, but until it clicked open the lock he was wasting his time trying to identify it.

It was not until six o'clock that he listened to the last small black chest and gave a tick shot to the last small white arm. It was twenty minutes past when he parked his car outside Blanton-Darrell Court. The afternoon at his legitimate profession had been as therapeutic for him as it had been for some twenty-seven mothers and their assorted offspring. He was whistling as he came through the iron gate into the Court, with a buoyant step and a cheerful mind.

"—Oh, hello. This is the second time I've been to see you."

Jonas came to an abrupt halt. If he had been tied to a B-29, walking away from it, he could not have been yanked back any more violently or with greater speed than the sound of Philippa Van Holt's voice and the sight of her tall slender figure yanked him back from a professional to a personal level. He'd been breathing the antiseptic atmosphere of another world, and been lost in it. In a split second he was back where he'd started from at half-past one, nothing settled, nothing changed.

She was waiting for him on the steps of the wing, Roddy wagging his tail beside her.

132

"Hi," he said. He looked at her a second time. "Been to California or going there?" he asked with a grin.

Philippa looked down at her cinnamon-colored slacks, beautifully cut and perfectly tailored, and smiled back at him.

"These are my working clothes. I should have told you I'm a writer. The words have to appear in letters of ink and gold come hell or high water. I guess I should have changed before I came out."

"You look okay to me. How are you?"

As a matter of fact she did not look particularly okay, not from the chin up. She looked tired and a little drawn. The discouragement in her sherry-colored eyes belied the smile on her red mouth and the little gaiety of her voice.

"Take that diagnostic glint out of your left eye, doctor," she said lightly. "I'm just pooped, is all. I've been to Baltimore, which always depresses me. It's so full of bricks. It always makes me think of an attic nobody's ever gone through and called the Salvation Army to lug the junk away."

"You're speaking of the city I love, madam."

"Then you can have it—but take it away, will you?"

She turned her head and looked up at the wooden dome of the State House above the trees.

"This I like. It's a lovely town . . . a sort of palace of green with enchanted towers. I never much liked it until I got back from Balitmore today and had to write five hundred words about it. But that isn't what I wanted to see you about."

She smiled at him again.

"I've got to go to dinner tonight, down at the Yacht Club. Some people are having a party, and the show's got to go on. I've got to cover the waterfront. I can't go alone—will you go with me? We don't have to stay late."

"Your hosts are casual, I take it," Jonas remarked.

"I was supposed to bring a man."

She didn't say the man she had expected to bring was dead. —Or was he? Jonas backed quickly away from the dilemma of which was Gordon, which Franklin Grymes, who was dead and who was not. He did not want to get into that supremely futile rat-race again. She looked unhappy enough just then, for him to feel a sudden compassionate twinge, and a small twinge of conscience at his own reluctance to say, Sure, I'll go with you. Instead he said, "Let me give you a call. I want to look at my book first."

"Okay."

133

The book he wanted to look at was the Annapolis Telephone Directory. Inside at his desk he turned it quickly to the "D's" and dialled the Darrell number, with neither hesitation nor compunction. He felt sorry for Philippa, but it was Elizabeth Darrell he needed to see and had to talk to. The painful lump that had been in his heart, and that had disappeared while he was on the job at the Clinic, was back again. He was like one of the mothers out there who had the misery all over. He had it almost unbearably as he listened to the ringing signal at the other end of the wire, hoping so intently it would be her voice that answered that Wetherby said "Professor Darrell's residence" two and one-half times before he said who he was and could he speak to Miss Elizabeth. And he couldn't. She and Miss Jenny were out, to a tea, and they were going to stay out for dinner.

"But Miss Olive, she's here, doctor. She up playin' double Canfeel with the Professor. You want to talk to her?"

"No, thanks," said Jonas hastily. "How is the Professor this evening?"

"Better. Right smart better, if'n Miss Olive jus' go home. She goin' to drive him to the Black Bottle if'n she don't. She *wears* him to the bone."

Jonas put down the phone, the smile that started to break out dying still-born as he stood, perplexed, thrown back into the quandary that had bogged him down so inexplicably on the side of the Ferry Road on his way to the Health Center. There was something almost maddening about it, something he ought to be able to reach out and take hold of but that eluded and escaped him, like playing hide and go seek with a phantom in a boxwood maze. The small spark that Wetherby's protest at Miss Olive's constant presence struck in his mind was useless to kindle any fire that would enlighten him; he had no idea whether it was something new, or the habit of years that had only then become an irritant to them all.

It was a futile search in a barren field. Jonas shrugged his shoulders, turned to the "O's" in the phone book and dialled Miss Olive's number.

"Philippa? Jonas Smith. I'll be glad to go with you. I'll pick you up. What time?"

"Oh, good—you're a lamb. I don't know what I'd do without you. Seven-thirty."

Then Philippa Van Holt laughed. It was an irrepressible lilting flicker of mirth.

134

"She's out, isn't she? Too bad, sweetie. If you'd just asked me, I could have told you."

"You devil."

Jonas laughed too but without the same kind or degree of amusement.

"—She devil. If you must quote my brother-in-law please do it accurately. He said worse than that today. Okay, I'll see you at seven-thirty."

Jonas put the phone down, his brows contracted into a heavy scowl. Her brother-in-law? He began seriously to try to take one logical step in the confused relationship of the Brothers Grymes. If the one in Baltimore was Gordon, and he was Philippa's brother-in-law, she was married not to Gordon but to Franklin. That was a simple statement of it. Whether she knew it or not was a different matter. Then, suddenly, he had a flash of intelligent memory. She did know it. He closed his eyes to shut out everything but the scene he was reconstructing in his mind's eye. It was at Miss Olive's, in Papa's sanctum. Philippa Van Holt was introducing him to Franklin Grymes.

"—my brother-in-law Gordon—I mean Franklin—Grymes . . ." He had thought then it was a slip of the tongue, the two of them being so extraordinarily alike. Now he wondered. He opened his eyes, and looked absently in front of him. Unless . . . she really was married to Gordon Grymes, and Gordon Grymes had, in some way, changed places with Franklin . . . and Franklin being killed left Philippa Van Holt, in that case, not a widow but a woman whose husband was pretending to be engaged to Agatha Reed.

Jonas rubbed his hand slowly across his forehead to try to smooth out some of the creases in the confused grey matter behind it. None of this made sense. Nevertheless, there was something going on that had the strong smell of decayed and sinister fish. No wonder, he thought, they were all in such a panic of apprehension and despair, shouting ruin at the top of their collective lungs. Jenny Darrell's shot had torn far more than a lethal hole in the body of one Franklin Grymes.

135

18

At quarter past seven Jonas, clad, suitably he hoped, in a freshly laundered white linen suit, closed his front door behind him and went along the brick path under the rose-covered trellised arch toward the gate, to get his car to go to Miss Olive's to pick up Mrs. Gordon, or was it Mrs. Franklin, Grymes nee Philippa Van Holt. As he rounded the mass of great old box on the other side of the rose trellis he half-stopped, and continued on.

She was coming home. She and Jenny were coming through the iron gate into the Court. He scarcely saw Jenny, except as a dark foil for the softly golden sheen of the girl beside her. They were laughing at something, and as Jonas readjusted his momentarily dazzled and enchanted vision, he saw they were laughing because Jenny was spilling water out of the glass bowl she was carrying in both hands. It was a goldfish bowl, and Jenny, seeing him first, said, "Hello, Dr. Smith. These are for Miss Olive. She can't bear to be without her fish. I think she feeds them to her cat when nobody's looking."

Her voice trailed off as voices do when they are telling a story to someone whose attention is obviously somewhere else. She looked quickly from Jonas to her sister. Her eyes widened, her laughter was gone. Elizabeth had stopped even more abruptly, and she and Jonas were face to face, the tension between them so electric it was almost tangible.

"Wetherby said you were going out for dinner."

It sounded as if he were accusing her, not Wetherby, of deliberate intent to deceive him maliciously.

"We did go out. We went to Gregory's, to make less work at home."

She spoke abruptly, her cheeks flushing.

"And I have a message for you from Cousin Andy—Sergeant Digges. He tried to get you out at the Health Center, but you'd left. He said to tell you he had to go to Baltimore, so you don't have to worry about him being around tonight."

She took Jenny's arm and started to go past him and on to the Blanton-Darrell House. Then she paused an instant.

136

"And I'd like to tell you I'm sorry I had to dash off before you got back this morning. I had to help Wetherby with Grandfather. And I won't be able to come any more, but I have a friend who'd like a job. I'll ask her to come and see you if you want me to."

"Thanks, you needn't bother," Jonas said stiffly.

He was angry, and she was angry. Jenny, holding the goldfish bowl in both hands, looked blankly from one of them to the other, not understanding any of it.

"And I've got something to say to you," Jonas added. He knew he was being a tactless fool, and went ahead. He turned to Jenny. "Go on, will you, Jenny? I want to talk——"

Elizabeth tightened her grip on Jenny's arm.

"No, stay here. Dr. Smith hasn't anything to say to me that you can't hear."

Her eyes were stormy, the flush deepened along her cheekbones.

"What is it you'd like to say, Dr. Smith? We're in a hurry . . ."

"It won't take long."

Jonas controlled a desire to take her by the back of the neck and shake some of the nonsense out of her.

"It's just this. I was back there, when you left this morning. I heard you talking to your brother Tom. I eavesdropped. And I'm not apologizing. I'm just telling you."

"I wouldn't expect you to apologize, Dr. Smith. And I'd expect you to eavesdrop. You seem to have a genius for it."

Jonas flushed, his irritation heightened by her obvious references to Saturday night at the Milnors' cottage on Arundel Creek.

"That's a little below the belt, isn't it, Miss Darrell?" He forced himself to speak evenly and coolly. "What I'm trying to tell you, if you'd shut up and listen, is that you're making a bad mistake. You knew what I meant last night when I was talking about a *coup de foudre*. You knew who it was I meant, and you knew it wasn't Philippa Van Holt. It's you, and you know it."

"That's not——"

"Elizabeth—don't! Oh, Elizabeth!"

Jenny holding the goldfish bowl still was able to shake her sister's arm holding on to hers. "He's telling you, Elizabeth . . . he's telling you he's in love with you! That's what he means by——"

"You keep out of this, Jenny. One thing you ought to have

137

learned is not to believe every man who tells you he's in love with you. I thought you'd learned that the hard way, sweetie."

She looked swiftly back at Jonas.

"I'm sorry if I was wrong. I was just giving you the benefit of the doubt, after I saw you and Philippa Van Holt saying good night here in the Court. I'm leaving out the girl in the office this morning. But let me assure you, Dr. Smith, that I'm neither touched nor flattered by your *coup de foudre.* You're at liberty to make love to every girl you see, which is what you seem to do. But not to me. I didn't like it in Gordon Grymes, and I don't like it in you. And as for my brother, I might as well tell you right now. Nothing I said made any difference to him. He's going to be out of the Navy, and we're going through with it. I'd hate to have to testify that I saw you kissing Gordon Grymes's widow, but I'll do it if you force me to."

Elizabeth Darrell flashed quickly around. Her slim body went taut, her chin came proudly up.

"Here comes one of your friends now. Will you let us by, please. Come on, Jenny."

"Oh, don't go, Elizabeth." Philippa Van Holt quickened her step. "Don't let me interrupt. We're in no hurry, are we, Jonas? I'll just run in and say hello to your grandfather."

"I'm sorry." Elizabeth made a startling reversal from fire to ice as she moved aside, ignoring Jonas Smith's large presence in the middle of the driveway. "Grandfather can't see anyone after supper. It gets him excited and he doesn't sleep. Some other time would be better. I'm sure Dr. Smith doesn't want to be kept waiting anyway. Come on, Jenny. Good-bye."

Philippa turned to Jonas, standing there motionless. Being put in a class with Gordon—or was it, he thought even then, Franklin—Grymes was hard to take. Having Philippa appear just when he was getting the *coup de grace* in his self-elected role of good Samaritan was even harder.

"Dear me.—I hope I didn't upset anything."

Philippa spoke with a curdling mixture of triumph and contrition.

"I just thought I'd come by and maybe we could walk down to the Club. I adore the Market Space, and you never really see it in a car. But I'm frightfully sorry. You look as if you'd like to throttle me.—Or is it Elizabeth? Or both of us?"

"Both of you," Jonas said curtly.

Especially, he thought, Elizabeth Darrell. In a sort of de-

138

layed visual reaction he was seeing Jenny, breathelss joy star-lighting her face, before she shrank back in stricken silence at Elizabeth's cutting reminder of what she should have learned the hard way about protestations of love at the Milnors' cottage on Arundel Creek. It was a searing lash applied to a glowing tender heart at its most vulnerable moment . . . and from the hand that had symbolized the only secure and protective love the small heart knew. It was a cruel thing to do, and as much his fault as Elizabeth's, for goading her into it, and undoing in a single flash everything they both had done to try to restore Jenny's faith and confidence in herself. She would be sure, now, that she was destructive and malign, a blight on the lives of all the people she loved and had no wish to hurt.

Jonas turned silently and looked at her, following her sister across the garden to the front door of the big house. Elizabeth was like a burning golden arrow. Behind her Jenny moved pale and wooden-limbed, holding the absurd glass bowl of goldfish in both hands in front of her, like an enchanted priestess blindly performing the ritual of some curious and unearthly cult. Jonas could feel his heart moved with pity and compassion for the kid. And anxiety. He felt a sharp twinge of anxiety, a sickening sense of utter helplessness in the face of it.

19

"Relax, Jonas. It can't be as bad as all that, angel."

Philippa put her hand on Jonas's arm. "Come on. A walk will do you good."

Jonas gave his head a shake to free it from foreboding and dark presentiments.

"I'm sorry," he said brusquely. "The hell with it. Come on."

He looked down at Philippa then. She was still in her cinnamon slacks, but the chunk of rose tourmaline set in a gold lotus leaf at her brown throat, the chartreuse corduroy jacket embroidered with brown and rose woolen birds and tropical flowers, gave her a festive dressed-up air.

"Pretty snappy outfit." He surveyed it and the figure it did nothing to conceal with a critical and appreciative eye.

"Thanks.—You know, it's a damned shame, really."

"What is?"

"The Darrell temper. They've all got it—except poor little Jenny. I guess it was stomped out of her from birth. Or driven underground . . . so she'll probably be the one to go berserk and really do somebody some damage some day."

Jonas gave her a quick sidelong glance. She was going calmly on, unconscious of the startling statement she'd made.

"If you believe in the psychology of frustration, that is. It's born in people. I'll bet you didn't know that. Miss Olive clipped it out of a paper. It has something to do with your brain cells. But God help anybody who marries one of them. The Darrells, I mean. I used to wonder why some smart gal hadn't copped off Grandpa and the Blanton-Darrell House—when I first came. Not now. It wouldn't be worth it, having to put up with all their foul tantrums."

"Oh, I don't know," Jonas said. Until she said it he had virtually come to the same conclusion.

"Okay. Let's skip it. Isn't this sweet?"

They were coming out of the foot of Cornhill Street into the Market Space. The fishing boats were crowded together side by side in the small rectangular basin between the two arms of the Square. Above the disfiguring signs and garish lights of pool halls and taverns, the roof lines of the Eighteenth Century were still pure, of simple dignified charm.

"There used to be an old slave block here, and the Space was open. I don't know why the City Fathers thought Ye Olde Colonial Type comfort stations were more important, except that City Fathers never recognize historical treasures until it's too late. However, I suppose honky-tonks and comfort stations are the stigmata of our age."

Off Compromise Street the Yacht Basin was as crowded as the harbor. Philippa and Jonas walked along the cinder road to the Club House, four great colonial mansions within fewer blocks of them, enclosed in their quiet twilit gardens, a contrast in peace and lost tranquillity with the roving restlessness all around them.

"Oh," Philippa said. She stopped abruptly inside the door of the Club. "I made a mistake. It isn't tonight. It's tomorrow. The dining room's closed tonight."

She nodded at the sign over the passage entrance leading to the dining room door. Jonas looked at her. Her mouth had tightened. For the first time he saw something in her face that was unguarded and very like chagrin.

"I'm terribly sorry. It was stupid of me. But let's go up and have a drink and then I'll feed you somewhere, just to make up for it."

"—You didn't really have a dinner date—either tonight or tomorrow, did you?" Jonas asked pleasantly.

They were seated on the long covered gallery looking out over the rippling water. The yachts below them were a beehive of music and laughter, people calling and visiting back and forth. Cars whipped by, going and coming over the hunchbacked bridge over Spa Creek from the foot of Duke of Gloucester Street to the Eastport side. The corner of the gallery was cool and quiet, strangely remote for all the noise and restlessness around them. Jonas sipped his Tom Collins and looked at her with a lift of his brows.

"Come clean. Why did you do it? You're not this fond of my company."

For a moment Philippa sat in silence, looking out at the liquid carpet of moving light and shadow in the open channel.

"Perhaps I am," she said at last. "Or maybe it's just my maternal instinct trying to keep you from making a fool of yourself. You're quite right. I didn't have a date. I thought it up on the spur of the moment after I stopped in Gregory's to get some cigarettes and saw Elizabeth and Jenny in there eating their dinner. Maybe it's a form of jealousy. Maybe I can't bear to see the only intelligent and attractive man I've met down here prefer somebody else to me. Which is a mistake, isn't it?"

"I'd say it might be."

"Oh, you make me tired!" Philippa struck a match sharply, held it to her cigarette and threw it down on the deck. "Why anybody like you wants to bury himself down here, and fall for the first pair of blue eyes he meets . . ."

She relaxed suddenly against the yellow woven plastic back of her deck chair. "Dear me. That's really none of my business, is it? You don't think I'm falling in love with you, do you? It certainly sounds like it. Maybe that's really it."

"Oh, nuts," Jonas said. He smiled back at her.

"Or maybe I wanted to ask your advice about something."

"What is it?"

"It's about my husband and my brother-in-law," Philippa said. The smile died out of her eyes. "You might as well know it now as later."

Jonas waited silently. The moisture dripped from the cold glass in his hand. He waited a long time. Philippa sat smoking

141

her cigarette, her head bent forward, her knees crossed, one foot absently beating time to the music from a radio coming up from one of the yachts in the Basin.

"Jonas," she said at last. "You were out there. Do you think they killed him? I've got to know about that. It's terribly important for me to know . . . for lots of reasons."

"Who do you mean by 'they,' Philippa?"

It took him some little time before he finally asked it.

"My brother-in-law and that girl, Agatha Reed."

"Agatha says not. So did he, didn't he, at Miss Olive's on Sunday?"

"That's not much help, is it?" Her voice had sharpened. "When all I'm trying to do is be decent about things." She got abruptly to her feet and shook herself as if she would like to tear everything to pieces. "This is driving me crazy. But let's skip it. Let's go get something to eat and go home. I'm a wreck. I've had what we call a gruelling day. And I think I'd like to see Sergeant Digges. Will you go over to see him with me?"

"He's in Baltimore."

"Okay, in the morning will do. Come on, I'm hungry. I'll go powder my nose first."

When she met him at the top of the steps to go down and out of the Yacht Club she was smiling again.

"I'm sorry I was irritable," she said lightly. "I keep forgetting Agatha Reed is an old friend of yours."

Jonas smiled back at her. He glanced at her chin.

She laughed. "That's not powder. That's just one of my mosquito bites. They even get me down here. I guess they know I'm a city girl, born and bred."

It was nearly quarter to twelve when they walked back from a restaurant on lower Main Street, across the Market Space around the rectangular basin of small boats nosed into the quay like fat obedient ducks waddling gently with the motion of the water.

Philippa slipped her hand into his arm and slowed his pace down.

"—Do you see who I see?"

They were coming up Prince George Street from its dead end at the water's edge. It was silent and empty, the rockers on the small wooden front porches of the painted frame houses deserted for the night. It was not entirely empty. Jonas had not seen the dark figure slipping rapidly along ahead of them. He saw it then, not recognizing it, and admitting his eyes would never be as sharply seeing in the external world of persons and places as the shrewdly observant and highly trained eyes of Philippa Van Holt.

"Who is it?"

"Tom Darrell," she whispered. "I saw his face when he turned just then under the street light. I'm sure it's him. It's his size and shape, and the midshipmen's gait. He must have come out around the end of the wharf. What on earth do you suppose for?"

She spoke softly, glancing behind them. "I don't see any jimmylegs on his trail. I guess he's got smarter with experience."

Jonas was watching the boy ahead of them. He saw him glance around, duck between two parked cars and disappear on the other side of the street.

"You know, it's a funny thing," Philippa said. "My father told me once that nobody ever went any place without somebody he knew or who knew him seeing him. He said it wasn't coincidence, it was an established rule of fate.—Or have I lived with Miss Olive too long so I'm beginning to quote my Papa too?"

"He seems to have been right in this case," Jonas said soberly.

"I don't suppose it matters much, with Tom, I mean. He's out flat on his rear anyway. I guess he figures he can't be any outer or flatter. I was talking to one of the executive officers at Bancroft, one of the Commandant's assistants. He says they'd give him a break if they could but they can't. He's a striper and a Navy Junior, and they've got to be tough or somebody'd start yelling favoritism. I gather Tom isn't doing much to cooperate."

Jonas was silent, all the way up Prince George Street and along College Avenue, silent and disturbed. If Tom Darrell frenched out of the Yard a second time, when he was confined to his room under a kind of technical arrest, it was a very serious matter—if he got caught. It was serious if he did not, serious on another level. There was no doubt in Jonas's mind that his frenching out the second time was the net result of his conference with Elizabeth in Bancroft Hall before noon meal formation. What he hoped to gain by it was hard to see, except to talk to his sister again, if as Elizabeth had said he was still determined to carry on the way they had started.

"Don't be so glum, Jonas."

143

They were coming up to the small yellow house covered with silver moon roses in St. John's Street.

"If he wants to be a fool, it's not your problem. Don't take it so heavily to heart, dear."

"I take any kid's wrecking his whole career pretty much to heart, if you want to call it that," Jonas said quietly. "Especially when it's not necessary."

"How do you know it isn't necessary?" Philippa asked easily.

He felt the slow flush that came up from under his collar and spread over his face. He looked at her intently, wondering how much he had given away. Her shrewd bright eyes were fixed on him. He shrugged and turned to open Miss Olive's gate for her.

"Nothing's that necessary."

He opened the screen door. "Do you want me to go in with you? Or have you got used to Papa's ghost?"

"Oh, we're great friends," Philippa said calmly. "But he's a little worried about Miss Olive. He doesn't believe maiden ladies should sleep in strange beds. He doesn't think it's nice for her to keep the Death Watch on poor old Professor Darrell."

The Death Watch. . . . The words lingered unpleasantly in Jonas's mind as he switched on the light on the desk in his consulting room. He gave a start of surprise at the object, or objects, he saw in the middle of his blotter. It was a bowl of water there, with two startled goldfish in it, and by its side a note in a spidery lady-like Spencerian hand.

"My dear Dr. Smith," it said. "Martha tells me you often plan to dine on the terrace. As your window was open, I took the liberty of placing my small gift of welcome inside, although the fish will not be harmed by the warm summer nights. The article I clipped from a paper and am leaving with you tells you about fish, and their proper feeding and care. Cordially, (Miss) Olive Oliphant."

"—For the love of all the saints," Jonas Smith thought. He put the note carefully down on the desk and picked up the bowl. His first impulse was to hurl it fish and all through the open window onto the terrace, let the chips fall and the fish flounder where they might. He thought better of it. Maybe Martha would like them. He took the bowl out through the pantry, put it on the kitchen sink and came back into the room. Roddy, lying sleeping on the cool brick hearth, opened one eye, gave his tail a tentative wag and went back to sleep.

"What's the matter? The heat got you?"

Jonas put his foot out and stroked the dog's back before he took out his pipe and filled it absently as he moved restlessly back and forth across the room, morosely trying to make up his mind as to what he ought to do. He wanted to see Tom Darrell. What good it would do he didn't know, but after a few moments of indecision he made up his mind, strode across the room and out the wicket across the garden.

He stopped and looked up at the Blanton-Darrell House. It was dark except for one light in the upper hall and the dim glow through the fanlight over the door to the back porch. If Tom Darrell was home, he and Elizabeth were taking care not to have him seen by inquisitive eyes prying through the shutter slats. Nor was it his business to pry. It was some time before he came to that quite simple and rational conclusion. It was practical, furthermore, he reflected, so far as tactics were concerned. In his white linen suit with the moonlight full on him he had probably been seen already, and with a front door handy Tom was no doubt well on his way back over the Naval Academy wall.

It was one of the times that it occurred to Jonas Smith he might not be as bright as he thought he was. He looked up at the house, a slightly ironic grin at his own expense on his face, and gave it an airy salute before he strolled back across the garden to his own place and sat down at his desk.

"What," he thought, "am I getting all steamed up about? Why don't I try minding my own business for a change?"

He had plenty of it to mind, including the report he had to have done before morning on the afternoon clinic at the St. Margaret's Health Center. He opened the desk drawer and took out his papers. Miss Olive's letter and the clipping were still in front of him. He picked them up, glanced through the letter again and ran his eyes down the clipping. Fish, it seemed, were extremely useful people to have around—if you liked fish and liked having them around, which Jonas Smith did not. He tossed the letter and clipping toward the wastebasket, missed it and leaned over the arm of his chair to pick them off the floor.

He heard simultaneously the crash of the shot, the shattering of the pane of window glass, the rip of lead into metal as the bullet tore through the lamp on his desk. The room was in staggering darkness then, and with an unconscious reflex he reached his hand up to his left shoulder where the bullet had seared its way through the pad under the white linen a quarter

145

of an inch from his flesh and bone. It all happened at once, in a flashing simultaneous instant that but for the guardian angel standing by him could have spelled another and deeper darkness than that in the room, the infinite and eternal darkness. He held his breath, his heart pounding, the cold sweat in living moving beads on his forehead, crawling through the hair on the back of his hands and clammy in his palms. The shattered light was a blinding after-image still in his retina in the intensified blackness the room had been pitched violently into. As Jonas blinked to erase it, he was seized with a sudden fury that drove all fear and shock out of him.

"The bastard, the little son of a——"

He jumped up to his feet and ducked down again as a flash of instinctive caution warned him not to let his broad white linen back be a shadowy second target for a murderous young fool. He shoved his chair back, crouched down and moved around the desk, straightening to his feet behind the solid brick wall. The whole thing had a fantastic kind of clarity that was almost as much of a shock as the hot lead ripping past him into the desk lamp. If he had read one more line about the ways and uses of goldfish it would have ripped through the base of his brain instead. But Jonas was not thinking of that. He was thinking of the pattern that it was to have been the finish of, and that he ought to have seen when he saw Tom Darrell slipping up Prince George Street. It had a kind of hideous rationale, hideous in the profound simplicity and ease that it must have presented itself with to anybody with so much at stake and so little to lose.

One Jonas Smith was the solitary witness against them. He was nothing to Tom Darrell, nothing to Elizabeth Darrell but a source of terror and danger, as against Jenny's honor and reputation and freedom. With Tom's distorted code, no sacrifice was too great. And he could not have been safer. If he got back in the Yard and back in his room at Bancroft Hall he had an alibi as unimpeachable as the prestige and dignity of the United States Navy. It was as perfect a set-up as any human being could demand. Especially as Elizabeth could pass Sergeant Digges's message on, that he'd be in Baltimore and not prowling around to disturb him.

Jonas took a step toward the desk and stood in the shadowy darkness, his brows drawn together, trying to look at this on somebody else's terms, somebody like a member of the Darrell family . . . passionate, violent-tempered, ruthlessly protective

146

of their own, young, terribly torn, emotionally, from the strange unhappy life they'd been decreed as wards of their grandfather and buffers between him and the dark elfin child he couldn't abide. He touched his shoulder again, exploring the bullet track through the freshly ironed linen, listening with intent ears to the silence around him. Roddy was snoring undisturbed, which was a little strange, and no one in the Blanton-Darrell House seemed to have heard, or cared to come out if they had heard. Jonas grunted an ironic and amused laugh, reached over and pulled the telephone to the corner of the desk. He counted the numbers with his fingertip from One at the top and dialled the Darrells' number in the dark.

He heard the ringing signal once, and once again, before he heard her voice say "Hello." She could not have been far from the phone, and there was no tangled mesh of sleepiness in her voice that he could detect.

"Miss Darrell, this is Jonas Smith," he said.

He heard her draw her breath in and let it out, in what seemed to him otherwise might be called a pregnant silence, which he was the one who broke.

"I'd like to speak to your brother Tom," he said deliberately.

Her breath was caught this time in a quick gasp. "Tom? I . . . I don't understand you, Dr. Smith. Tom isn't here. He's in the Yard."

For an instant Jonas hesitated. She sounded sincere, perfectly truthful . . . surprised, of course, but surprised at the idea of Tom's being there and his asking for him. And it might be so. It suddenly occurred to him that it probably was true . . . that she would be the last person Tom Darrell would tell he was frenching out to kill someone, and make her thereby a second time accessory after the fact. But he wasn't sure. It was axiomatic that the fairy gift laid in every female crib is the gift of lying with a straight face, calm voice and not the slightest sense of guilt.

"Okay," he said casually. "I'll just call him there. It's 2611, isn't it? What's the Bancroft Hall extension number?"

He heard her breath caught while he was speaking.

"Oh, no! Don't call him! You can't do that, it's too late. Dr. Smith, you mustn't call him!"

"Why not, if he's there?" Jonas said.

The desperate urgency in her voice came again over the wire. "Oh, please don't call him!" she implored.

"All right," Jonas said. "I guess you mean it's okay if he

147

takes pot shots at me through the back window."

"—*Shots?* Oh, no no . . . I don't believe it!"

The shocked incredulity in her hushed voice had an authentic quality. But so it had had before.

"Oh, Dr. Smith . . . I . . . I *can't* believe it!"

"Can't or don't want to, Miss Darrell?" Jonas inquired. "Tell him in the morning, will you? Tell him I'm still alive and I plan to stay that way. Good night."

20

He put down the phone. "Well, that's that," he thought. "That's telling 'em." Then, in a moment or two, the bitter glow of satisfaction he felt at so telling them lost its glow and left nothing but the bitterness prompted by a sneaking suspicion that he Jonas Smith had acted like a first-class skunk. If she hadn't known about the shot, if she'd heard it and thought it was a car back-firing in the street, he'd certainly done a fine job telling her. A skunk, a louse, he thought—the victim of wounded ego trying to get even.

It was a filthy trick. He reached for the phone again, wrung by a sharp contrition, and let his hand drop to his side. There was nothing to tell her. The damage was done. He couldn't make her stop worrying now that she knew. And maybe it was best she did know. She could keep Midshipman Tom Darrell from having the blood of Jonas Smith on his hands and head.

He edged away from the desk over to the wall switch by the door, to turn on the overhead light, felt his way and found when he reached it that there was no light. The fuse had been blown. He felt for the switch in the reception room, with the same result. He made his way back, closed and locked the terrace window, and went back into the vestibule to go upstairs. As he put his foot on the bottom step, he stopped, listening. There was a knock on the front door. He reached over in the dark, found the knob and opened it.

She was there, a cotton bathrobe thrown on over her pajamas, her hair pushed back behind her ears, her face white and unnatural, caught in the indistinct rays from the street light over the wall through the trees. Her breath was coming in quick short gasps. She stepped forward a little and put a shaking hand on his arm.

"Are you . . . are you all right? You're . . . not hurt, are you? He didn't . . ."

He looked steadily at her for an instant.

"Hit me? No, but it wasn't his fault. I happened to lean over and he hit my desk lamp instead. But I'm sore as hell, I'll tell you that."

She was shaking so that she reached out and took hold of the white door frame to support herself, and bent her head down on her arm.

"Oh, I'm so sorry! I just can't believe he did it. I knew he was terribly upset, and nothing like himself . . . and he said it would be the best thing that could happen to us if something happened to you. But I didn't think he meant it.—Dr. Smith, I just can't believe it! I didn't even know he had a gun. I was in bed when he came barging in. He said he came out of the Yard because he was afraid I was going to get cold feet and make a mess of things. He's just been up there in his room brooding over everything, and reporting every hour to the Main Office, and . . . oh, I just don't know. I was afraid yesterday he might do something crazy, but I can't believe he meant to . . . to kill you. If he meant to he would have. He's one of the best marksmen in the Yard. Maybe he just meant to . . . to scare you."

Jonas grinned suddenly. "He did that all right. He scared me plenty." His face sobered. "But I'm afraid he shot to hit. My head was right in front of the lamp until I just happened to lean over."

"Oh, no." She pressed her head against the door frame, shaking it back and forth. "It's so awful. I just don't know what to do. Have you . . . called the police?"

"No," Jonas said. "Nor Bancroft Hall. I shouldn't have called you. But I was sore, I guess. I figured you hated me enough to be in on the deal."

She had raised her white face and was staring up at him, blank and stricken. "Me? Hate you? I don't hate you," she whispered desperately. "After what you've done for us . . . how can you say anything so horrible? I wouldn't hurt you for . . . for *anything*."

"You're sure of that?"

She nodded.

"Then nothing else matters."

149

He wanted to reach out and take her in his arms, and tell her that nothing mattered except having her there. It didn't matter if her brother had tried to kill him. The intoxicating sweetness of having her there was making him light in the head. Only the solid fear that one mis-step might shatter the enchanted moment kept him firmly on his side of the threshold.

"It doesn't matter, Elizabeth. Nothing does. Because I love you. I meant it last night, and this afternoon. I mean it now. I love you so much that if it would help to have me shot I'd be crazy enough to say go ahead and shoot. Except that I couldn't see you then——"

"Oh, don't say things like that . . ."

"I'm not. All I'm saying is, I do love you, Elizabeth. As truly as I know how to say it. And I want you to believe it. I'm not joking. I love you, Elizabeth. You know it, don't you?"

"I . . . thought I knew it, last night."

She turned her head away from him.

"Then I thought I'd made a mistake and it wasn't me but her, because she's so much more exciting and everything than I am. And I thought I'd made a fool of myself because I felt the same way about you. I couldn't get you out of my head all day. That's why I had to call you up out at the Fergusons'. I was ashamed of myself, but I couldn't help it. And I was out in the garden so I could be alone, because I was so . . . so terribly happy, and then I saw you and Philippa . . ."

Jonas did not hear the rest of it. It was lost in the folds of his linen coat as he held her tightly in his arms, whispering her name, transmuting its syllables into the tender magic of all his song of love.

"—Elizabeth, I love you . . ."

She raised her face to his. He kissed her softly on the lips. Then he gently disengaged her arms. "I think I liked getting shot at, Elizabeth."

"Oh, don't . . . don't say that."

He kissed her again. "I'm going to take you home now. I don't approve of my wife calling on strange men in her pajamas and bathrobe. So come along. And you don't happen to have an extra fuse at your place, do you?"

She clung to him for a moment.

"Oh, Jonas, I'm so miserable, and I'm so happy. And we do. We have a whole box in the kitchen. And I meant to tell you if you don't like starched shirts you have to take them to the Chinaman on Main Street. Oh, Jonas! I couldn't have stood it if you'd been in love with her and not me!"

The fuse in his hand and all the stars in the firmament dancing to light his way to the fuse panel over the kitchen sink, Jonas found the restored electric current pallid stuff compared with the radiance from the airy clouds he walked on. He went through to the consulting room to turn off the overhead light he'd left switched on, and stopped to look around. The thing to do now was clean up the glass and put the shattered lamp out of the way so the bright investigating eyes of Sergeant Digges would not start another routine job. He went around the desk and picked up the wastebasket. Miss Olive's letter and clipping were still on the floor. He picked them up, started to crumple them and toss them in the basket, and decided that was pure ingratitude. Low opinion of goldfish as he had, they had saved his life that evening. He put both documents in his pocket. He might even write the memoirs of a village doctor some day.

He picked up the glass and the lamp, got a dust pan and a brush, made his way eventually down to the cellar and emptied all the mess into a box. He stuck the box behind a crate in a cobwebby recess in the old foundations of the house. When he went back up, put the empty wastebasket by the desk and looked around, the only thing left to repair was the window pane. That would have to wait till morning.

He went over to the wall switch.

"Come on, Roddy. Time for bed."

He whistled sharply. Roddy did not move. He slept heavily and peacefully on.

"Roddy, Roddy boy!"

Jonas went over to the hearth, knelt down and touched the spotted silken head. He raised the dog's closed eyelid, held it open for a moment before he let go of it and sat back on his heels, his face as sober as it had ever been in his life. Roddy was drugged. He was breathing rapidly, the pupil of his eye was dilated and unresponsive to the light.

Jonas sat there motionless for a long time. Someone had drugged his dog. Someone had wanted Roddy to sleep. That was why he'd got no bounding greeting as he came into the house. He remembered the opening eye and feeble tentative wag of the feathered tail on the hearth that he'd been too preoccupied, with the meaning of Tom Darrell outside the wall, to pay any attention to. He put his hand on the dog's body, feeling for his heart, absently stroking his head. At last he got up,

151

went into the tiny laboratory, prepared a shot of benzedrine, came back and gave it to him. Still on his knees on the hearth beside the dog, his eyes moved, disturbed, around the room. The window had been open. Anyone could have come in . . . anyone who knew there was going to be need of a sleeping dog.

He shook his head slowly. That meant someone must have known Tom Darrell was coming out of the Academy. Someone must have known what he was going to do. That in turn meant design and premeditation. It was someone Tom Darrell could appeal to, and trust. Not Elizabeth. And not Jenny. He was sure of both of them . . . surer of Jenny than he was of Elizabeth, about this thing, when he was faced squarely with it, but sure of Elizabeth too.

Jonas's hand moved slowly to his pocket. The letter there, he thought; the clipping . . . the bowl of goldfish out on the kitchen sink. It was a fantastic present, but it was a perfect excuse to come in the house—or to be seen coming in.

He got slowly to his feet. It was fantastic, it was absurd. But nevertheless . . . Miss Olive Oliphant. Miss Olive with her cat, sending Jenny out to buy goldfish on her way home from a tea. Miss Olive with Tom Darrell's picture on the mantel of her father's memorial room, Miss Olive's pride and devotion to the Darrell family. Her accumulated store of disconcerting and curious information gleaned from magazines and newspapers. Her carefully cut-out knowledge of fish, and cats, and . . . other animals?

—And Miss Olive, over there now, keeping the Death Watch.

Jonas Smith shook his head. A chill passed over his heart nevertheless. He was seeing the child-like china blue eyes, the fresh rosy cheeks, hearing Miss Olive's child-like voice prattling away. Papa's child who had never grown up.

As he bent down to pick up Roddy and carry him upstairs, Jonas was wondering a little grimly if Miss Olive Oliphant had not suddenly become a sinister and very frightening child.

His uneasiness was not diminished in the morning when he came downstairs to breakfast, Roddy eagerly ahead of him as if a heavy night's sleep was exactly what he had needed. Martha had put his coffee and toast and a large dish of ripe red strawberries on a bridge table on the terrace.

"—Wasn' broke when I *lef'* here. Somebody mus' have broke the lamp too. It ain' on the desk, an' there's fine glass to get in my vacuum an' ain' do it no good."

Jonas heard as he came out, thinking it was Roddy or herself

152

she was talking to, until he saw Wetherby leaving the terrace and saw a whole pane of glass where there had been the jagged remains of one when he went up to bed.

"Morning, doctor, sir." Wetherby was as immaculate and dignified as glazier and handy man as he was as major-domo, nurse and games companion. "Miss Elizabeth told me there'd been an accident. I came over before the Professor he wakes up. He say another glass get broke over here, he going to block the place up with brick and mortar. He sick and tired of replacements. Bes' he don't know, then he don't get all upset and nervous. Bes' nobody say nothing about it."

He looked at Martha, who gave an offended grunt and went back to the kitchen. Jonas sat down and poured himself a cup of coffee. He wondered with a sardonic lack of amusement what they would all have done if it had been his carcass sprawling across the desk. They'd probably have disposed of it neatly and said nothing about it, not to disturb the Professor and make it awkward for the Darrells generally. Which of course was not fair. All it meant was he was jealous that Elizabeth's waking impulse should be toward protecting her wretched brother and keeping her grandfather from getting nervous and upset, leaving Jonas a poor third in order of importance. He was also a little annoyed at himself for not having considered that Martha would notice the desk lamp was gone, that he hadn't cleaned up as well as he thought he had, and that he hadn't met her with a plausible story before she had formed some dark explanation of her own, which from the murky look she gave him obviously had to do with bacchanalian vine leaves in his hair.

Nor was there any sign of a lifting of the moral ceiling when the door bell rang and she came back outside.

"It's that woman again," she said stonily. "That woman in pants. You want me to let her in 'fore you've——"

A door was only a door to Philippa Van Holt, its purpose to open and admit her when she wanted in.

"——Jonas!"

"You'd better bring a cup, Martha," Jonas said. "Hello, how are you?"

Philippa stopped in the open french window. "Gee. Struggling young doctors sure have it tough around here, don't they?"

She fished a cigarette out of her scarlet linen jacket pocket, lighted it and pulled a chair from the end of the terrace. She flopped down in it, took a long drag from the cigarette and let

153

it feather from her red lips as she leaned her head back against the canvas and closed her eyes.

"What a night!" she groaned. "Gosh, what a night."

Jonas looked at her face in profile across from him. To say it was haggard would have been untrue, but the lines of strain were there, beside the closed lids and the drooping tense line of her mouth.

"I don't suppose you'd like to give me a cup of coffee, would you?"

"Coming up."

He pushed the cream and sugar over to her as Martha came in with her cup and saucer.

"Thanks," Philippa said. She poured herself some coffee. "I'm an absolute wreck."

"What's the matter?" Jonas had not asked her, having the odd feeling in some way that he would rather not know.

She put her cup down. "I wish I knew. I'd like to think it was Papa walking. I'm not scared of ghosts."

She stopped an instant. "At least I say I'm not. I don't know. I was certainly scared last night." She looked at Jonas. "You won't believe it. I was literally just too damned scared to go downstairs and phone you . . . or the cops. You can't turn the hall light on from the second floor, and if I'd gone down in the dark I know I'd have died. I know I would have. I don't know what got into me. You know what I did?"

Jonas shook his head. He felt the slight chill in his heart again.

21

"I pushed the dresser across the door," Philippa said. "It's one of those big heavy Empire jobs and I don't think it's been moved for a hundred years. I tore off one of my fingernails." She held her hand out. "And I damn near broke my back, getting it away this morning. Last night I was so petrified I could have moved mountains. And then . . ."

She looked away and made an unsuccessful attempt to laugh it off.

". . . I slept with the shades down and the light on. What

154

little sleep I got. I said I don't believe in ghosts, but I didn't take my eyes off the door, even with that monstrous object in front of it. I never was so glad to see daylight in my life."

"Was somebody in the house?" Jonas asked quietly.

"That's it—I don't know. I don't know whether it was somebody in the house, or out in the back garden. Or whether it was somebody, or . . . something. I know that sounds cockeyed now, but last night it was the most hideous feeling. Maybe the creaks were just the old boards and plaster. Maybe what I thought I heard outside was just the shutters needing oil and the dead branches that needed pruning. I don't know. If I'd had any sleeping stuff or a bottle of whisky I'd have slugged myself out. But why don't I shut up? What I'm saying is I was scared and I didn't get much sleep."

She put her head back and closed her eyes again. Jonas sat silent, looking at her.

"And don't just tell me it's nerves, doctor, I'm not a nervous woman."

"I wasn't going to," Jonas said. "I don't know what to say."

It was the truth. It was too disturbing to make any statement. He knew one thing only to be true. They could leave the ghost of Miss Olive Oliphant's Papa at rest, in St. Anne's Churchyard or wherever it lay.

"When I first went in, I had an odd sort of feeling," Philippa said. "Like some people do about cats. I put the chain on the door—one of those sliding arrangements, only Miss Olive's must have come off the *Constitution*—it's big enough to hold up the anchor of the *Missouri* and it's been there forever. I got to the bottom step and went back and took it off. I had a queer feeling I might want to get out of there quick. Once when I first came I'd dreamed I was struggling with it. And then I was too scared to take advantage of my foresight."

She got abruptly to her feet. "Can I use your phone? I'm going to see if I can get a room at the hotel."

Jonas nodded. He sat there staring in front of him.

"What's happened to your lamp?" Philippa asked as she came back through the window.

"What?"

"Your desk lamp. You know. The thing on your desk that gives artificial light, for you to read by."

"Oh," Jonas said. "It's out of order. I've got to get it fixed."

He could have known her sharp eyes would not miss that.

She sank down in the canvas chair again. "That's too bad. It

155

was a nice one. I was going to ask you where you got it, but I'll wait till they're perfected, as the man said about the motor car."

She sat there for a moment, her brows together, chewing at her lower lip, snapping her gold cigarette lighter off and on. "Jonas," she said at last, "I don't believe in ghosts. The ordinary kind, I mean. Some kinds I do. I believe in ghosts of people's past actions, that start haunting them and driving them sort of nuts, making them do pretty strange things. Things they wouldn't do in their right minds. I'm just wondering. I'm wondering if my brother-in-law is mad enough——"

She stopped again, holding her lip in her white even teeth.

"——Or haunted enough, to think that if he got rid of me . . ."

She gave her head a quick shake. "Anyway, I'd like to tell you—just for my own protection—why my brother-in-law, and Agatha Reed if the idea of her being in on it doesn't offend you . . . why they were in such a desperate and frantic dither to see my husband Saturday night."

Jonas stirred his coffee in concentrated silence. He was thinking, "—It's funny she never calls them Gordon and Franklin. She always says 'my husband' and 'my brother-in-law.' She hasn't mentioned their names since . . ."

It came back to him suddenly. ". . . since Sunday afternoon at Miss Olive's, when she said 'Gordon—I mean Franklin—Grymes.' "

He had thought it was a slip of the tongue because the two of them were such extraordinary replicas of each other. He listened now, his mind going back over the various conversations he'd had with her, and out at the Milnors' cottage when she was talking about them to Sergeant Digges. She never used their given names.

"It was because my husband——"

Philippa broke off. She raised her head sharply. At the Blanton-Darrell House a screen door banged shut. There was the sound of feet racing across the wooden porch and down the steps, running wildly across the dry ground toward the hedge.

"Jonas! Jonas!"

"My God, don't tell me Grandfather's had another stroke."

Jonas dashed for the wicket. Before he got half-way across the garden Elizabeth had come through it and was running to meet him.

"Jonas! Jenny . . . she's done it! She's—oh!"

She stepped back with an involuntary gasp wrenched from

156

her throat as she saw Philippa relaxed cosily at the table on the terrace. "Oh!" Her face, already shockingly pale, turned a dead sick white. She turned and ran back. Jonas caught her as she reached the bottom step of the porch. He took her shoulders with both hands.

"Stop it, Elizabeth!" he said curtly. "Stop being a . . . I can't kick her out when she walks in."

"But what's she there for? What's she there for? Why does she always come!"

"Cut it out, Elizabeth. Jenny . . . what's she done?"

"She's gone to Sergeant Digges."

Jonas's hands dropped from her shoulders.

"She wrote me a letter, before she left for school. Then she sent it back by a colored child after she'd gone, so I couldn't stop her. It's my fault, Jonas. She thought she was ruining my life too! And she's gone, to tell him she killed Gordon——"

His name froze on her lips. Her eyes were fixed and bright, staring past Jonas. He turned sharply.

Philippa Van Holt was at the corner of the hedge behind them. She was standing rigidly immobile, her face an expressionless mask . . . a woman alone, withdrawn and intense, strangely moving in some way, and at the same time profoundly disturbing . . . a woman who had been a friend and had become an enemy.

Jonas put his arm out and drew Elizabeth to his side, a protective gesture, involuntary, instinctive. Philippa dropped the cigarette between her fingers onto the ground and rubbed it into the dry grass without taking her eyes from them.

"I'm sorry it was Jenny."

Her voice was quiet and dispassionate.

"I've been thinking it was you, Elizabeth. I figured it must be you Jonas was trying so hard to cover up for. I'm sorry it was Jenny. I wanted it to be you, Elizabeth."

She looked at them steadily for an instant, turned and disappeared behind the hedge.

"What's she going to do?"

Elizabeth's lips were dry, her voice a muted whisper. Jonas felt the convulsive tremor shiver through her body as he held her.

"Where's she going? What's she going to do?"

She whispered it again, her eyes still fastened on the corner of the hedge where Philippa had stood and had vanished from almost without the sensation of physical movement. The

157

crushed cigarette, a scarlet smudge of lipstick on a mutilated bit of white paper, was the only evidence that she had stood there . . . stood there and heard and spoken, and disappeared.

"—I don't know," Jonas said. "I know what we're going to do. Was Jenny going to Digges's house, or the Police Station?"

"The station."

"Come on. My car's out in the street. We can't stop her, but we can see he doesn't throw her in the cooler. He'll have to let us get a lawyer. Come on . . . quick."

"—I'm afraid of Philippa. I've never liked her, but now I'm afraid of her."

Elizabeth said it twice . . . as she huddled down in the front seat of Jonas's car and again as they passed the Yacht Club crossing the bridge over to Eastport. The rest of the time she sat tense and silent, staring sightlessly in front of her. Jonas Smith was silent too, silent and absorbed. It would have been better, after all, to have made a clean breast of it at the very beginning, before Philippa's malice and anger had been roused. It would have been better for all of them—Jenny, Elizabeth and Tom. And for Agatha Reed and the other Grymes, Gordon or Franklin, whichever one it was still alive and quaking in some abject fear, haunted, as she said, by some ghost from his own past.

"There it is." Elizabeth pointed to the small wooden shack with "Anne Arundel County Police, Eastport Station" on a sign over it. Jonas stopped the car, they went in.

"I'm Elizabeth Darrell. Is Sergeant Digges here?"

The officer at the desk turned down the radio. "He's not here."

"Miss Darrell's sister was coming in to see Sergeant Digges. Did she come?"

"The little dark-haired girl? Yeah. Heard him say they were going out in the country some place. It was about that Grymes deal out on the Creek."

"Thanks," Jonas said. He took Elizabeth's arm. She was trembling again. Out in the car she slumped down in the seat and closed her eyes.

"I can't bear it," she whispered. "The poor little kid. The poor baby . . ."

Jonas took his hand off the wheel and gripped hers.

"Take it easy. We've got to face it."

They crossed the bridge again. On the right, across the sea of small craft in the Yacht Basin and the red tin roofs and brick end chimneys of the old house on the waterfront, were the green athletic fields and massive stone buildings of the Academy. Elizabeth turned her head away.

"Poor Tom," she whispered. "What'll he do now?" Then, remembering what Tom Darrell had missed doing by a fraction of an inch, she shook her head quickly. "Jonas—I just can't believe he did it . . ."

The music of the band was coming over the wall as Jonas turned up King George Street . . . the work and pageantry of a Service school going on its efficient routine. Somewhere in it, carrying his own burden of knowledge, Tom Darrell was moving, a depersonalized unit, waiting for the end to come that would cut him out as the Brigade closed in and went on, with nobody but a classmate or two to miss him and none of them to know why he went and what his going meant to him. But what would happen now, when Jenny had refused that sacrifice along with the others? Jonas was thinking of that as they rounded the bend at the Post Graduate School.

"He'll resign now, I suppose."

Elizabeth said it as if he had asked the question aloud.

"He's so proud I don't think he could stand having the whole Brigade talking about her. They wouldn't mean to be cruel. But he'd feel responsible. He'd feel he'd never live it down."

"That's silly, of course."

"No, it isn't. He's young. It would always be on his record. Everything goes down. Every time he comes up for duty, or selection, some officer would have to read it again. You just don't forget things in the Navy. And if the papers have gone up to the Secretary, it doesn't matter. It would take an act of Congress to put him back in. There'd have to be a hearing. That would be worse, really."

She closed her eyes and shook her head wearily. "I'm so sorry for him. A lot of boys come to the Academy because their families get them the appointment. They don't really care. It's all Tom ever dreamed of doing. When we came back here from China, after Mother died when Jenny was born, he'd come over to the Yard and watch the midshipmen march. One day the Superintendent stopped and said 'Are you going to be a midshipman, son?' Tom said, 'No, sir, I'm going to be an admiral.' Now he won't even be an ensign. But it's Jenny I'm frightened about. I don't even care about all the . . . all the mess it's going to be. I'm just terrified she'll do something awful to herself. Oh, when Grandfather hears about it . . . oh dear, oh dear!"

Jonas had been thinking about that too.

They drove on in silence for a while. Elizabeth put her head down in her hands and covered her eyes. "We're almost there, Jonas—Jonas . . . what *are* we going to do?"

He shook his head as he turned the car into the white oyster-shell road that branched down across the marsh to the Milnors' cottage. It had a kind of grim inevitability that made words of his futile.

As they made the last wooded turn into the clearing, and saw the cottage down on the point, Elizabeth straightened up. She put her hand quickly on Jonas's arm.

"That's *her* car. She's out here."

Jonas had already seen the maroon convertible through the trees.

"What's she doing out here?"

He shook his head again, and stopped his car behind Philippa's on the road half-way down to the cottage. There was an empty police car near the house, where Gordon Grymes's car had been that Saturday night. The whole place was strangely quiet, the only movement around them as they went toward the point the rippling of the water and the slow flap-flap of a pair of white herons winging their way toward the Fergusons' shore.

"—Say that again, Jenny. You were inside here?"

Sergeant Digges's voice came through the open kitchen window as they passed it. Elizabeth ran around the corner of the cottage and tore open the screen door. "Jenny! Jenny!"

Jonas came up behind her. Jenny was standing by Sergeant Digges. A uniformed officer was sitting at a small table in a corner, his notebook open, pencil in hand. Philippa Van Holt was sitting on the raised hearth, her face pale above the scarlet linen of her jacket.

As Elizabeth ran forward Jenny drew back, her face bloodless in the cloud of dusky hair. There were deep violet circles under her eyes.

"I've already told him, Elizabeth," she said. Her voice was hardly more than a whisper, but it was clear and firm. "I should have done it right away. So please don't say anything now, Elizabeth. I had to do it. I've told him everything."

She looked past her sister at Jonas.

"Make her go away. I don't want anybody to worry about me,

160

any more. I've made just too much trouble for everybody as it is."

From the doorway Jonas looked across the room at Sergeant Digges. His grey uniform shirt with the blue chevrons was drenched with sweat. Jonas had never envied any man his job less. He felt a sudden feeling of pity for this man with the job that was his to do.

Sergeant Digges nodded at them.

"I'm as sorry about this as you are, Elizabeth," he said stolidly. "Now you're here you can stay if you want to. You'll have to stand outside and not make any trouble.—Miss Van Holt, I've already told you to keep quiet."

His voice rose harshly. Philippa relaxed against the brick fireplace with an impatient shrug.

"You can shut up or get out of here. There's no use talking to me—save it for the State's Attorney. I'm neither judge nor jury. I'm an investigating officer. You needn't keep on yelling about self-defence. I'll tell you frankly you'll do a better job to let Jenny tell her own story and you keep out of it. I'll do everything I can for her. My God, what do you take me for?"

He looked from one to the other of them and turned back to Jenny Darrell, his manner changing instantly.

"All right, Jenny. Don't pay any attention to anybody else. What I want you to do is try to think as clearly as you can, and tell me exactly what you did. Everything that happened. You came in here to telephone. Go on, Jenny."

She had turned her back on Elizabeth and Jonas, and stood erect and still, speaking quickly and clearly. The terror she had lived with had died, and left courage to face everything and be through with it.

"He told me to come in and phone while he turned off his lights so the battery wouldn't run down. I didn't think then that they didn't have a phone. Then I thought maybe they'd got one in. I started to look in the galley when he came in. He said I knew there wasn't a phone."

"Where were you then, Jenny?"

"I was half-way to the galley door. He came in. He was taking his flask out again. I was afraid of him then, and I wanted to get back close to the door, but he'd locked it. I didn't notice that till he went to the galley to get a glass and I tried to get out. He laughed and showed me the key in his hand and said I could get out if . . . I don't want to say what he said. He said a lot of things. I didn't understand the words but I knew what

161

he meant. Then he put the key on the arm of his chair and said if I wanted it I could come and get it."

"Where was he then?"

"Over there."

She pointed to the chair in the middle of the room.

"He was there. I was right here on this side of the table. I kept trying to make him see he had to let me go home. He'd finished his flask and started to fill it up out of a bottle on the bar there. Then he took out his gun and said I meant so much to him he'd kill himself if I didn't, and I'm so frightened of guns, because Grandfather always said I'd kill somebody if I got my hands on one, and then he lurched up and I thought he was coming after me. I didn't know what I was going to do. That's when he threw the gun on the table. It slid over and hit me and I grabbed it. All I know is I had hold of it and he was saying 'All right, shoot me,' and all sorts of things, and all of a sudden I . . . I shot him. He made a funny sort of horrible noise and that's what happened. He was down on the floor, and there was blood, and . . . I don't know, I must have got the key, because I got out, but I don't remember that. All I remember is I stumbled down the beach. I don't know what I did, really, here, after I got the gun in my hands and he was talking and—"

"All right, all right," Sergeant Digges said. "Take it easy, Jenny. Just take it easy. All I want to know is this: you were standing right here?"

"Yes, sir."

"I don't mean somewhere near here, but right here?"

She nodded.

"And he didn't take any steps, or move, before you shot him? He was standing right there, the other side of the table, and he just doubled up and went down?"

She nodded again.

"Just where, exactly, Jenny? Help us out here, doc, will you? Stand over there where this fellow was standing. Is that it, Jenny?"

"Yes."

"All right. Take this, now."

As he thrust the revolver into her hand she recoiled with a sudden cringing horror, her eyes screwed shut like a child's at the taste of some bitterly loathed medicine. Her arm was out rigid, her hand shaking, the muzzle pointing dangerously not at Jonas Smith's heart but at his knee-cap, her thumb fumbling for the trigger.

"Shoot it, Jenny! Pull the trigger!"

"I can't shoot it! I don't know how! I'm afraid of guns . . .
I don't know how to shoot it!"

The revolver fell out of her hand to the floor. She clutched
at the table, sobbing hysterically, and slid quietly down. Sergeant Digges took a quick step forward and caught her.

His eyes moved grimly from Elizabeth to Jonas.

"You people thought for one minute this kid shot somebody?"

He put Jenny on the couch and turned back.

"Let me show you damn fool amateurs something," he said
bitterly. "You're standing right where Grymes stood when he
was shot, doctor—and the position of the body showed he really
was standing there. Now do a right-face."

Jonas turned. He was directly in front of the door to the tiny
kitchen, and he was looking through it, for the second time,
directly at the kitchen window through which he had first seen
the Darrells close-up Saturday night.

"Now, about-face, doc. Your back's to that window. Look
straight ahead of you. On the wall, right of the fireplace. You
see that hole? That's where we found the bullet that went
through Mr. Grymes's body.—I tried to tell you, doc. I told
you, right in this room, as much as I could, the guy was shot
from through that window. You figured we were saps. You
figured we never looked into *anything*. You believed an hysterical frenzied kid. Maybe she should have shot this guy, but she
sure didn't."

Sergeant Digges turned and looked down at Jenny. "Take her
out, doc, and bring her to. That's your job. Leave me do mine.
You crazy fools, it's a wonder you didn't drive the kid *clear*
out of her mind. Get her out of here onto the porch. Get some
water, Elizabeth—or do I have to do your job as well as my
own?"

22

"—You didn't do it, Jenny! It wasn't you, baby . . . you just
thought you did it! It was somebody else, it wasn't you!"

Jonas, back inside the cottage, could hear Elizabeth saying it

163

over and over again. Jenny out on the porch was still white and dazed, still not understanding. Inside, Sergeant Digges was still tight-faced and hard-jawed.

"It went straight through his heart on a line from that window ledge and into the cinder block there next to the fireplace.—I asked you about my taking out an appendix, doctor. Maybe you'd better study something about ballistics."

The stinging sarcasm, the realization of his own folly, brought Jonas Smith out of the stunned daze he'd been moving in.

"—And I'm sorry, Miss Van Holt," Sergeant Digges said. His voice was a shade more gentle. "I know it's not pleasant for you to have to——"

"I'm just glad it wasn't Jenny, Sergeant. It's . . . oh, the pattern was all so recognizable. It . . . it has some kind of justice. He had no right to bring a kid out here. That's all I was trying to say to you . . . that she shouldn't have to pay for . . . for that. And now it's somebody else, isn't it. I don't understand. It's . . . frightening."

She looked silently at Jonas. It was the way she'd looked that morning, telling him about the night at Miss Olive's. "It means somebody else was here. I don't understand."

"There's only one person known to have been present," Sergeant Digges said moodily.

Jonas shook his head. "You're just wasting your time if you still think it was me, Sergeant. I'd never seen either of them. I just came over after the shot woke me up, to see if I could help out. I didn't know she'd shot him or thought she'd shot him until I heard her tell Elizabeth and Tom. Then I looked in the kitchen window and saw him."

Sergeant Digges nodded. "Sure, that's all you did. You just stood in the mint bed with your size twelves and tramped out all the tracks that were there before. Or that's what you're telling me now you did. If you're telling the truth now——"

"He is telling the truth."

Elizabeth had come to the door and was listening, her eyes bright.

"Because he was at the Fergusons'. He had to be there, to see Jenny put her dress and shoes in Natalie's beach bag. He brought it in town and it's in the wing now."

"Or he went back after he'd shot him, saw her footprints going to that closet and got the bag out then," Sergeant Digges said. "We'll skip it for the time being. Maybe the doc never did see Grymes before. It sure wasn't any stranger Grymes saw looking in that window at him with a gun aimed at his heart. The doc mentioned that surprised look on his face. It's in the pictures we took of him. He was standing there, after he'd tossed the gun to Jenny, and he heard a noise, or something. He turned and saw somebody he knew and didn't expect to see, and it surprised the hell out of him. And they fired and killed him just when Jenny thought she did, and when she ran out they came in, took the gun Jenny'd had and put theirs down on the floor."

"Jenny dreamed someone else was here," Elizabeth said slowly. "It was a . . . a kind of nightmare she had. Maybe she really knows . . ."

"Isn't there some drug you can use, to help her to remember?"

Sergeant Digges looked reproachfully at Philippa Van Holt. "Truth serum? They use that in the movies. If Jenny knows any more, now you experts are through with her and she's not going on having the liver scared out of her for something she didn't do, it'll come back of its own accord."

He went out on the porch and put his hand on her shoulder. "They're going to take you back to town now, Jenny."

"I . . . I don't have to go to jail?"

Sergeant Digges stroked her hair back from her brow with his callused fisherman's hand. He shook his head. "No. Come on, now. Elizabeth's going to take you in."

"Why don't I take her?"

Philippa came to the door. "Elizabeth must want to go and see Tom at the Academy. I should think this would make some difference to him." She smiled faintly at Jonas. "He won't have to break any more regulations to see this girl I never believed he had."

"Oh yes, of course!" Elizabeth went forward swiftly. "Thank you, Philippa!" She put her hand out. "And thanks for trying to help Jenny. I didn't——"

Philippa Van Holt's hands stayed in her jacket pockets. Her brows raised. "Don't thank me, Elizabeth. Not yet. We still don't know who was at the window. You may not want to thank me—if we find out."

She lowered her voice. Jonas could not hear what she said, but he saw Elizabeth's cheeks flushed as she stepped onto the porch. "You'd better come with us, Jenny," she said quietly. "You want to see Tom too, don't you?"

"Not very much." Jenny shook her head slowly. "I'll come if

you want me to. If Jonas doesn't mind."

"I'd like to talk to you, Miss Van Holt," Sergeant Digges said. "I want some information about your brother-in-law."

"Which won't help very much," Philippa remarked. "He and Miss Agatha Reed being on their way to Baltimore when my husband was killed. However . . ." She shrugged her shoulders and smiled at him. "There are a few things I'd like to talk to you about. I've moved from Miss Olive's."

Jonas heard that as he opened the screen door for Elizabeth and Jenny, before Philippa turned and went back into the cottage.

"What does she mean?" Elizabeth whispered. "What's she going to tell him?"

Jonas shook his head. "I don't think Digges will believe in ghosts."

"Ghosts?"

Jenny was ahead of them, getting into the car.

"Somebody was around Miss Olive's house last night. That's why Philippa moved out. She seems to have an idea it might have been her brother-in-law.—Could it have been Miss Olive?"

She didn't answer, and as he glanced aside at her she quickened her step. "Don't ask me, Jonas. I don't want to talk about it, not in front of Jenny. And we've got to hurry. We've got to see Tom."

In front of the magnificent marble staircase in the great rotunda of Bancroft Hall, Elizabeth put her arm around Jenny's shoulder and gave her a quick squeeze. "I'm going to see the Commandant. You take Jonas to the reception room and wait till we come."

She touched Jenny's cheek lightly with her lips and gave her a smile. She looked back at Jonas. "I didn't intend for her to go see the Commandant, or to see Tom, till he knows. I just didn't want Philippa to have a chance to do a pumping job about . . . about all of us."

. . . About Miss Olive Oliphant, she was saying, Jonas thought. He watched her hurry across the empty rotunda toward the corridor at his right. Jenny touched his arm.

"This way," she whispered. "You tell them at the Main Office we're waiting for Midshipman Darrell."

She drew him left toward the opposite corridor. "I'll be in the reception room. I'm all right—don't worry about me."

He was worrying about her. She looked bloodless and fragile, huddled in the corner of the sofa, when he came across from the Battalion Office and sat down beside her. She didn't look up until he took her cold small hand and held it tightly.

"You know, it's a funny thing," she said. Her voice was hardly audible. "I mean, dreams are funny things, aren't they?"

"Very."

"Wetherby has a dream book. He's always dreaming something and explaining it, but I don't think he believes it. I think he just uses it for an excuse to explain things to Grandfather and all of us. He told me he dreamed he saw me walking by a pit that was full of scorpions, and in the book that meant there was some wicked man I should look out for. I guess he heard from somebody I was being foolish, and wicked. Do you think it could have been a dream?"

"I don't know, Jenny. He could have dreamed it, I guess."

"And I had a dream last night, all sort of mixed up and crazy. I was asleep but I didn't seem to be, and I heard a shot. I tried to get up, but I couldn't, and I was trying to run but Miss Olive's cat kept getting in my way, and the leash got all tangled around my feet, and Grandfather was pointing his finger at me and making a horrible noise trying to make me drop the gun. But I didn't have it, then, and I kept trying to make him understand I didn't have it. Then a bell started ringing, and I knew they were coming to get me and take me away. Grandfather was laughing and Miss Olive was crying, and it was terrible. I couldn't move because I was tied with the cat's leash. And Elizabeth was crying too sort of way off by herself, but I knew that was because I'd seen her crying yesterday when we came in. It's the only time I've ever seen her cry. That's why I decided to go and tell Mr. Digges this morning."

"It's all over now," Jonas said gently. "She's going to marry me, pretty soon."

"Grandfather won't let her. That would just leave me, and he wouldn't like that."

"You can come and live with us, Jenny."

"Then there wouldn't be anybody to take care of him. I don't think we could do that."

"—The hell we couldn't," Jonas thought. It was the first time he'd felt like laughing since he found Roddy drugged the night before. His feeling was short-lived. Jenny's body tensed suddenly. She swallowed and moistened her lips as she heard them coming. She drew herself together, her eyes on the door.

"Jenny!"

Tom Darrell was there, erect and stiff-backed. She pulled

167

herself unsteadily to her feet as he hesitated an instant.

"Jenny, baby!"

He came quickly across the room and put his arms around her.

"Oh, Tom, you don't hate me!"

She hadn't been sure. Not till the moment he came toward her had she been sure of anything. Jonas, studying the inscription under an old print of the *Constitution*, wondered how insecure you could be and not have your dreams a nightmare of binding cat's leashes and terrible laughter, interpreting even the reality of the shot fired at him and the phone ringing when he called Elizabeth as accusatory echoes of a tortured soul.

"I thought you'd still be mad at me even if it wasn't me that did it. I didn't think you'd ever forgive me . . ."

Jonas turned. Elizabeth was beside him, her hand on his arm. Her eyes were shining.

"It's going to be all right. The papers have gone, but the Commandant says he'll stop the messenger and review it again. He's still on Class A offence. Jonas—he told the Commandant he frenched out last night. He told him himself."

Her hyacinth eyes were grave and full of meaning. She turned around.

"Tom," she said quietly. "Did you shoot at Jonas last night?"

Tom Darrell took a step toward them. "Did I what?" he asked.

"Did you shoot at Jonas last night?"

"—Did somebody . . ."

"You be quiet, Jenny. I'm talking to Tom. Did you——"

His face flushed with anger. "Of course not. I may have felt something like it, but I didn't happen to do it."

"Sorry," Jonas said. "My mistake." He went over to him. "I seem to make quite a few of them. I apologize, Darrell. I got the idea, last time we talked, you'd regard it as a pleasure. But as I plan to marry your sister, should we perhaps bury the hatchet?"

He put out his hand. Philippa had refused Elizabeth's, and for an instant he thought Tom was refusing his. Then he relaxed and put his hand out, with a half-grin.

"I think she's crazy, but it's her hard luck."

He grinned more broadly then, and added, removing the sting but not the barb, "Have either of you mentioned it to Grandfather?"

"I think you're both very cute," Elizabeth said. "It seems to

168

me it's beside the point. The point is, if Tom didn't shoot at you, Jonas, who did? I think it pretty serious, myself."

Jonas had already thought of that. He was still thinking about it, in the back of his mind, when he deposited Elizabeth and Jenny on the front steps of the Blanton-Darrell House. It was quiet inside, except for a black-and-gold bumble bee buzzing angrily inside the screen door, trying to bully his way through it.

He gave Jenny an encouraging pat on the shoulder. Her face was still drained of any lively warmth and her knees not too steady, but it was nothing that couldn't be put down to intense emotional and physical fatigue. "Try to drink a big glass of milk with some sherry in it and get some sleep, will you?"

He let off the brake and started up, looking back as he turned at the end of the drive to wave at Elizabeth. She waved back and went on in with Jenny.

"—Hi, there."

He was just getting out of his car, parked outside the Court, to go back through the iron gate to the wing, when Philippa's maroon convertible came alongside of him. She pulled in to the curb ahead and leaned across the front seat, her motor still running.

"Did you settle all that?" she asked easily.

As she saw him looking at tht back seat she said, "It's just the rest of my gear from the vine-covered cottage."

There were a couple of suitcases, a typewriter and a brown paper carton of grimy oddments that bore the unmistakable stamp of the village antique shop.

"—And so that's that," Philippa said. Her brows lifted ironically. "Neat, I'd say."

"What do you mean?"

He was startled in spite of himself.

"Oh, Jonas, my friend." She looked at him with patient amusement. "You know, Jonas, you'll do very well as a doctor, but you ought to go some place where there are a lot of rich women. You'd make a fortune. Sympatico, I believe is the word. Or romantic. You haven't an ounce of the realist in you, have you?"

Her full red lips curved in an ironic smile.

"Still, far be it from me. I think it's divine she's going to get away with it. I'll certainly remember if I ever get into trouble to pick a town where the—what was it he called himself?—the investigating officer is a first cousin once removed. I thought he

169

handled it very well."

Jonas stared at her. "For God's sake, Philippa . . ."

"Let's not go into the righteous indignation routine," she said wearily. "And don't be a dope. Use your head, angel. I told you little Jenny was a Darrell through and through. You should have seen her when I gave her a word of friendly advice. Still water runs deep, as Miss Olive has often said, or will when she gets around to it . . . and it runs underground, Jonas. I told you she'd probably blow her top some day. You can't be that repressed and frustrated without it's coming out some place. And I like her, don't forget that. But any gal who had the courage, and the presence of mind, to go whipping over to a presumably empty house and change her clothes and come back to where there was a man she even thought she'd killed, would certainly have what it takes when it came to the pinch with a gun in her hand."

She smiled pleasantly at Jonas. "It was a good show. She lives here, and we're outlanders. It doesn't make much difference what happens to foreigners in a hide-bound hole like this. So, the hell with it . . . only, I feel a little bitter—as you no doubt see, my lamb. I'll bet you a million bucks Cousin Digges writes it off as a terrific unsolved mystery nobody'll ever solve. It wouldn't be the first one in Annapolis, Jonas. I could tell you several I've had whispered in my pretty ear. Ah well, what the hell. It was his own fault. A guy that gets tight and forgets Annapolis isn't Hollywood, and hasn't found out there are still girls who aren't pushovers for the quick take. . . . Or maybe he'd promised her Hollywood, and she knew he was going to renege."

Philippa slipped the car into low and moved forward.

"—But me, I'm not quite sure yet whether I'm going to let them get away with it. I think I'll break down and have a talk with my brother-in-law. I'll let you know what I decide."

23

Jonas Smith stood staring at the flash of the sun of the maroon car as it rounded the corner of the Court.

"Oh, Dr. Smith!"

He turned. Martha was calling him from the gate. "Dr. Smith, there's a lady with a child in here who wants to know is you engaged in the practice of medicine? I tol' her I don' know, but you was out here and I'd see if I could find out."

Jonas winced, and grinned. "Touché," he thought. Now that the point had come up, he wondered himself. "I'll be right in," he said.

The child had fallen and sprained her ankle. Before he had finished taping it another child appeared, still dripping wet from a swimming party where she had dived and cut her knee open on an oyster shell. Her brother who was with her had climbed a tree covered with a handsome poison ivy vine. Martha's niece was fourth in line with an infected ear. If it was not a series of diseases a young Osler might dream about, it at least kept him busy for an hour and a half and anaesthetized the gnawing anxiety Philippa had left unhappily with him.

He had just closed the front door on his last patient and stepped into the reception room on his way back to his desk, when the door into the kitchen opened. He glanced around, expecting to see Martha. But it was not. It was Miss Olive Oliphant.

"—Oh, I thought I heard you go out, Dr. Smith."

Miss Olive tried unsuccessfully to back into the kitchen again, dropping a paper bag, embarrassed, her pink cheeks getting pinker as Jonas, picking up the bag, felt a splash of water on his shoe and looking up quickly saw that what Miss Olive was trying to conceal, imperfectly wrapped in newspaper, was the glass bowl with the two unhappy goldfish in it. She dropped a second bundle to the floor.

Jonas grinned at her.

"Indian giver!" he said.

"No, indeed, Dr. Smith. I was just going around the house, and I saw the fish in the kitchen window in the hot sun. I felt they were not getting the proper care. So I——"

"Maybe you're right," Jonas said.

The child's china-blue eyes were so full of distress that even if he had dearly wanted the goldfish he would have been delighted for her to take them. He smiled at her again.

"You said the other day you wanted to see me? I'm free now, if——"

"Oh, no, Dr. Smith. I didn't have that in mind at all. I was just on my way home, and I——"

She dropped her knitting bag, her hairbrush and comb falling out of it on the floor. Jonas recovered them and took the bowl out of her hands. "Why don't you let me walk home with you, and carry some of this stuff?"

"That would be very kind of you, Dr. Smith. I'm afraid I have more than I can comfortably carry. And I do want to get things straightened around."

"I take it you've decided Professor Darrell is going to get well?"

"That isn't kind in you to say, Dr. Smith." There were sudden tears in the child's voice. "I never had any other thought, or wish. It's just that now we don't have to . . . to worry about things any more, I felt it was my duty to go home. If you'll hold my bag a minute, my cat's right over there by the tree."

She stuffed her knitting bag under Jonas's arm. The cat was secured to a branch of a crape myrtle. Jonas watched her release it. He and Miss Olive and the cat on its red leather leash continued through the iron gate to the street.

"It's just a step, as you know," Miss Olive said. "And we haven't walked much lately. It isn't that I mind losing money to Tinsley, when of course he doesn't accept payment. But it *is* provoking. Thirteen per cent of the people of America who buy playing cards play pinochle. But now it's decided that Jenny had nothing to do with that dreadful thing out on the Creek, I don't feel they need me any more. I suggested to Elizabeth that Jenny could come stay with me, but that upsets Tinsley too. He's very aggravating, Dr. Smith. However, I think now we can take it for granted Mr. Grymes *did* kill himself, and I'm sorry if I've mentioned anything I should not have. Least said soonest mended, was one of Papa's favorite sayings. Now if you'll take the leash, I'll get my key out of my bag."

She gave Jonas the leash and took her knitting bag from under his arm.

"It's all a great relief to me, I assure you, Dr. Smith. Come in, won't you? Just take the bowl out and put it on the kitchen table."

She closed the screen door, fastened the hook, closed the door carefully and took the leash off the cat.

"Miss Olive, why did you think Jenny was mixed up——"

"I'd much prefer not to talk about it." Miss Olive turned on the tap and added fresh water to the bowl.

"But I'd like very much to know."

"Would you care for a glass of sherry, Dr. Smith?"

"Thank you," Jonas said.

The sherry was in Papa's sanctum. He followed the plump white-haired little lady in and watched her as she poured them each a glass. She sat down by the marble-topped table and crossed her feet.

"I really think you ought to tell me."

"Well, I'm sure it's very simple, Dr. Smith. Jenny is a sweet child but very aggravating. She takes after her mother, who was a delightful woman. All her trouble was that she didn't stand up to Tinsley. If she'd simply put her foot down, Tinsley would have admired her. She was afraid of him, and it provoked him. Jenny's the same way. Papa always said to me, 'Olive, stand up and say Oh, pshaw! and you'll always get along with Tinsley.'

"You see, Dr. Smith, Jenny had an engagement with this man Saturday night. She admitted it to me when she changed her plans and brought her frock over to me the last minute to cut off the skirt where the net had stretched. She came by for me to see her with her midshipman on the way to the hop. I normally retire early when I'm home and haven't company. When my cat is restless, I sometimes take him across on the College Green, which I did Saturday night. I saw a big car go in the Court, and I was curious, so I walked over that way. I saw Jenny and this man. I wouldn't have hesitated to stop them, but I wasn't properly clothed to speak to a gentleman, and my hair was up in curlers. But they were talking about the St. John's dance, and I knew Elizabeth intended being there, so while I was worried, I didn't wish to be unreasonable. But that explains why I felt it was my duty to say something Sunday after church. Of course I was not aware, Dr. Smith, that Miss Van Holt was married to the man. That surprised me very much."

She took a sip of sherry and put her glass down.

"Can you shoot, Miss Olive?"

He asked it casually, watching the rosily flushed cheeks and the bright indignant blue eyes.

"Oh, yes, Dr. Smith. Papa was an old-fashioned gentleman. He felt it was every young woman's duty to know how to protect herself. He——"

Miss Olive stopped suddenly, and got to her feet with surprising agility. "——I'm not expecting any callers." She hastily rearranged the white ruffles in the front of her dress. Her ears

173

were sharper than Jonas's. He had not heard the gate till it closed and Miss Olive was half-way to the front door.

He heard her open it and give a startled gasp.

A man's voice asked, "Is Miss Van Holt in?"

Jonas went quickly to the hall. Miss Olive Oliphant, deserted at once by her child-like poise and her early training, had recoiled a couple of steps from the door. As Jonas had done on Sunday in the room behind him, she must have felt she had conjured up the ghost of the man she had been talking about.

"Hello, Mr. Grymes," Jonas said. He moved in beside her. "Miss Olive, this is Miss Van Holt's brother-in-law. Mr. Franklin Grymes."

"Oh," Miss Olive said. "—Miss Van Holt has left my house. I expect you'll find her at the hotel."

Jonas thought she was about to shut the door hurriedly in the handsome face of whichever Grymes brother it in truth was. He put his hand on the door and reached for the screen hook.

"I'll just go along, Miss Olive." He would have liked to talk to her longer, but he wanted to see the other Grymes. Mr. Grymes was a different man now. His pallor was gone. He was no longer a picture of frenzied despair as he had been on Sunday in Papa's sanctum. He was debonair, assured and confident to the point of smug self-satisfaction.

He put out a suntanned hand. "Dr. Smith, isn't it? Glad to see you again, sir," he said cordially. "My car's down the street. Can I give you a lift?"

"I'm just a block or two away," Jonas said.

He closed the gate and looked back to smile at Miss Olive. She was standing in her doorway. Her eyes were curiously distressed, the roses in her cheeks faded to a mottled bluish-grey. She seemed almost to be appealing to him, in some way he could not make out. As he hesitated for an instant, as if to go back, she closed the door quickly. He heard the chain rattle as she fumblingly barricaded her door.

"Funny little old lady, isn't she," Grymes said. "—You know, doctor, I think I'd like to explain——"

"You don't have to explain anything to me," Jonas replied. "It's none of my business."

Grymes shrugged. "Well, now it's all settled, I'm frank to admit I had a pretty bad few hours. And I feel damned sorry for the girl. Jane . . . Janey, what was her name? My sister-in-law called me this morning and told me she'd confessed."

174

Jonas started to speak, and stopped.

"I'd have gotten down here sooner, but I had to go into a huddle with my lawyers. If there's anything I can do for her, of course . . ."

They had come to the gate to Blanton-Darrell Court. There was a patronizing air to Mr. Grymes's offer that made Jenny Darrell sound in some way like a common tart and made Jonas Smith suddenly boiling hot under the collar. He stopped.

"There is some reason to believe she——"

He broke off as he saw the shiny green car at the curb a little ahead of his own and Sergeant Digges getting out of it.

"There's the Sergeant," he said stiffly. "He can probably give you the latest."

Grymes turned his head sharply. From the expression on his handsome face it struck Jonas he would have preferred getting it somewhere else. But Sergeant Digges was already coming toward them.

"Howdy, Mr. Grymes. I heard you were expected down. Thought I might run across you. I'd like to talk to you a few minutes."

He turned to Jonas. "Could we drop in your place, doctor?"

Grymes looked at his watch. "My time's limited, I'm afraid. Glad to see you some other day. I have an important business engagement——"

"—With Miss Van Holt," Sergeant Digges said politely. "She'll wait, I imagine. I won't keep you long."

He went through the gate and up the path to Jonas's wing without a backward glance. In the consulting room he ignored Mr. Grymes still further by going first to the desk, and out on the terrace. He came back, dropped his hat on the floor by a chair and stood leaning on the chair back, looking steadily at Jonas.

"What happened here last night? Miss Van Holt tells me your lamp's gone and you had a new piece of glass put in."

"Somebody took a shot at me. I didn't report it because I thought I knew who it was. I understand it's out of your jurisdiction anyway, and I didn't see any use calling in another set of policemen. So I just kept my mouth shut."

Sergeant Digges nodded in ironic approval. "And you found you were wrong again. I told you to look out, I wouldn't be here."

He turned to Grymes. "Where were you last night?"

"In Washington. I had a business appointment. Miss Reed

says she explained that to you. From what my sister-in-law has told me, I shouldn't think you'd have to look far for the people who'd be interested in shooting Dr. Smith. I understand——"

"You can let me worry about that. It's you I'm interested in right now. You've got some explaining to do, Mr. Grymes. What is your first name?"

"Franklin."

"I believe not. Your name is Gordon Darcy Grymes. Your dead brother was Franklin Grymes. Is that right?"

There was a tense silence in Jonas's consulting room. The man standing by the fireplace flushed, and went curiously putty-colored. His color returned slowly, his eyes lighting with anger.

"My sister-in-law . . . ?"

Sergeant Digges shook his head. "The FBI and the Los Angeles Country Police, Mr. Grymes. Your brother's fingerprints are on record in both places, from January 18, 1940 . . . seven months before you took his name and came to Baltimore.— You didn't know such a record existed, did you, Grymes?"

"Not until—" Grymes checked himself quickly. "No. I didn't know it. I'd never have let myself out on——"

"You'd never have let yourself out on a limb if you'd known it?"

Sergeant Digges looked at him curiously.

"You mean you wouldn't have killed him if you'd known the record existed, and he could prove ownership——"

Grymes's voice rose hysterically. "I didn't kill him! And he didn't own the Foundry!"

"I think he did, Mr. Grymes.—Your uncle left the Old Foundry to Franklin Grymes. It's in the deed and it's in his will. He deeded one half of it to Franklin Grymes in August, 1940 and left the other half to him in his will in 1942. You, Gordon Grymes, took your brother's name and took his property."

"That's a lie. I didn't take it—my brother gave it to me. He didn't want it, we agreed on it. He'd never done any business, he didn't want to have anything to do with it. It was a liability when my uncle tried to give it to him. He'd have gone bankrupt waiting for the old man to die before he could sell it to some museum or historical society. I wanted it. I could use it. I've built it up to a five million dollar plant. But my uncle wanted to keep the name Franklin Grymes. He wouldn't give it to me. That's why we switched names, and my brother dropped

176

the Grymes because Darcy sounded better in Hollywood. It was a friendly agreement. The old man couldn't tell us apart, and nobody else could have if he hadn't been arrested before we switched. I never knew it, and he must have forgotten about it."

"You're sure he forgot? Are you sure that isn't what he reminded you of when you had dinner with him Saturday night?"

Gordon Grymes had controlled himself. "He knew it was my brains and my work that made something out of it. I was willing to make a deal with him. That's what I came back for. I didn't kill him, Sergeant. There was never any idea of fraud——"

"You're sure of that too, Grymes?" Sergeant Digges asked shortly. "I'm not. Seems to me there's a little matter of draft evasion you've forgotten? Or have you? Your brother Franklin was an obvious 4-F. If you hadn't taken his place in the Foundry, you'd have been drafted back there. You sure the Department of Justice wouldn't be interested in you?"

Grymes' face was grey.

"I was deferred. I was in an essential occupation. The statute of limitations——"

"You were deferred by fraud, under another man's name. And you've had your lawyers look up the statute of limitations? You'll be glad to hear there's some question about that. But what I'm telling you now is that Saturday night, here in Annapolis, you and your five million dollar plant were at the mercy of your brother. You didn't know till Saturday that he had legal proof to establish his identity as Franklin Grymes, and it wasn't merely a matter of his word against yours. You were down here in Annapolis——"

"I tell you, I didn't see him the second time I came down. I went to his hotel room. He wasn't there. A woman called and I got out. I went straight back to Baltimore. I'm trying to keep Miss Reed's name out of this, but she——"

Jonas Smith, sitting at his desk, absently turning over the cards he'd filled out on his variegated young patients, tossed them aside and got up. He felt an intense annoyance. For a man who was trying hard to keep Miss Reed and her name out of it, Grymes certainly managed to bring her and it in, johnny on the spot, whenever he thought they would do him any particular good.

"Excuse me," he said. "I think I'd like a little fresh air."

He strolled out on the terrace and through the wicket into the Darrells' garden. Even a glimpse of Elizabeth would clear some of the murk out of his mind. He looked up at the big house. The doors and windows were wide open, but it seemed strangely quiet. He glanced up at the Professor's window. His chair was there, but the card table was closed and leaning against the wall in front of the window. The place was too quiet. Jonas had a curious sense of malease as he wandered toward the kitchen wing. The gravelled space behind the old carriage house was empty. Elizabeth's car was gone, and so was Wetherby's dilapidated vehicle that usually stood there.

He went around the kitchen to the front of the house. The drive was empty. The black-and-gold bumble bee was buzzing on the outside of the screen door, trying to bully his way in. He hesitated an instant and went up the steps. The screen door was hooked. He knocked tentatively. Someone was inside; he could hear the murmur of voices coming from the living room. He knocked again.

"Hello!" he said. "You were supposed to be in bed asleep."

It was Jenny who appeared in the hall doorway. He didn't like the hard white flesh at the sides of her nostrils, or the too-bright, too-fixed look in her eyes. "What goes on?"

"Nothing. I was in bed, but I got up. Elizabeth had to go out, and Wetherby took Grandfather to the Club."

She spoke quickly, drawing the door half-shut behind her to exclude him, pointedly not asking him to come in.

"Who's here, Jenny?" he asked quietly.

"Nobody."

But there was somebody. Through the space between the heavy iron hinges of the old door he could see the light from the back garden windows. He caught a scarlet flash as someone moved noiselessly across it, moving back, out of the way. It was Philippa, in there talking to Jenny.

"Sure?" he asked.

Jenny's eyes brightened and two red spots came out on her pale cheekbones.

"I'm allowed to have anybody I want to come to this house, Jonas Smith," she said hotly. "You don't have any right to ask me questions. I'm talking to an old friend of mine, trying to see if I can remember if I saw anybody out at the cottage that night. I have a perfect right to talk to anybody I like."

"Sure you do, Jenny. I beg your pardon. I'm sorry."

Jonas looked at her intently a moment before he moved back.

He raised his voice. "By the way, if you should happen to see Philippa, tell her her brother-in-law's over at my place talking to Sergeant Digges. She might——"

"Sergeant Digges? Is he over there too?"

Jenny caught her breath. He saw her hand tighten on the door knob.

"Yes. He's there. Would you like to see him, Jenny?"

"No."

He had the impression she'd quickly changed her mind, and that that was the impulse she'd had. She moistened her lips as she moved back.

"No. What would I want to see him for?" She was closing the door slowly. "I'll . . . tell Elizabeth you were here. And if I see Philippa, I'll tell her what you said."

He went down the steps and toward the wing. He was profoundly disturbed. Philippa Van Holt was a shrewd, bitter and determined woman. Her friendship and sympathy for Jenny, in contrast with her antagonism toward Elizabeth, had been one of the best things about her. He was worried now. Maybe she did believe Jenny had killed her husband, and was going at it here, in some way, to find out for sure. Or perhaps she'd given up that idea and was working at it through her own special brand of truth serum, trying to make Jenny remember.

He was worried, nevertheless, worried at the way Jenny looked. He went in the wing. The door of his office was open. Digges was standing at the window, his head down, his hands in his pockets, absently rattling his change and keys.

"Where's the Apollo of the Old Foundry?" Jonas asked.

"I let him go. He won't go far." Sergeant Digges shook his head. "If this Reed woman sticks with him, and gives him an alibi . . ."

He relapsed into moody silence. Jonas sat down at his desk. He picked up his record cards and sat staring down at them.

"But if he did it, I'll get him. He'll make a mistake. They all do."

Jonas Smith, thinking about Jenny over at the big house, automatically shuffled his cards, sorting them into alphabetical order. He started to reach out to put them in his file box, and suddenly stopped short. The top card was the one he had made out for his third patient, the little boy who had come with his sister who'd cut her knee on an oyster shell. Two words he had written on it leaped out at him, and for one instant, oblivious to Sergeant Digges there in the room or to anything else, he sat staring down at them as they burned in his mind. He felt again the cold chill at his heart as other things raced suddenly back into his consciousness.—The urushiol, he thought . . . the goldfish bowl . . . He could have kicked himself for being a blind fool . . . but he knew now, at long last, all about Miss Olive Oliphant.

As he jumped to his feet, he saw Sergeant Digges staring at him curiously. "What's the matter, doc?"

Jonas pushed the telephone across the desk. "Get Miss Olive over here—quick."

He started for the door.

"Miss Olive? Look, Smith. I talked to her yesterday. She's bats. I've known her all my life. She has a mental age of two."

"Get her over here," Jonas said urgently. "Not here—get her to the Darrells'. Don't tell her I'm there, but get her. Don't let her give you any of the childish flim-flam either."

He stopped at the door and looked back. Sergeant Digges had a reluctant finger pressed tentatively on the telephone dial.

"For God's sake, Sergeant——"

"I tell you the woman's bats."

"Sure she's bats," Jonas said quietly. "Jenny's over there, trying to remember who she saw out at the Creek. If anybody. Miss Olive can drive a Model T, she can shoot, she lives next door to the St. John's campus. Get her, quick."

24

Jonas walked quickly up on the back porch of the Blanton-Darrell House, looked to see if the screen was hooked as it had been in front, saw it was not and held the door open a little, waiting for Sergeant Digges.

"Elizabeth was over there," the Sergeant said, coming up the steps. "She answered the phone. I told her to bring Miss Olive over. I didn't say why. Sure you know?"

Jonas nodded. He went quietly into the hall, opened the door to the back parlor and went in. Jenny was in the front room, on the love seat where she and Elizabeth had sat, mute and frozen, on Sunday morning while Miss Olive babbled out her startling news. It was Philippa Van Holt with her now, gripping her hand as she flashed to her feet in sudden white-lipped panic.

Philippa rose too as Jenny's hand flew to her throat, her eyes moving from Jonas to Digges.

The Sergeant went forward. "Jenny," he said, "the doctor tells me you're trying to remember who it was you saw out at the cottage. Do——"

"Sergeant Digges." Philippa came around the end of the love seat. "If you don't mind, I'd like to say something before you go on."

She spoke quietly but with determination.

"Go ahead, Miss Van Holt."

"It's simply this, Sergeant. You have no right to walk in here this way. You and Jonas Smith think you're being Jenny's friends. Well, you're not, and I'm not going to let her talk to you until she has some legal advice and protection. This isn't Russia. It's Annapolis in the Free State of Maryland, and——"

She looked swiftly around behind her. Elizabeth and Miss Olive were coming up the front steps. Jonas crossed the room and opened the screen door. Miss Olive Oliphant gave him a startled look and tried to draw back as she saw past him into the house.

"Come in, Miss Olive. Come in, Elizabeth."

He held the door open. As Elizabeth looked questioningly at him he shook his head. She went quickly into the big room.

"Jenny—what is it, baby? What's happening here? *Jenny!*"

The girl drew back, shrinking away from her. "Please, Elizabeth! Go away . . . don't touch me. I don't want anybody. And I don't want a lawyer. I just want to tell the truth."

Elizabeth moved toward her.

"No! Please—let me alone! Everybody let me alone. I lied, this morning. There wasn't anybody there. It was just me. I shot him. I wasn't telling the truth. I did move. I didn't stay where I said I did. I . . . I'd gone out in the kitchen. I had the gun in my hand. I knew I couldn't get out the door. I thought maybe I could get out of the bathroom window. But he started after me. That's when I shot him. That's the truth. That's——"

"Jenny," Jonas said. "Who was out there? Who did you see at the kitchen window?"

"Nobody. Nobody was there."

"Was it Elizabeth?"

"Oh, no!" She gave him a startled terrified glance. "No. It wasn't anybody."

"It was somebody who'd come out in the old car I saw in the back road," Jonas said. He looked over Elizabeth's pale golden head at the plump little woman. Miss Olive had managed to find a chair and was sitting bolt upright in it. Her gloved hand nervously opened and closed on the clasp of the white leather bag in her lap. "—Was it your grandfather, Jenny?"

"No!" she cried desperately. "No! It wasn't anybody! I did it myself! I tell you, there wasn't anybody else there!"

"—Miss Olive," Jonas said.

As he spoke her name, she gave him a startled look out of her innocent blue eyes.

"I . . . I'm very upset, Dr. Smith," she said unsteadily. "—And oh dear, here he comes. It would have been very much nicer if he'd stayed at the Club. It's very hard to explain things sensibly when Tinsley's around. I may be an old fool but I don't enjoy being constantly called one."

If Miss Olive's heart had sunk at the sight and sound of the lord of the manor returning, it was not hers alone. Jonas groaned as he heard Wetherby's car rattle up the drive. He felt Elizabeth's arm taut as a bowstring. But Jenny, whom he had half expected to slip down in another small lifeless heap behind the chair, curiously did not. She drew herself together, her chin up.

"I don't want to worry Grandfather, Mr. Digges." She spoke in a tight controlled little voice. "He hasn't been well. I've told you the truth. I'd like to go away now."

It was too late. Professor Darrell was at his front door.

"Take that blasted junk heap off the steps, Wetherby, and bring me a drink. You hear, you scoundrel—and whisky, not branch water."

"Yes, sir, Professor. That's jus' what was in my very own mind."

The screen door slammed, Professor Darrell came in. He stood in the living room doorway. Professor Darrell had lost weight. His fey horse's eyes glared as before, but his linen suit hung in baggy folds around him.

"What the devil . . . Olive, I thought you'd gone home. Philippa, how do you do, my dear."

Professor Darrell bowed to Philippa. He looked at Jonas.

"Elizabeth, what's the horse doctor doing in my house? And who's that? Digges, I told you——"

"Grandfather!" Elizabeth put her hand on his arm. He shook it off.

"I'm not getting excited." His voice rose dangerously. "I'm asking for information! Elizabeth, I will not have my house infested——"

"Tinsley, you'd better be quiet," Miss Olive Oliphant said. "You're making a donkey of yourself is what you're doing, and Elizabeth is going to marry Dr. Smith so there's no use at all in saying he's a horse doctor."

"Elizabeth . . ."

Jonas, holding his breath, tensed himself to catch Professor Darrell as he fell.

"Elizabeth, going to marry . . ." Professor Darrell spoke in a dazed and quiet voice, looking around at her as if he had not seen her for a long time. "Elizabeth . . . Is my granddaughter old enough to be married? And she's going to marry a horse doctor?"

"Yes, Grandfather." Elizabeth moved closer to Jonas. "But he's not a horse doctor."

Her grandfather shot a baleful glance at the little woman beside him. "It's that fool Olive. She said he was a horse doctor."

"I never said he was a horse doctor, Tinsley. And that has nothing to do with it. I'm just trying to tell Sergeant Digges that I do not believe Jenny shot Mr. Gordon Darcy Grymes."

Jenny Darrell's hands tightened convulsively on the damask chair back as she braced herself for her grandfather, as he turned slowly to acknowledge her existence and her presence there in the room.

"Jennifer . . . shot Grymes?" His glance moved back to Miss Olive. "Bilgewater and potato peels! Look at her. She couldn't shoot off a Christmas cracker. What blasted fool says she shot Gordon Darcy Grymes?"

"I say it, Grandfather! I say it!"

"Great . . ." Professor Darrell felt for the black ribbon that secured his black horn-rimmed nose glasses. He put them on and looked at her. "I'm drunk," he said. "I'm drunk or I'm crazy."

"You're probably both, Tinsley," Miss Olive said. "And I would have preferred it if everybody just said it was suicide and let it go at that. It would have been nicer for all of us. But I will not stand here and let Jenny say something I know is not the truth. Tell the truth and shame the devil, is what Papa——"

"Olive, your father was a——"

"Tinsley, my father was *not* a——"

183

"Go on, Miss Olive," Jonas said. "You weren't asleep, Saturday night, were you. You were out walking your cat. You saw Jenny and Grymes leave the Court. You saw something else. What was it, Miss Olive?"

The fresh pink roses in Miss Olive's cheeks were a faded mauve, her blue eyes round with appeal, as she nervously snapped and unsnapped the catch of her white bag.

"I'd rather not say, Dr. Smith. As long as Jenny did not do it, it doesn't matter really, does it? He's dead. He can't come back."

"—What is urushiol, Miss Olive? Why did you give me the piece about urushiol? And why did you give me the bowl of goldfish, Miss Olive?"

"Because I saw somebody come off the College Campus in that old automobile. I was very much surprised, because . . . well, it was very surprising to me."

"Who was it, Miss Olive?"

Miss Olive was trembling.

"Of course, I don't like to make trouble for people, and I don't like to say people aren't telling the truth, and I didn't know what to do, because I . . . I was afraid. But I tried, all along, over and over, to tell Dr. Smith I was troubled with insomnia, and up a great deal of the night. And goldfish eat mosquito larvae, doctor. I thought you ought to know that. And urushiol is named after a Japanese scientist and it's what our Navy friends find in lacquer poisoning out in the Orient, and it is also the blistering compound in poison ivy. I gave you the fish so you'd understand there are no mosquitoes in my back yard, Dr. Smith, and I gave you the clipping about the urushiol so you'd see that anybody who is all covered up with calamine lotion and says she is bitten by mosquitoes, and suddenly starts wearing pants instead of skirts to cover up her legs, because she's got poison ivy, isn't telling the truth, and anyway Miss Van Holt did take the old car, and I saw her go, and I saw her come back. Because she was the one who——"

"Watch it!" Jonas said.

Philippa Van Holt's hand was moving slowly down in the love seat. Sergeant Digges took two steps and caught her wrist. She straightened up sharply.

"That's a . . . a stupid lie," she said. The sherry-brown eyes were burning coals. Her face was hard, her jaw tight. "It's a lie. For God's sake, Miss Olive's——"

"Why, Miss Van Holt."

184

Miss Olive's cheeks were flushed an indignant pink.

"I think that's most ungrateful . . . You ought to be ashamed, after I've gone out of my way to say nothing to Sergeant Digges. You know you have poison ivy, and you know you got it Saturday night, because you didn't start complaining about mosquitoes and scratching till Sunday, and littering up my bathroom with calamine lotion till the middle of the afternoon. I know poison ivy when I see it, and I keep goldfish just so I won't have mosquitoes in my pool. And you know as well as I do that Mr. Darcy called you up at ten o'clock Saturday night, and you answered and said 'Wait till I see if the old bat's asleep,' and you came up to my room and opened my door and spoke my name. I pretended I was asleep, because I didn't enjoy being called an old bat, and if you had anything to say over my telephone you were afraid for me to listen to, then you had no right in my house, using my telephone, and I intended to ask you to leave the very next morning."

"Why didn't you?" said Philippa Van Holt.

"Because I didn't dare. After the unladylike way you talked over the phone, about seeing people in hell first, and getting your cut of the property, and anybody being fool enough to throw away millions of dollars that belonged to them and they could prove it, and not caring whether they played around or didn't as long as you got your share, I didn't feel I wanted to cross you when you were in a bad mood. And especially after I saw your face under the street light, I was so alarmed I got up and took my cat out, and I saw you in the old car, and I heard you when you came back and looked in my room to see if I was still asleep. And then what you said about being married and pretending to be in love with that young man. And saying I had mosquitoes in my pool. I just don't like people that——"

Miss Olive broke off as the she-devil unleashed blazed out of Philippa Van Holt's burning brown eyes. Sergeant Digges's hand closed harder on her arm, and Jonas stepped protectively closer to the plump frightened old lady.

"I was just dumb, lady," he said to her. "It wasn't till a few minutes ago after Digges put Gordon Grymes on the spot about changing his name and finding out there was a record, so it could be proved the Foundry belonged to Miss Van Holt's husband, that I got your word about urushiol and the goldfish. I don't know that I'd have got it then if I hadn't just had a kid in the office with his legs covered with poison ivy, and happened to notice his card, and remembered the dab of calamine Miss

Van Holt said wasn't powder but lotion for mosquito bites on her face, down at the Yacht Club the other night."

He turned to Philippa.

"You overplayed it, Miss Van Holt. I swallowed your gag about somebody in the house the night you tried to shoot me, knowing Tom Darrell had frenched out of the Yard again and knowing I'd blame it on him. It was flattering. You must have thought I was catching on to you when I wasn't."

"The Sergeant could have," Philippa Van Holt said coolly. "And you did swallow it, didn't you?"

"I did, and that's okay. I forgot you called yourself a fourth-rate actress, and I forgot you're a writer used to making up stories. And that's okay too. But it wasn't okay to dope my dog, and it wasn't okay to pretend you're a friend of Jenny's and try to make her take the rap. How did you do it?—She told you you were saving your grandfather, Jenny?"

Jenny Darrell, frozen behind the chair, her face a deathmask, was staring at Philippa in dumb stupid horror.

"She . . . she said it was Grandfather. She said she knew. It . . . he'd thought it was Elizabeth, out there with Gordon, and that's why he shot him. She said she saw him take the car from St. John's. She said . . . oh, Philippa, how could you do such a thing!"

"All right," said Miss Van Holt. "So what? I told you to leave him alone. You said I was jealous. Okay, maybe I was. No high school brat's going to walk off with my husband. I shot him. What do you think? And I've been almost crazy, but not for reasons the horse doctor thought. It's this damned poison ivy. How should I know the place out there's full of it? I never saw the stuff before. I knew he was going to take you out there. He liked to tell me the places he was going and who he was taking and what he was going to do. It was old stuff. I should have killed him a long time before this. But when he calls me up and tells me he *likes* his precious damned brother, and the Foundry really belongs to him, and he feels sorry for him, and he's not going to bother about the property that's willed to him and in his name, then that's really it. He forgot he'd made a will himself, and I'd made him make it in his own name, when he first told me about the switch—in the days I first married him and he hadn't started picking up every gal he saw."

"I don't believe it! I don't believe it!"

Jenny Darrell put her dark head down on the back of the chair.

Philippa looked at her with a curious expression of pitying contempt.

"Your grandfather's right, Jenny. You'll go through life trusting a lot of heels. You trusted my husband and you trusted me. And your grandfather here, who's never spoken a decent word to you—what do you do for him? You'll go to jail to keep him from going . . . the blustering old fool. That's the kind you are. So you don't believe me? Take that bag, Jonas."

She motioned to her handbag in the love seat. Jonas picked it up and opened it.

"Give her that little object in there. See if she remembers it."

It was a beautiful thing of ivory and mother-of-pearl, chased silver and deadly steel. Jenny closed her eyes and turned away as Jonas thrust it into her hand. She gripped it and held on to it for an instant, opened her eyes and looked at it.

"That's it. I remember the feel of it now. Oh, Elizabeth!"

She flung the revolver from her and threw herself into her sister's arms. "Oh, I thought it was Grandfather . . . I thought he did it for you!"

Elizabeth held her, staring down at the gun on the floor. "That's it—that's the one he had the night he gave it to me . . ."

"Of course," Philippa said. "It wasn't loaded. It wasn't loaded Saturday night either. My husband was a fool but not that big a fool. He was also afraid of going to jail again. He gave me his other one."

She turned to Sergeant Digges.

"You're pretty smart, aren't you. I did stand outside the window, and he was surprised when he saw me with the gun in my hand. He was tight but not so tight he couldn't see I'd had enough of . . . of everything. And that, my friends, will be Miss Van Holt's defence. I dare say my brother-in-law will be glad to help me make it stick."

Jonas had reached down and picked up the lethal bauble of chased silver and mother-of-pearl from the floor.

"I'll take that, please," Philippa said. "I'd like it as a . . . a souvenir."

Sergeant Digges' hand reached out. "I'll just keep that, doc," he said tranquilly. He broke it open. "You say your husband carried it empty?" He let the shells slip into the palm

187

of his hand. "There's a little charge of the attempted murder of Jonas Smith you've got to face too, Miss Van Holt. I got a bullet—from this, I guess—out of his wall this morning. It's not going to be as easy as you think, Miss Van Holt."

He dropped the ornate weapon into his coat pocket.

"If you'd stuck to your line, and told me about this poison ivy, doc we'd have got there sooner. But no hard feelings, doc." He looked at Miss Olive. "You hadn't ought to have tried to hoodwink me the way you did, ma'am. Last Sunday you swore up and down she never left the house, and I never figured a lady like you would deliberately lie to me. That was before I knew about her husband and his brother switching names, so the only motive I figured on then was her husband being out with another girl. I didn't get around to him being the legal owner of the Foundry and her being his heir at law till last night. You being a respectable witness and giving her an alibi like you did sort of foxed things up, Miss Olive. You could get yourself in a lot of trouble doing a thing like that."

Miss Olive tightened her lips and blinked the tears out of her eyes like a child who had been unfairly rebuked.

"I thought it was better if everybody just decided the man had done away with himself, Mr. Digges," she said. "I didn't think anybody would think it was Jenny who did it. And I didn't want her to shoot me. That's why I left my house until she got out. I know I haven't been welcome here, but I thought even Tinsley would rather have me here than have me dead."

"Not at all, not at all." Professor Darrell came out of a dazed fog, and bowed to her. He turned and looked at Sergeant Digges and Philippa Van Holt as they went out. "Too bad, too bad. Handsome woman. Called me a blustering old fool."

He stood unsteadily in the middle of the room a moment, and turned to his granddaughters. "Elizabeth, are you going to marry this man Olive calls a horse doctor?"

"Tinsley, I did not call him a——"

"Yes, Grandfather. I am if you don't mind."

"I don't mind. I don't mind if Jenny'll stay with me. If Jenny don't mind putting up with a . . . a blustering old fool."

"Oh, Grandfather, I'd love it! I'll take care of you! I'll do my very best!"

Her starlit eyes, the breathless poignancy of her voice, startled even Professor Darrell. He looked at her as if he was seeing her for the first time in all the years of her life.

"Good girl," he said. "Good girl. I didn't care for your

mother, but I dare say she was a good girl, or my son wouldn't have married her."

He patted her head clumsily. "You've got the Darrell eyes."

As he looked at Jonas, the Professor Darrell glare was coming back into his own.

"You two plan to go on living in the wing?"

"Yes, sir. I imagine so."

"You plan to go on paying the rent?"

"Yes, sir. Of course."

Professor Darrell put his hand out and shook Jonas's cordially.

Elizabeth gave Jonas a quick mischievous smile. "But we've got to have a new furnace, Grandfather. And the hyphen. So we can have a dining room."

Her grandfather glowered at her.

"You don't either, Elizabeth," Jenny said. "The furnace is old, but it's perfectly good. You can have the hyphen, but you'll have to pay more rent for it. Grandfather can't afford to do anything more over there. Can we, Grandfather?"

Professor Darrell put his arm around his new granddaughter. "Good girl," he said. "Sensible girl."

Jonas grinned. "Elizabeth, let's go over to Gregory's and eat. Do you realize we've never had a meal together?"

Elizabeth Darrell caught up her bag. On the front porch of the Blanton-Darrell House she stopped and smiled up at him. "Jonas—I'm the fledgling . . . they've pushed me out of the nest. But I have some place to go, haven't I?"

"Oh, darling, forever and forever."

He bent down and kissed her. From out of the living room, he could hear Miss Olive's plaintive voice:

"Tinsley, I never said Dr. Smith was a horse doctor."

"Olive, I heard you with my own ears.—Wetherby! Where's that black scoundrel? Wetherby, we need a drink.— Olive, you called my grandson-in-law . . ."

Jonas and Elizabeth ran down the steps.

"You'll never get over it, Jonas. It's something new for them to quarrel about . . . I hope you don't mind."

Wetherby was in the kitchen door as they went around the corner of the house.

"Congratulations, doctor! Congratulations, Miss Elizabeth!"

He shook hands with both of them.

"Doctor, the Professor he's in there. He's callin' for his liquor. Do I give it to him, or do I not?"

"You do not," Jonas said. "You certainly do not. The Professor is off liquor."

"Yes, sir, doctor. The Professor he don't know it, but he's off his liquor till you say he's back on."

Wetherby made a discreet bow and backed into the kitchen. "Thank you, doctor, sir."

Jonas grinned at Elizabeth. "That, Miss Darrell," he said, "that will teach your grandfather to call me a horse doctor."

He bent his head and kissed her again.